MURDER
in CLICHY

Cara Black

Published by
Soho Press, Inc.
853 Broadway
New York, NY 10003

Library of Congress Cataloging-in-Publication Data
Black, Cara, 1951–
Murder in Clichy / Cara Black.
p. cm.
ISBN 10: 1-56947-411-7
ISBN 13: 978-1-56947-411-2
1. Leduc, Aimee (Fictatious character)—Fiction.
2. Women private investigators—France—Clichy—Fiction.
3. Art—Collectors and collecting—Fiction. 4. Jade art objects—Fiction.
5. Clichy (France)—Fiction.
I. Title.

PS3552.L297M796 2005
813'.54—dc22   2004048242

10   9   8   7   6   5   4   3   2   1

Dedicated to all the ghosts,
past and present.

My heartfelt thanks go to so many for their patience and knowledge to fan the spark into a fire!

Deep appreciation goes to Li He, Chinese Department, Asian Art Museum, San Francisco; Musée Cernuschi, Paris; Dr. Terri Haddix, MD, Renee Slon, RN, Dr. Jan Gurley MD, and to Béatrice Trang, a huge debt; Carla Chemouni, who made it happen; Thiên Ly Buu Tòa and the Cao Dai Temple, the lady in Vientiane, Barbara Serenella, Marion, Warren, Bill, Don Cannon, on computer patrol, Erick Gilbert; Grace Loh, Jean Satzer, Dot Edwards, Barbara McHugh. In Paris, the generosity, wisdom and *esprit de mes amies*: Anne-Françoise Delbègue for her warmth, Sarah Tarille *toujours, la Tunisienne*; Gilles Fouquet his excitement, Jean-Damien his support, and Chris. For Jim Frey who spurs me forward, Linda Allen who holds my shakey hands and Laura Hruska who guides them with sure ones. My son Tate Shusei and always, Jun.

"The true heroes stay anonymous . . ."
—overheard in the Paris Métro

". . . there is always something absent that torments me."
—Camille Claudel, sculptress, in a letter to Rodin.

MURDER

in CLICHY

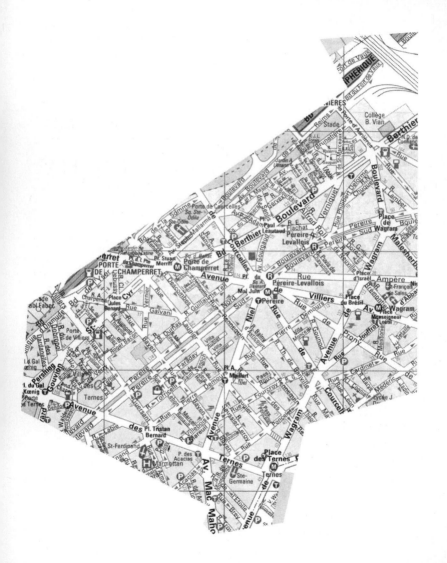

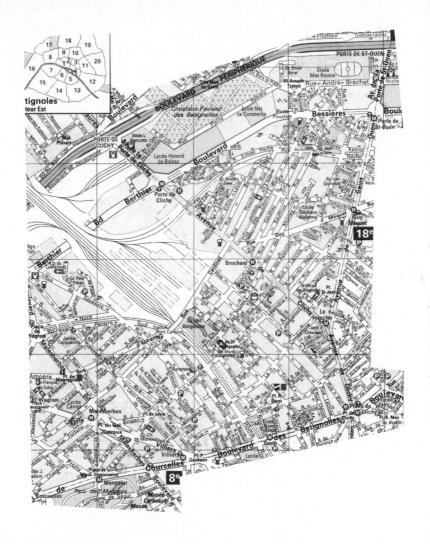

PARIS

NOVEMBER 1994

PARTS

Tuesday

IN THE STOREFRONT CAO Dai temple under the red
lanterns, her foot asleep, pins and needles up and down her
legs, Aimée Leduc struggled to keep her spine straight, thumb
and pinky together, in the half-lotus position. Her partner
René, a dwarf, sat with a look of total concentration, in perfect Lotus posture, in the men's section. But Aimée's brain
flashed with lines of computer code and throbbed with an ache
for an espresso. No blank slate of tranquility for her with sirens
hee-hawing on the quai and the Seine fog curling over the skylight. As the blue-robed priest struck the gong, the sigh of
relief she exhaled mingled with the mindful breaths and musk
of incense surrounding her.

"Three weeks, René," she muttered, "and I still can't
meditate!"

She'd tried and failed breathing exercises, a new practice she'd
begun with René Friant, her business partner, after her optic
nerve had been damaged the previous month during an assault.
It had seemed like a good time to begin to live healthily.

The ten or eleven women in yoga pants, from the nearby
Université de Paris, grabbed their books and headed for the
door. Ripe fruit scents from the tiered altar offerings clung to
the velvet curtains that kept out the cold. The swish of a
broom wielded by Quoc, the temple custodian, an older
Vietnamese man, filled the foyer.

"Mindfulness," René said, rolling up his meditation mat,
"think of it like that. Try to concentrate. Don't give up,
Aimée."

René was right, of course. But the calmness and tranquility
she sought remained as elusive as a wisp of smoke, even though

her bouts of blurry vision had receded. She had her sight now, most of the time.

From the rear came Linh, a slender Vietnamese nun, in a Mandarin collared white *ao dai* tunic with matching trousers, smiling, her palms together in greeting. Middle-aged, her black hair in a bun, crows feet lines fanned from her eyes as she smiled.

"Forgive me, we've worked on this before," Linh said, an undertone of sibilance just perceptible in her accented French. "Next time, Aimée, be open to the divining board; that's a form of meditation."

Like a large wooden ouija board, the divining board stood near the all-seeing divine eye, the Cao Dai's symbol, a huge globelike eyeball suspended over the altar. Mediums used it to communicate with the spirit world in séances and in prayers to a pantheon of divine beings, including the Buddha, Confucius, Lao Tzu, and Jesus Christ. Crystal candelabras, brass drum bowls, yin and yang symbols, and peacock feathers adorned side altars.

"*Merci*, Linh," she said, grateful for help from the nun she'd met only last week.

Pictures of Victor Hugo and Sun Yat-sen lined the walls. They were venerated as saints in this esoteric sect, whose philosophy was a potpourri of Hinduism, Christianity, Taoism, Islam, and Buddhism. A sign reading VAN GIAO NHAT LY, meaning "All religions have the same reason," faced her. Aimée inhaled the peacefulness of the small, makeshift temple, wishing that tranquility would stay with her.

She paused with René at the table littered with leaflets describing meditation courses and a solicitation for signatures to a petition.

"We're hoping to build a real temple," Linh said, watching Aimée. "Our lands were confiscated in Vietnam. Members of our sect were executed."

"We'd like to help, of course," Aimée said, after signing. "I'll pass around your petition."

"But there's something more important," Linh said. Her face crinkled in worry; there was a slight tremor in her eyelids. "Your application says you have a detective agency. Can you contact someone for us?"

"On a good day we contact encryptions, viruses, and hackers invading computer systems," René said, grinning.

Linh pulled a creased paper from her sleeve. "What about this man?"

Aimée saw the scribbled name Thadée Baret; no address, just the 17th arrondissement, and a phone number.

"He's sympathetic . . . he helps our cause. Can you give him something from me?"

"As I said, we want to help," Aimée said. "But Linh, you don't need us to telephone him or to meet him . . ."

"Politics," Linh interrupted, shaking her head. "My father was a judge years ago in Saigon. The regime denounced him and blacklisted our family, which still remains under surveillance. My younger brother's in prison for 'political dissent.' His children have been denied visits to him. Even here, in Paris, *they* watch me."

Watch her?

"Please understand," Aimée said, wariness intruding. "I want to help, but what our firm does is computer security."

"How much?"

"*Non*, Linh, it's not a question of money, it's simply not my field," Aimée said, feeling awkward. Linh had helped her, a novice, in her struggle with meditation, and now. . . .

"But I read about you . . . how you found a killer in the Bastille while you were *blind*."

Embarrassed, Aimée wished the newspaper articles had never appeared.

"It's complicated . . ." Linh continued, eyelids once more fluttering nervously.

"In what way?" Aimée said. The meditation room was becoming chilly.

Linh pulled an envelope from her robe and said, "In my country we suffer anonymous denunciations by a network of informers, detentions without trial. Priests and nuns from our sect, or anyone with a political agenda that could threaten the government, live in fear. Please, just give him this from me."

Aimée tried to catch René's eye, but he'd bent down to tie his shoes.

"I'm new to Paris," Linh continued, twisting the amber prayer beads on her wrist. "Mostly I fund-raise at Cao Dai meditation seminars. And I am petitioning the International Court of Justice and Amnesty International for my brother's release."

"Doesn't that conflict with your vocation?"

"Not at all," she said. "As the Dalai Lama says, 'There are many paths all leading to the same place.' My mission and our practice glide together."

Aimée heard sincerity in Linh's voice. But corporate security was the bread and butter of Leduc Detective. After last month's incident when she'd been assaulted, she'd vowed to steer clear of anything else.

"Think of it as our donation, Linh," René said. He gestured to the envelope. "May I take this? We will deliver it for you, gladly."

Surprised, Aimée shot René a look.

"No problem," René continued, "we'll make the phone call . . ."

"And you will arrange to give this envelope to him? He will have something for me." Linh put her palms together again, a gesture of greeting and farewell.

René returned her gesture. "We will try."

* * *

"WHY GET us involved, René?" Aimée asked as soon as they were outside on the narrow street, lychee seeds crackling under their feet. She hitched her bag onto her leather-clad shoulder. "Trying to earn good karma?"

René pulled on a Burberry raincoat, tailored to his height. In the weak afternoon light a flurry of windswept brown leaves and Chinese candy wrappers swirled from the gutter. "What's a half-hour to meet this man, Baret, to give him this envelope? *Et alors*, you're going to the seventeenth to check on the Olf project anyway. And a little good karma wouldn't hurt, would it?"

She nodded. Maybe he was right. All she ever did was over-tip taxi drivers, hoping to earn late rainy night taxi karma.

Apart from the oasis of the nearby Buddhist temple, in the midst of a mind-numbing sea of concrete tower block build-ings, in this polyglot *quartier* of Vietnamese, Chinese, Laotians, and Cambodians, the thirteenth arrondissement had little charm. It was impersonal, its gray uniformity punctuated only by bright red Vietnamese *pho* noodle restos, Asian video shops, and hairdressers' salons.

She paused at the bus stop by *Armée du Salut*, the ferro-concrete Salvation Army building, designed by Le Corbusier: a treasure trove of cheap, used armoires.

"See you back at the office, René," she said, and caught the bus.

RAIN PATTERED on the windows as dusk descended over Avenue de Wagram. The chic *quartier*, off one of the streets radiating from the Arc de Triomphe, lay in the seventeenth arrondissement. Hopeful, Aimée wound the black wool scarf around her neck, signed in, and mounted the stairs spiraling up to Olf's state-of-the-art corporate headquarters, located in a wood-paneled *hôtel particulier*. A mixture of steel and curved aqua glass-walled offices constituted the mansion's top two floors.

But the project management staff dealing with her proposal had left for a trade show outside Paris. A wasted trip! She wrote a note and left it in the *chef des opérations* box.

Downstairs, the concierge's post was vacant. Where was the security man she'd seen? Shadows from the pillars crisscrossed the black and white floor. As she wrote her initials by her name on the sign-out log, the timed lights shut off.

In the darkness, she felt her way, her boot heels echoing on the tile, her shoulders tight with apprehension. She sniffed. Only the smell of cold stone and floor wax.

Then a rustling and the click of a door closing.

"Is someone there?" she called.

Silence.

She felt a *frisson* of fear. And for a moment it was as if she were blind again, groping in darkness, her only guide sounds, odors, and the currents in the air. Panicked, holding her breath, she kept going and felt the cold, smooth marble of a pillar. Seeing the dim glow of the streetlight, she let out a sigh of relief.

With a quick step, she made her way through the door to the street. She looked back but saw no one following her. A few blocks away, she turned into rue de Lévis, glad of the bustling street market marking the tony *quartier*.

In the chill dusk, horns beeped. "*Crevettes, un kilo!*" shouted a fishmonger standing by the tubs of bright pink shrimp, frost framing his words in the evening air. Lighted stalls with every kind of cheese and produce filled the narrow pedestrian *rue*, an old Roman road once used by Jeanne d'Arc and her army. Shoppers jostled Aimée on the rain-slicked pavement.

She punched in Thadée Baret's number on her cell phone

which rang and rang. She was about to hang up when someone answered.

"*Allô?*"

"Monsieur Thadée Baret?"

"*Un moment.*"

She heard what sounded like the *télé*, the whoosh of an espresso machine in the background.

"*Oui?*" A man asked, "Who's this?"

"Aimée Leduc here. I'm trying to reach Thadée Baret. The nun Linh gave me this number.

"About time," said the man, urgently. "I'm Thadée. You have something for me?" His suspicion had vanished.

"An envelope, we should meet . . ."

"How long will it take you to get here?" he interrupted.

"Where's here?"

"Near Place de Clichy." He spoke fast. His breath came over the phone in gasps.

"Say ten minutes, by the Métro. But can't we meet at my office?" Aimée asked.

"No. Come here. Stand in front of the *boulangerie*," he said. "Across from Sainte Marie des Batignolles church."

Odd. But she knew it was a crowded, busy place. It should be safe. Easy to melt away in the crowd if this man turned out to be even more strange than he sounded.

"How will I know . . . ?" she began.

"I'll find you."

Why all the mystery? she wanted to ask. But he'd hung up.

She knew Clichy, the less-chic part of the many-faced seventeenth, a district containing two worlds: Aristocrats with *de la* before their name, whose children attended the local *école primaire* and later ENA, school of the elite, before nabbing a government post. And immigrants with *-ski*, *akela*, or *khabib* at the end of their names, destined for the short BAC exam, a trade school, and a factory job. The seventeenth was an arrondissement of elegant consulates and the best closet-size Turkish kebab shops this side of the Seine. Now, noticing the Mercedes parked between trucks on the street, Aimée became aware of a newer cross-section of moneyed bourgeoisie and hip *médiathèques* added to the traditional working-class population of Clichy.

Clichy? Only a few called it Clichy these days: the *flics*, kids, and old gangsters who'd gone to the Gaumont cinema palace and thought it was classy. It was the area Henry Miller had tramped through, fringing the Place de Clichy, with its Boulevard des Batignolles and its boules players and narrow streets. Nowadays, the kids who sold drugs called Clichy and its boulevard bleeding into Pigalle their place of business. From the chic Avenue de Wagram and Arc de Triomphe *quartier* to the double wide Boulevard Pereire, nicknamed the *maréchaux*, lined with foreign sex workers, the seventeenth now held something for everyone.

Aimée ascended the Place de Clichy Métro steps, slipping on her leather gloves against the chill November wind. Late afternoon commuters surged around her. Darkness descended before six this time of year. The Café Wepler, a Wehrmacht soldiers' canteen during the German Occupation—(earlier immortalized in Vuillard's painting)—glowed in the dusk. Its awning sheltered a stall displaying Brittany oysters on ice to passersby.

She rushed to a taxi stand, anxious to get her errand over with. But Place de Clichy traffic was at a standstill. Klaxons honked and the Number 95 bus shot diesel exhaust at the Maréchal Moncey monument, commemorating peasants who defended Paris at the end of a Napoleonic campaign. She gave up on a taxi, left the busy Place fronted by cinemas and brasseries, and hurried through the narrow Clichy streets.

She passed *la Fourche*, the fork, that divided the *quartier* into the "good" seventeenth and the "bad." More than in any other part of Paris, the architect Haussman had stamped his signature here in the last century. The image the world thought of as Paris: broad tree-lined boulevards riven by the classic gray stone five-storied buildings with metal filigreed balconies and chimney pots like organ pipes on the rooftiles.

She reached Batignolles Park with its rolling lawns and black swans gliding across the small lake. The fretwork of plane trees, puddles, and clumps of wet leaves faced real estate offices and antique shops. A gunmetal sky threatened; she hoped Thadée Baret wouldn't be late. Beyond lay the derelict train yards, part of the 19th century *ceinture*, the railway belt circling Paris. Their walls were bright with silver graffiti.

She entered a cobbled crescent that had a village feeling. Two-story buildings lined the street and old people congregated on the green slatted benches beneath the clock tower of the columned church: a pocket of "old" Paris.

Aimée saw a thirtyish man, wearing black pants, his thin white shirt whipping in the wind, scanning passersby from under an awning over the *boulangerie*. He had a pale face, wore thick black-framed glasses, and held a backpack by its strap. An arty or political type . . . Baret?

She waved and saw recognition in his eyes. And what looked like fear.

Around him on crowded rue Legendre mothers pushed strollers and old women walked their dogs by the acacia trees. Fresh-baked bread smells wafted from the *boulangerie*. As she approached, she saw how thin his arms were, and how he kept picking at something on his wrist and wiping his nose with his sleeve.

She waved again, wrapping her scarf tighter as she hurried toward him. Coatless, wasn't he cold? An old woman huddled under an umbrella near the glass phone cabinet by the blackened stone buildings.

"Monsieur Baret?" she asked. "I'm Aimée Leduc. We talked on the phone."

He reached out and grabbed her arm.

"Do you have it?"

She nodded and handed him the envelope Linh had entrusted to her. He put the strap of the backpack in her hand.

"For Linh. Sling it over your shoulder."

She did.

"They're following me," he said in his breathless way.

"Who?" She looked around. She saw only busy shoppers. Slush from car tires rolling over the cobblestone street sprayed her boots.

"But you must know," he gasped into her ear.

"*Tiens,* wait a minute," she said. "I don't understand what's going on here."

He registered her surprise. His eyes darted around the crowd; he glanced across the street. "They're here." He clutched her coat, a wild look on his face. "But Nadège and Sophie depend on me . . . if I don't. . . ."

"What do you mean?"

She saw his terror as a motorcycle gunned its engine, drowning his answer.

"Look, I'm just helping a nun . . ."

The words disappeared in the crack of rapid gunfire. Baret's body jerked. Someone yanked at the backpack on her shoulder. But she grabbed the strap and held on to it. A motorcycle engine whined. The sound of a bullet's ricochet echoed off the stone buildings. Then there was the screech of tires.

"Get down!" Aimée yelled.

Little balloons of stone dust grit burst on the pavement ahead of her. She ducked, pulling open the nearby phone cabinet door for shelter. As she pulled at Baret, he collapsed onto her, his shattered glasses red with blood mist. An exhalation, smaller than a sigh, escaped his lips.

Panic flooded her as she saw that red-black holes peppered the back of his white shirt.

He sprawled on top of her as she heard the roar of the motor-cycle engine gunning away. Her arm stung. She saw blood and realized it came from her. Shouts and cries erupted around her.

Crows cawed, their nest above the *boulangerie* doorway disturbed.

The old woman ran, then tripped; her baguette launched onto the glistening cobbles in a slow motion arabesque. Aimée tried to pull Baret into the shelter of the phone cabinet but his hand caught on her pocket. Someone screamed. And screamed.

Aimée's knees trembled as she felt for his pulse. None. Her fingertips traced ribbed scars and scabs, the needle tracks on his arm. Bluish purple, old marks. Blood trickled down his pale chin onto the rain-slicked cobbles.

"*Mon Dieu* . . . call the *flics*!" She couldn't reach the pay phone. Where was her cell phone? In the silence someone was sobbing, and a child howled.

Then there were voices. "*Terroristes!*"

"*Non*, she did it . . . she fought with him," Aimée heard someone say. "She pulled him down!"

"That one," the old woman sprawled on the wet pavement whimpered, pointing her out. Someone pulled the body off Aimée, and tried CPR.

Aimée struggled to her feet. A man grabbed her shoulders. "Hold on, Mademoiselle, we saw what you did," he accused.

"What do you mean?"

The old woman was shaking her, grabbing at her scarf. A dog barked. Aimée looked around in panic.

"Let go! Don't you understand . . . someone on a motorcy-cle shot him!" Aimée said.

Aimée saw a woman's face in the tall window opposite, her

mouth open in a silent scream. And then she heard the approaching police siren. Warm blood dripped from her arm.

A large green and white garbage truck had stopped in front of them, blocking the street. She saw the motorcycle at a distance, stuck in traffic.

"Stop that motorcycle," she shouted, but no one listened. She broke past the throng and tried to run, the backpack bobbing on her good shoulder, the bloodstained envelope she had tried to give Baret now clenched in her fist.

The motorcycle shot down a narrow street on the right, weaving between the cars. Aimée ran, trying to keep up, for half a block. The helmeted, black-leather-clad figure looked like every motorcyclist on the street. She collapsed against a dented Citroën, panting. Tried to catch her breath.

"Stop her," someone shouted. Then the motorcycle turned, jumped the curb, and aimed for her.

The hair rose on the back of her neck.

She scrambled to her feet, slipped as her heel caught in a cobble, got up again and ran into an open courtyard. Panting, she raced down a narrow slit between buildings. No exit, just doors. All locked. She pounded on several until one opened.

"We don't let patrons into the laundry this way," said a woman, plastic hangers in her hands. She eyed Aimée's black fishnets, boots and black-leather-belted coat. Behind the woman were steamed-up windows and the roar of industrial dryers.

"My ex-husband's on a rampage." Aimée said the first thing she could think of. "Please, I need to come inside before he sees me."

Another woman, bent over a pressing machine, glanced up. "Eh? This isn't a public thoroughfare," she said.

"Just this once, please."

The woman shrugged and stood aside.

Aimée edged past the crisp white sheets piled on the

counter, careful not to let the blood from her arm drip on them.

"Next time, use the front entrance," said the woman.

But Aimée had pulled on a wool cap over her spiky rain-drizzled hair and gone out the front door. She wrapped her wool scarf around her arm. An ambulance and police cars came to a screeching halt by the *boulangerie*. She headed over to the next narrow street, her heart thumping. Keeping her head down she walked close to the buildings. On rue Boursault she huddled in a doorway until the Number 66 bus disgorged riders, then entered it by the rear doors. Trembling, she pulled her coat close around her and sank into the seat, thrusting the envelope into her coat pocket.

The few passengers on the bus read or sat with eyes closed, ignoring her. She set the backpack down on the next seat and felt inside it. Her hands touched something hard. A gun? She felt again, rummaged within, touching soft silk and hard smooth carved surfaces. She located a small, intricate object.

She peered inside. The absinthe-green of a jade monkey's face stared back at her.

Late Afternoon Tuesday

IN THE APARTMENT, NADÈGE pulled her bag from under the bed. The duvet stank of cat piss; feathers floated in the last of the November light slanting through the tall window. Techno pounded on the Radio Liberté station.

She had to make her legs move or her uncle Thadée would find her like this, hollow-eyed and shaking. Waiting for the next pipe of life. He'd throw her out, like her father had.

She'd slipped. Again.

Her little Michel, only five years old, needed milk money. But she needed money more. Well, *Grand-mère* would take care of him. *Bien sûr. Grand-mère* always did.

The phone chirped. *Merde!* She hunted under the piled *Le Parisien* newspapers, around overflowing yellow ashtrays with RICARD printed on them, beneath the leather jacket on the soft wood floor. Where was it?

She wound her thick silky black hair in a knot and held it in place with a tortoise-shell comb.

"*Allô?*" she said finally when she had retrieved the phone.

"Where's Thadée?" asked a deep voice.

"Playing pool at Académie de Billard," she said. More likely, buying smokes at the café-*tabac*, she thought, wishing she had one herself. He was supposed to meet her here. Why hadn't he come? He'd left his jacket.

"Then I'm the Queen of Hungary," said the voice.

"Very funny," she said.

"Tell Thadée I'm waiting."

"Maybe I will," she said, throwing her makeup into her bag, scrabbling into her shoes and her shearling parka. "Maybe I won't. Tell me what you want."

"No candy then. Kiss those bonbons goodbye."

"Wait a minute, Thadée's straight . . . what's . . . ?"

He'd hung up. Arrogant *salaud!* She had other sources. But she didn't want Thadée to know about them. If he found out, he wouldn't let her stay here again.

Monsieur Know-it-all! the Bonbon King . . . what did he know? Not much unless Thadée had confided in him. Thadée had gone to clinch the deal. The deal, he'd told her, that would settle his debts, hers, and more.

Taking the two hundred francs she found in Thadée's jacket pocket, she slipped down the winding back stairs. Passed through the gate to the cobbled courtyard with its decaying vegetable dampness and rotten wood molding smells, a repository for vats of used cooking oil re-sold to cheaper restos. A Romanian flophouse, doubling as a sweatshop in the day, faced onto it.

As Nadège exited onto rue Truffaut she saw a motorcycle take off, spraying gray splinters of ice and wetness. Her eyes rested for an instant on a stroller with a crying infant, an old woman huddled on the pavement, and then on Thadée's body sprawled against the phone cabinet. Gasping, she edged toward the crowd. She tugged the red silk cord around her neck feeling for her lucky piece. Saw the blood, the *flics*, medics, and one of the Bonbon King's henchman edging into the throng. She ducked before he could see her. Her hands shook. It didn't make sense, this wasn't supposed to happen!

Could she help Thadée? But she knew he was beyond help.

She backed up, shaking uncontrollably. Where could she go? And what about Thadée's stash that he said would clinch the deal?

She ran back to the courtyard, her heels echoing on the soot-blackened stone. In the rear, behind an old staircase, she loosened a stone and felt behind it for the hollow in which Thadée had once hidden dope: only bits of brick and old paper wrappers. Dirt got under her fingernails. Then she felt something cold. Metallic. She scraped it out. An old-fashioned key. But to what? Sirens wailed. She dropped it into her vintage Versace bag and ran.

Tuesday Early Evening

AIMÉE'S HEART POUNDED. STILL shaken, she stood at the eye clinic reception desk in Guy's private consulting office on rue de Chazelles. The freshly painted, high-ceilinged suite overlooked the old metal foundry in whose courtyard the Statue of Liberty had been forged. Now, the courtyard stood deserted, gray and beaded with rain.

The last evening patient had passed her as she came in. Guy smiled, pushed his glasses onto his forehead and set his stethoscope on the reception counter.

"Doctor Lambert," his receptionist said as she put on her coat, "I'm sorry but I'm late picking up my daughter from day-care. Do you mind . . . ?"

"Go ahead, Marie," he said. "I'll close up."

Marie smiled at Aimée and left.

"Lock the door," Aimée told him, "I may have been followed."

"Kind of jumpy, aren't you?" Guy said, coming forward and kissing her on both cheeks. Lingering kisses. "I've missed you. Geneva was boring without you." He ruffled her hair.

"Sorry," she said, inhaling his Vetiver scent. "Perhaps it's force of habit."

"But you've given all that up, haven't you?" he said. He put his hands inside her coat, ran his warm fingers down her spine.

"You think I'm overreacting?" she asked. "Just before I came here . . . there was an incident."

"*Quoi?* Criminal work again? You know your optic nerve's delicate, that stress could cause a rupture. You have been warned."

She didn't need him to tell her this again. She hadn't seen him since he returned from the medical convention in Switzerland and already they were off to a bad start. Maybe she should leave.

He looked at her coat. "What's this? Blood?"

"I think I need stitches."

"What's going on, Aimée?" he asked in alarm. He pulled her into an examining room. "You're paler than usual." He took her coat off, rolled up her sweater sleeve. "I'm so stupid . . . tell me about this incident . . . what happened?"

"I thought it was a graze but. . . ."

"Looks deep."

A black-red slit, the length of a toothpick, oozed below her elbow.

He lifted her onto the cold examining table. The white paper crinkled. "What happened?" Antiseptic smells of alcohol and pine soap wafted over her.

"A man died in my arms. Shot."

He stared at her, then pulled out disinfectant, surgical tweezers, needle, and thread.

"I should report this," he said, swabbing her arm with topical anesthetic. "What about your promise to stay out of trouble?"

She gritted her teeth.

With deft movements, he probed, pulled out a sliver of gray metal, and cleaned the wound. "Your leather sleeve protected you, it could have been much worse. What do the police say?"

She tried to ignore the stinging and his question as he sewed her up.

Outside the window, the half-moon hung over the foundry, bathing it in a pearlescent sheen. The glowing orb reflected on the glass roof.

"Guy, you make it sound as if I invited a bullet," she finally said, pulling back after his last stitch. She shivered, feeling cold.

"Four stitches. I suppose, for you, it's all in a day's work," he said.

"But it's not like that, Guy," she said as he taped a bandage to her arm.

"Take this for the pain," he said, handing her a glass of water and a pill. "Tell me what happened, Aimée. You trust me enough to come here to get stitched up, tell me the rest."

"I didn't want to get involved in anything. The Cao Dai say

giving back is as good as receiving. I just wanted to help." She downed the pill with water, took a deep breath and told him how she had tried to "give back" by doing Linh's errand.

"Then when you deliver this backpack to the nun, you're finished?" Guy asked.

"I better be," she said.

His gray eyes softened. She felt his tapered fingers on her neck, his wonderful long fingers.

"If I promise to be good . . ." she said.

"*Ah oui?* If you promise to be bad, that's another matter," he said, kissing her neck.

"Guy . . . no lectures, promise?"

"Lectures? That's all I've had for two weeks," he said. "I have other ideas in mind."

"Now that," she said, pulling him close, "won't be a problem."

"You know I missed you. Couldn't stop thinking about you."

"You told me. You're not on call *this time*, are you Guy?"

"At least not for another two hours," he said. "Even if there were a nuclear attack."

At least that's what she thought he said before his lips found hers. And then his fingers were massaging her spine, his breath in her ear. His scent in her hair.

"Now that we're together," he said, "I don't want to let go."

The paper crinkled under her. She ran her hands through his hair.

The phone rang and Guy kicked the examining room door shut with his left foot.

"Shouldn't you get that?"

"That's why I have an answering service."

"You do this often, doctor?"

"You're the first," he said, nibbling her ear.

Her skin tingled and warmth spread all over. She didn't want his hands to stop exploring.

"I've always loved your tattoo," he said, his breath on her back.

"The Marquesan lizard, the symbol of change, with the sacred tortoise inside?"

He grinned. "Why haven't we ever done it like this before?"

"Your old office was too small," she said and she nibbled at the nape of his neck.

He took off his white coat. "Is this better?"

"We'll have to find out, doctor," she said, pulling him on top of her.

GUY'S WATCH beeped in her ear. Her eyes opened to the examining room, bathed in the moon's dim reflection on the stainless steel. His arm shifted under her head and she remembered what they'd been doing. And how wonderful it had been.

"I have to hurry. I have hospital rounds in thirty minutes," he said, kissing her, then dressing hastily. "Sorry, I hate to leave you. Let me find you more medication before I go."

She sat up, found her shirt, and stretched.

Her cell phone rang.

"*Allô?*"

She heard a crackle and then Linh's voice. "Aimée, don't you have something for me?"

The nun's words brought it all back. The bullets ricocheting, Baret's lifeless body.

"*Oui*, but Linh," she said, "Thadée Baret's dead. Shot . . . there's more to this than. . . ."

She heard Linh gasp. "I can't talk now. There are men outside. Watching me."

"You mean . . . Linh, I'm surprised you entrusted me with . . ."

"Keep it safe," Linh said, her voice agitated. "I can't come now. We'll meet tomorrow."

"Wait a minute—"

But she'd hung up. Aimée hit the call back number. Only a buzz. Probably Linh had called from a public phone.

If people were watching Linh, and they had shot Baret . . . soon they'd be after her. If they weren't already.

She reached into the backpack to see what else was inside. What someone had tried to grab, what Thadée had been killed for. She loosened the buckles and lifted out several burnished silk-enfolded objects. She carefully unwrapped them and gasped. Jade animal figures. She took them out, one by one, and set them down on the stainless steel examining table. They looked like the animals of the zodiac she'd seen on the poster at the Cao Dai temple. The jade was intricately carved, and its opaque green milkiness radiated in the light. Exquisite. Eleven figurines, each no bigger than her palm.

Guy's office phone rang again. "Hold on, Aimée," he said from the hallway. "Let me take this call."

Aimée stared at the jade pieces. Even to her untrained eye, they seemed to belong in a museum. Small, slender jade disks crowned each figure, except for two which showed old breaks.

She fingered the smaller of the two loose jade disks. Worn lines, just visible, were carved into the jade. A kind of hexagram? She peered closer, realized the lines formed a primitive dragon.

She re-counted. Eleven zodiac figures: the Rat, Ox, Tiger, Rabbit, Snake, Horse, Goat, Monkey, Rooster, Dog, and Pig. Weren't there twelve zodiac signs? One was missing. The Dragon.

There was no way she was going to carry these treasures on the Métro to her office. She had to stow them somewhere safe, until tomorrow. Somewhere no one would think to look.

The moonlight suffused and softened the hard lines of the examining room. Surely they'd be safe here overnight. She could nip into the office early and tell Marie she'd forgotten something. Meet Linh outside, and deliver the backpack, with its contents, to her.

She opened the doors of white office cabinets filled with boxes of gloves, disposable syringes, and Steri-strips. Guy's office staff must stock them regularly. She opened the cabinet under the small sink. Flush with its side was a piece of white particle board, perhaps intended to be installed as a shelf. She removed the containers of bacterial soap, stuck the backpack inside, fitted the particle board in front, rearranged the soap and closed the cabinet door.

Guy walked in and handed her some pills. "Antibiotics to prevent infection and a stronger anti-inflammatory medication for your optic nerve. And go to the police. Doctor's orders."

He pulled on his raincoat. "Sorry, I have to rush to hospital rounds," he said, helping her into her coat. "You know, my apartment lease is ending and I'm looking for a new place. Bigger, in the suburbs." He touched her face, cupped her chin in his hands. "Wouldn't you like a modern place . . . somewhere near the Neuilly park for Miles Davis to run about in and bury bones?"

Where had this come from? Give up her seventeenth-century apartment on Ile St-Louis, with its pear tree in the courtyard, temperamental electricity and sparse hot water? For the suburbs and a commute to work?

Guy traced his fingers down her neck. "You could work from home. Do consulting."

Surprised, she pulled back. He was going too fast. "Guy, I'm a Paris rat, born and bred. I need to keep close to the sewers."

She still hadn't told him that she was half-American, afraid it would raise questions: questions she didn't know the answers to, about her American mother who had disappeared when Aimée was eight. Who had been linked to radicals and German terrorists in the 1970s.

"I like riding my bike to Leduc Detective," she said, neglecting to mention that her bike had been stolen the previous week. Again.

"My colleagues want to meet you," he said. He stared into her eyes, feathered her brow with kisses. His tone had turned serious. "Their wives keep busy in the suburbs and they wouldn't dream of moving back . . . the crime, pollution, the traffic and noise."

"Then I wouldn't have the Métro strikes to complain about," she said, keeping her tone light. Or the *grisaille* image of a Paris winter, light reflected off the roof tiles with a bluish hue, to enjoy outside her window.

The way this conversation was going disturbed her. Was he hinting at domestic *duties*?

He looked at his watch, then back at her and grinned. "To be continued later. Remember where we left off."

AIMÉE TOOK the Métro, changed twice, and waited by the Louvre-Rivoli kiosk until she felt sure no one had followed her. She took a deep breath, walked the well-lit half block to Leduc Detective, and found René at work on his computer. She hung up her coat and made espresso.

"I thought you drank green tea now," he said. "Part of your 'regimen' ".

He meant for her condition; she was still recovering from loss of vision caused by injuries inflicted in the vicious attack she'd suffered in the Bastille district.

"I drink that, too, René."

Homeopaths and Western medicine . . . she tried them all with an impatient wish for a miracle pill to strengthen her optic nerve. Time and tranquility—Guy's prescription—were what she didn't have.

Invoices were piled high on her mahogany desk. The office, apart from computers, scanners, and fax, had changed little since her father and grandfather's time. On the wall, old maps portrayed

Paris divided by arrondissement, one showing the ancient walls, the other the sewer tunnels webbing the foundations. The armoire containing her father's old uniform and her disguises stood by her grandfather's desk, his auction find, which had belonged to Vidocq, the former thief who had become Paris's first Police Inspector. The room was full of memories, the only history she had.

What had she gotten into now? She didn't want to lose all this. Or her livelihood.

"Things smell, René. Bad."

"How's that?"

"Sit down, René."

"But I am sitting," he said.

The yellow glow of the streetlight slanted across the parquet floor as René leaned back in his customized orthopedic chair. She sank into the Louis XV chair in need of re-upholstering, put her feet up on the *lit à la polonaise,* a Second Empire daybed, another auction find of her grandfather.

"Thadée Baret was shot. He died in my arms," she said.

René's large eyes bulged. "Were you hurt?"

"Just a graze. Guy stitched me up," she said. "I'm fine."

"Let me see," he said.

She flashed her bandage and told him the rest.

"Take that jade to the temple tomorrow, Aimée."

"I intend to," she said.

"I had no idea . . ." René's voice trailed off. He shook his head. "But we're in a crunch, I need help with the stats to clear this report by tomorrow's deadline."

"Bien sûr," she said. "Don't forget you encouraged me to do this favor for Linh."

"Aimée, I thought it would be simple. Don't forget your promise to stay away from this kind of thing," he said. "The promise to yourself. And me. Your new regimen and meditation."

She bit back a retort and stared at the statistics pile on her desk. Better make a dent in it. She worked silently for a half hour, preoccupied. Then she stopped.

Should she confide in René? She'd always dumped her love problems on him and asked his advice. "Guy wants us to move in together. In the suburbs!"

"You . . . living a doctor's wife's life, doing lunch?"

René turned away but not before she saw an odd expression on his face.

"What's the matter René? Are you afraid it spells disaster for our relationship?"

"Do you think it's your style, Aimée?"

She rubbed her eyes. Funny, he'd encouraged her to see Guy, her one-time eye surgeon, until their relationship grew intimate.

"The truth? I always thought. . . ." His words trailed off.

"Thought what, René?"

But he'd shut his laptop case and pulled on his custom-tailored raincoat. He avoided her gaze.

"I'm late," he said. "My Firewall Protection class at the Hacktaviste Academy starts in twenty minutes." He supplemented Leduc Detective's income by teaching hacking safeguards. Her guilt increased, knowing how the damp air aggravated his hip dysplasia, something he never mentioned.

"Saj will help us fine-tune the Olf project," he said. René had raved about his student Saj, the encryption genius. With work mounting, they needed help. And Saj, according to René, was a find. "Will you be all right, Aimée?"

"Look, René," she said, holding up the smallest jade disk, which she'd put in her pocket. Its milky-hued translucence shimmered in the light, mirroring René's green eyes.

René shook his head again. "I don't feel good about this."

"There's more, René. Linh said men were watching her and the temple."

"Call the *flics*."

"And say I ran away from a murder scene?" she interrupted. "That I may have been a target? And someone chased me?" She sat down, wishing her arm didn't still sting.

He paused at her desk, his laptop in his bag. Hurt, and something else, showed in his eyes. "You have to make up your own mind. Think of your future, your health, a relationship . . ."

"You're part of that, René."

But she spoke to the closed office door.

Why had she blurted out her dilemma about Guy? Was René afraid she'd give up Leduc Detective? She began to wonder . . . was *he* preparing to move on, to form an alliance with his friend who had a computer shop, or to go corporate? Tears welled in her eyes.

He'd get bored in a week. He'd hate corporate life. She imagined the snide remarks he'd endure about his size, told herself he wouldn't really do it, and buried her head in her hands.

The office, quiet for once, echoed with memories; her father's old typewriter in the corner and Leduc's first detective license, circa 1944, framed on the wall bearing her grandfather's prisonlike photo, the one where he looked like he had sucked a lemon.

All of her life was here.

Tears wet the Post-its on her desk. Could she walk away from all this, consult from a home office as Guy suggested? Could she run Leduc Detective by herself?

And what about René, who'd saved her life, and fought at her side when her world had fallen apart and she couldn't see? Taken up the slack, kept the agency running. And fed Miles Davis.

Why hadn't she seen it coming? Made him talk about it, listened to him?

So unlike René . . . he'd hesitate to tell her but . . . she

couldn't imagine not talking with him or sharing sushi take-out
when they worked late at the office.

She wiped her eyes, downed her pills. Took a deep breath and
switched on the computer. She couldn't lose René. Besides her
godfather Morbier and her dog, he was all the family she had. But
she had to put that aside; she'd call him later.

She booted up her computer and searched. Twenty minutes
later she found one entry specific to Cao Dai temple lands. A
1958 article, posted on an obscure mining website, by a
Frenchman named Gassot of the Mining Engineer Corps affiliated with the Sixth Battalion. This article, on geologic excava-
tions in Indochina, briefly mentioned a Cao Dai Temple and
nearby emperor's tomb that had been looted of national treasures. Chinese underground forces claimed that the missing
hoard, objects from the fourth century, belonged to them. But
Ho Chi-Minh and the French colonials laid claim to them, too.

The Vietnamese government blamed the Cao Dai, who were
safeguarding it—as Linh had said. The theft had occurred as
the 1954 Battle of Dien Bien Phu, the death knell for French
colonial rule in Indochina, raged. Aimée read between the
lines and figured the French had wanted the treasures for the
Louvre.

She found a Nicorette patch and stuck it under her clothes,
near her hip. Her mind spun. Jade, and a junkie dying in her arms
. . . what was it really about? Was the jade she had hidden part of
the looted treasure she'd just read about?

Her hands trembled. Time to go home.

"WORKING LATE again, Aimée?" asked Nico, the bald-
ing owner of her local café.

She kissed him on both cheeks. "How else can I keep Miles
Davis in dog food?"

He wiped the zinc counter as he set a glass down in front
of her. Worn stools and warmth from a working heater

accompanied by the pings of an old pinball machine in the corner gave the café a comfortable feeling.

"The usual?"

She nodded and he poured a glass of red wine. The dense garnet-red wine left a sediment in the bottom of the ballon-like glass. Nico was the kind of *mec* who listened to her stories when no one waited for her in her cold apartment under the sheets. A *mec* who would stifle a yawn and share a bottle at the zinc counter.

"Aimée . . . how are your eyes?"

"*Pas mal*. Haven't stopped me yet, Nico," she said.

"Not even the TGV can stop you when you get going, eh? As your papa used to say." He wiped his wet hands on his none-too-clean apron and untied it. "Share a *verre* with me, my treat?"

"Next time, Nico," she said.

He jerked his thumb toward an entwined couple nestled in the corner.

"They can't decide between a rough little Sangria or a smooth Veuve Clicquot." He winked. "Two ends of the spectrum. Do they want to dance on the table? Or feel it tomorrow, behind their eyeballs?"

The man in the far corner pointed to the champagne.

"*Excuse-moi*, a decision." He reached for the champagne flutes and a tray. "Back in a minute."

Aimée sipped her wine.

How could doing a simple favor for Linh have gone so wrong? And what should she do now? But the full-bodied wine with a smoky aftertaste had no answers.

She tried René's cell phone. No reply.

She set five francs down, bid Nico *à bientôt* and turned the corner to her apartment on quai d'Anjou. Fingers of fog curled under the Pont Marie and spilled over the wet, cobbled quai.

A figure walked a dog along the riverbank below. Two men

in wool overcoats stood by her door. Another joined them as she approached.

She gripped the pepper spray in her pocket.

"Mademoiselle Leduc?" said the one smoking a cigarette. Pale-faced and with dark, darting eyes, he emitted a bristling energy. The stubble on his head could have used a trim, or maybe he was growing out the shaved-head look.

"Hasn't your mother taught you manners? How to introduce yourself, and apologize for accosting a young woman alone?"

"Guess she forgot," he said, with a narrow-lipped smile. "In my job, it's not required."

"And what would that be?" She scanned the quai, saw one man behind the trunk of a plane tree, another against the stone wall, the barge lights silhouetting his cap. Not exactly a subtle show of force.

"I can't speak officially. Let's say I'm employed by someone who guards the common good. . . ."

"Someone with nasty methods?"

"It doesn't have to be that way," he said. "Now, show me what's in your bag."

He'd seen too many old movies. And the way he watched her, his eyes intent on her mouth, bothered her.

"What common good?"

"We work in the national interest."

Typical RG talk. Straight out of the Renseignements Généraux manual. One of the men shifted, the gravel crunching under his feet by the wall.

"You'll have to show me some ID. I'd feel stupid if I were to be robbed on my own doorstep."

The two men moved closer and she backed up, pulling out her pepper spray.

"Back off or I start screaming and you get this in the face."

She wished she had her Beretta. But those days were over.

No more climbing over rooftops or hanging from rusted pipes. She'd promised.

"*Du calme*," he said, and flashed his card.

"I can't read it," she said pulling out a flashlight. At least she could smack one of them in the face with it and get the talker with the spray.

"Fabien Regnier, Renseignements Généraux," she read. "Guess you think that impresses people."

"Not you, I'm sure," he said. "But you've dealt with us before, on contract. In a ministry surveillance context, remember?"

She bit her lip. The ministry surveillance on which her father had been killed in an explosion. It had been five years ago, but was as vivid to her as if it were yesterday. She'd never known the RG were involved.

"So for old time's sake, hand over the bag," he said.

"Just like that, out here on the cobblestones? You've got more balls than you were born with, expecting me to . . ."

"We want what's ours," he said, lowering his voice.

"You have no authority," she said. "What do you mean, *yours?*"

"I think you know."

Two additional men drifted from the shadows, a stocky red-haired man and a lean one with a stringy ponytail down his back. They enclosed her in a tight ring. The red-haired one spread a much-thumbed *France-Soir* newspaper over the wet cobbles. Fabien Regnier, if that was his real name, gripped her bag. She winced as he emptied it, shining *her* flashlight on the contents as he picked through her Nicorette patches, ultra black mascara, a broken turquoise earring, her worn Vuitton wallet, cell phone, Chanel No.5 purse-sized atomizer, well-thumbed cryptography manual, Swiss Army knife, the holy card from her father's funeral, an Egyptian coin, and a letter containing Guy's poem.

"*C'est de la poésie, ça?*" asked one of the men reading the poem with a furrowed brow. "Calling you a wild orchid, your rose complexion's rough beauty . . ."

"That's personal," she interrupted.

"But it's very well written, Mademoiselle." Fabien Regnier grinned, passing it around. It infuriated her. They were looking through a window into Guy's soul and using it for a cheap laugh.

"Where did you put it?" he asked. His eyes were hard. He leaned close to her face. "The *jade*."

She had to think fast. "Since you know so much, how come you don't know it's gone?" she said, making it up as she went along. "*Pfft*, stolen from my office while someone barricaded me in the supply room."

"How convenient!"

"Not really, but it didn't belong to me. And I don't think it belongs to you."

"Stolen property must go back to where it came from."

Had Baret stolen the jade to sell to Linh?

"What do you mean? How does the jade connect to you at the RG?"

"That's not your concern." Fabien Regnier snapped his fingers.

As Aimée looked up she caught the eye of the hawk-nosed man who approached. Lean and in his late fities, his cap brim low over his hooded eyes: she knew him. Recognized him from the unit that had contracted for Leduc's services for the Place Vendôme surveillance. He'd been the one holding her back as she screamed, seeing her father's charred limbs on the cobblestones.

Tension knotted her shoulders.

"We don't want to have to mess up your apartment but—"

"Go ahead, it's a mess already. The contractor makes sure of that."

"Actually, we already have," he said. "You need a new contractor."

"What? Where's your search warrant?"

Fabien Regnier picked up his cell phone; it must have vibrated on his hip. And then she noticed the butterscotch colored plug in his ear. An audio amplifier?

"*Oui*," he said, turning to answer it. A moment later, he clicked off, nodding to the others who fell back. He whispered in her ear, "If, as you say, you don't have it, we want you to find it. That's your priority now. Your career here, in Europe, anywhere in the world, depends on it. Your agency, your apartment, even your dog's yearly rabies shots, depend on it."

She stiffened.

"Good evening," he said, giving her his card. "See, mother did teach me some manners." And got into a waiting car.

SHE FELT so weak she had to force herself to climb the worn marble stairs to her dark apartment. This stank worse than overripe Camembert. The RG's tentacles extended everywhere: their calling cards were intimidation, blackmail, and wiretaps. She never understood how people could refer to them as the good guys, likening them to the FBI or MI5. Then again, maybe it was apt after all.

Miles Davis, her bichon frisée puppy, greeted her with a wet nose and wagging tail. At least he was fine. She hit the switch of her hall chandelier and fiddled with the radiator. The only response was a dribble of heat and a sputtering, angry knock in the pipes.

She gasped at the mess they'd made, though the RG had a method to their ransacking. Neat piles of papers and her clothing sat in the middle of the rooms. Her computer lay untouched, thank God, but her armoires hung open. Drawers in several old chests were pulled out, too. Did they think she'd stash the jade in her apartment and leave it?

Thinking of Fabien Regnier going through her things made her sick. They'd dirtied everything by their presence.

Who was the black-leather-clad figure on the motorcycle?

Was he, too, with the RG? And where did the hawk-nosed man from the Place Vendôme, who'd witnessed her father's death, fit in? What did this imply?

She forked the last of the horsemeat into Miles Davis's chipped Limoges bowl. These days, a *boucherie chevaline* with the gold horse head above it, the sign of a horsemeat butcher, was harder to find in the *quartier* than a child without Nintendo.

She kicked off her boots, hung up her damp coat, reached in the pocket for a cigarette and remembered she'd quit. *Merde!* Papers crinkled. Her hand held something; the envelope she'd meant to give Baret. She remembered how he'd clutched her coat . . . what had he said . . . Nadège, Sophie? She slit open the envelope Linh had given her. Inside lay a cashier's check for fifty thousand francs.

Linh had been buying the jade! Stolen jade? If Linh had asked her to make the exchange, because she was under surveillance . . . well, now the RG were watching *her*.

She shivered and pulled on the ski parka she wore when the heater refused to cooperate. So far, it had happened every night this week. But the chill in her bones wasn't just from the cold.

She pushed aside the tool box. If only the contractor would sheetrock the rest of the kitchen wall. Two weeks and she'd only seen him once. And then she got to work, putting away her things, cleaning up the mess the RG left. A quick, cursory job. They must have been watching her apartment, known she hadn't returned. After an hour, her arm throbbed but she'd put away most of the piles.

She looked inside her small box of a refrigerator. Nothing except an expensive eye cream the woman at the Samaritaine cosmetics counter assured her performed wonders. So far, she hadn't noticed a difference. A runny Reblochon and *pain rustique* waited on the counter. But her appetite had disappeared. She hit the red blinking message-machine button. One message.

"Aimée . . . I thought you'd be home . . ." Guy's voice said. Unsure and annoyed.

A click, and he'd hung up.

Her heart sank. Regnier and the RG had heard this, too.

"Looks like you and me, Miles, and the brick."

She turned on the oven and stuck a brick inside to warm. In an hour, she'd put the hot brick in her bed and keep toasty all night: a trick her grandfather had learned in the war when charcoal was scarce.

She climbed into bed, weary, her arm aching, but she couldn't stop the thoughts spinning in her head.

Endlessly.

Aimée pushed the duvet down. She slipped on wool socks and an old bathrobe of her father's. Below, blue barge lights on the Seine reflected off the glistening wet stone Pont Marie. Pigeons, nesting in the pear tree below, in the courtyard, cooed.

In the dim salon, she powered up her laptop. Who was Thadée Baret? All she knew was he had possessed stolen jade— stolen from whom she didn't know—and needed money. One didn't go out in raw November weather without a coat unless to dash down to a nearby *tabac* or a café below one's apartment. Certainly not with a backpack of valuable jade. So she figured he had lived close by the place where he had died.

Start with the obvious, her father had always said. Sometimes it worked and saved time. She searched in the phone book. No listing.

Online, she hacked into the standard financial databanks, a practice she and René performed routinely to find someone's credit history. There was no credit card issued in his name. Talk about flying below the radar. Bank account searches required more time, so she put that aside.

He'd looked arty, had an *intello* air, a former junkie by the old marks on his arm . . . was he a *gauche caviar* who'd squandered the family wealth? Searching further, she checked university registrations for the past fifteen years. Ecole nationale d'administration, then of Political Science. Nothing. Not even at the Ecole des Beaux-arts.

If he needed money . . . drugs? But his tracks were old. Gambling? Wait a minute, she'd forgotten something. Paper had rustled in her pocket . . . why hadn't she checked it? She ran, her wool socks padding softly on the floor, to the coatrack in her hallway, and emptied her pockets. Besides the envelope, there was a half of a torn PMU—*Pari mutuel urbain*—horse race betting slip. She remembered the sounds accompanying his phone call. Like a café-*tabac* in the background, where bets were taken. It must have been a local place, where he awaited her call.

She'd investigate tomorrow. After she retrieved the jade from Guy's office. It would be a place to start. Getting the RG off her back was a bigger problem.

In her bedroom, she sat crosslegged and put the small jade disk on the window ledge. It glowed in the light. Ethereal. A circle of beauty. She closed her eyes, tried to empty her mind. Concentrate. Inhaling, exhaling, counting her breaths.

But the images of the jade animals floated above her, as if they were pulling her back to consciousness. She saw the mocking smile of the jade monkey, then the hawk-nosed man. And felt the stinging and smarting of her stitches.

She rubbed her eyes. The corners of her vision blurred. Nervously, she washed down a pill with bottled Vichy water. Her dreams echoed with the insistent cawing of the crows nesting over the *boulangerie* where Baret had been shot—loud and grating. Their flapping, glossy, obsidian-black wings tried to tell her something. Dawn found her on the floor, shivering.

Tuesday Evening

HERVÉ GASSOT DIPPED HIS fingers in the icy holy water font of the nineteenth-century church. He stuck his cap in his wool overcoat pocket, smoothed down his fringe of white hair and sat in the worn pew. He ignored the *tsk, tsk* of an old woman woman bent in prayer as he lifted his artificial leg onto the kneeler. His prosthesis, stiff on the cold unforgiving stone floor, had rebelled.

Candles sputtered by the saints' statues, their scent of burning wax as familiar as the low drone of prayer from the confessionals. He bowed his head and prayed for his stupid *camarade*, Albert, from his old regiment. Albert, who'd earned the *croix de guerre* at Dien Bien Phu, had gone to the *clinique*, between the plumber's and Communist party office, for a routine cardiogram and ended up on a cold slab in the morgue.

The priest made the sign of the cross, ending the evening rosary. Gassot stood and went to shake hands with the younger priest who wore a clerical collar and jogging shoes as he passed out the liturgy calendar.

"*Bonsoir, mon père,*" he said.

"Don't forget the sing-along liturgy tomorrow, *mon fils,*" the priest said.

But Gassot knew neither he, nor the church congregation, all over sixty, would make that a priority. Out in the vestibule, the white marble gleamed in the low light.

On the church steps, Picq, one of the few left from his regiment in Indochina, sidled up next to Gassot, lighting two unfiltered Gitanes. He offered one to Gassot, who accepted, inhaled the woody tobacco, and exhaled into the night air.

"The first one to go, eh?" Gassot said, shaking his head. "And in a careless way, but that sums up Albert."

"Not careless," Picq said. He wore a blue raincoat that

matched the hard blue of his rheumy eyes. He leaned close to Gassot's shoulder. "Lucie's upset, something strange with the doctor's report. I showed it to my nephew, the *médecin*."

Médecin? Picq's nephew had flunked out of medical school and made false teeth now. And a good living.

"Funny red pinpoints in his eyes," Picq said. "And bruising on his neck."

Gassot's shoulders tensed. "But he went for a cardiogram and his heart gave out!"

"Not according to my nephew," Picq said. His eyes narrowed. "You know what that means."

"But he was in a clinic!"

Picq jumped to conclusions. Always had. Still Gassot's stomach twisted.

Albert had always worried he'd be the first one they caught up with: Their miscalculations had wiped out the village near Dien Bien Phu, but it had been by mistake.

"Lucie said the strangest thing," Picq continued. "Albert's pants' cuff was rolled up when she claimed his body."

"Eh, so what?" Gassot said.

"Rolled up beyond the tattoo on his ankle."

Gassot stiffened. *The dripping knife.* They each had one.

"That could mean anything."

"Try convincing yourself after reading the report from the Préfecture," Picq said. "They're calling it suspicious, starting an investigation. It all began after the jade reappeared."

The jade?

"We've been looking for years. . . . How can you be sure?"

"Use your head, Gassot," he said. "We had a lead. Albert blabbed and shot it to hell."

"You call that rumor a lead?"

"Seems the *mec* took the bait. . . ."

"Wait a minute Picq, what bait?"

"We got to talking, I had every intention of telling you."

Picq shrugged. "But Albert challenged this guy. Told him 'If the jade's resurfaced in Paris, prove it.' To force his hand we offered him a cut if he discovered it. He doublecrossed us and took some bullets in the back."

Gassot clenched his teeth. "Why didn't you tell me?"

"It happened right over there." Picq pointed to the boulangerie.

Harebrained schemes. Imagining themselves rogue warriors but they were just foolish old men like himself.

"Did he have the jade?"

"We don't know," Picq said.

Gassot wanted to distance himself from his comrades but he had to know the extent of the damage they'd done.

"Tomorrow, meet me at the market," Gassot said. "Bring Nemours. We'll talk."

"Watch your back."

Gassot always did.

He rolled up his collar against the chill and limped through the shadows cast by sodium streetlamps' light filtering through the trees. He tried unsuccessfully to ignore his fears.

Fools! What kind of mess had they dragged him into?

The jade had belonged to them . . . they'd discovered it while surveying land, buried in a metal ammunition box by the old emperor's tomb. By rights it was theirs: To the victor belongs the spoils.

But at Dien Bien Phu they had been losers and the box had disappeared. Gassot clutched his phantom leg and leaned into a darkened doorway.

He closed his eyes but he saw the monsoon-swollen Nam Ron river, engorged with dark green silt and bloated bodies. Heard the crackle of gunfire, the drone of C-119s so low they whipped leaves off the mango trees, and the whimpering of someone in the bushes. And that's when it happened. Not the landmine half-buried in the red earth he avoided stepping on, but sniper fire, had shredded his calf and ankle. The piercing, tearing pain brought him to his good knee. His hands had come back covered with his own blood and gristle. Sniper bullets spit all around and he crawled, pulling himself toward the mangroves.

Adrenalin propelled him and then the chalky earth gave way and he was in a hole, a bombed out Vietminh tunnel on the warm, wet body of a moaning man. A Vietnamese holding his blood-soaked arm. "Help me and I help you," the man said. "I know a way out. To the temple. No fighting there."

What chance did he have? None by himself in the enemy trenches.

"Call me Jin," the man said, "My father worked in France. The Vietminh don't trust me."

Gassot had taken off his ammo belt, wrapped it tourniquet-style around Jin's arm, and staunched the blood. He unscrewed the canteen of Courvoisier that General de Castries had issued to the corps for courage, drank, and shared with Jin. Then he bit a morphine tablet in two, put half in Jin's mouth and swallowed the other half. He gritted his teeth and bound the loose muscle shreds of his own leg with his shirt. "Show me," he'd said. "We have to move while we can." While the morphine lasted.

Somehow he'd crawled and half-dragged Jin through the tunnel all afternoon—cries, cannon fire and earth-pounding explosions above them. The cognac had loosened Jin's tongue and he'd sung folksongs. In the evening, when the smoke settled by the river, the French troops had surrendered and he'd never seen Jin again.

Gassot had survived prison camp. Bamboo cages, and rice gruel if they were lucky. A concrete hole and all the rice paddy rats they could catch when they weren't. Gangrene had set in and a Parisian-trained Vietminh doctor had amputated his leg above the knee.

Gassot shook off the memories. What was he doing, reliving the past again, huddled in a doorway on a cold, wet street?

He headed home to where Avenue de Clichy intersected a maze of narrow streets. He lived in a hotel on the Clichy side, by the derelict marshalling yards of the old steam train line. Once the fief of Mérovingian king Dagobert and much later, home to Verlaine who taught at the nearby *lycée*; Manet and Renoir's ateliers; Georges Simenon's first Paris address; Captain Dreyfus's apartments, Proust's suite, Colette's despised aunt's bourgeois apartment; the area in which Zola found inspiration for Nana, the courtesan of his novel. And Ho Chi-Minh. Now, they wouldn't know it.

He entered his third-floor room. There was no elevator, but the stairs kept him in shape. Going down was the hard part. He opened the door to the back steps. Always keep an escape route, he remembered their commander saying.

Indochina had lain in rubble and the République ignored its soldiers. Gassot even had to fight for his pension. But the old Colonials, rich and fat with the spoils of Indochina, had thrived. Still thrived.

Gassot hung up his jacket, unstrapped his prosthesis, set it by the door next to his shoes, and lay on his cot-sized bed. He set his alarm clock and switched off the light. Only the occasional red blink of neon from the kebab shop sign below illuminated his wall giving the military calendar a blood-red glow.

Gassot put his hands behind his head on the pillow. The past invaded and permeated his thoughts. After the camp released him, he'd recovered, tended by Bao. He remembered the incessant *gyaow-gyaow* of the cicadas in the hot, still night and the black satin sheen of her hair brushing her slim waist. The aroma of the herbal cloths she laid on his fever-wracked head mingling with the tamarind scent wafting through the blown-out windows. They'd camped in an abandoned yellow stucco, green-shuttered colonial villa, its rococo interior pockmarked by bullet holes. Until the Underground—a ragtag alliance of Ho's deserters—found her. Took her on a forced labor march.

Repatriated to France, he'd done physical therapy in the army hospital in Toulon, been given a fake leg. Gotten an engineering job at the Citroën factory. Luckier than most, he always told himself. The old Indochina existed in his memories, revisited only via crackling newsreels.

Then he saw the paper napkin slipped under his door, the way the waiter let him know he'd had a phone call. Picq and Nemours never used the phone. His heart pounded.

Scribbled on the napkin were the words "You a dirty old man, Gassot? A *mec* called to tell you that he's going to roll your pants up."

Wednesday Morning

RENÉ PASSED THE LINE of people buying newspapers and Métro passes at his corner *tabac*. A man stood reading a newspaper and smoking in the chill gray mid-morning.

"*Bonjour*," René said as he opened the door of the shoe repair shop a few doors down from his apartment.

The new apprentice, whom René didn't know, affixed taps to a pair of heels. Loud grinding noises filled the narrow shop crammed with shelves of arch supports and insoles, shoes to be worked on, shoes to be called for.

The young man switched off the grinding wheel. He wore a blue work coat with FRANCK embroidered on the pocket, that was marked with glue smears, over patched jeans. He looked down at René, took in his short stature.

The usual stare.

"Picking up for someone?" Franck asked, rubbing his hands on his pockets. His gaze hadn't left René's long trunk and short legs.

René pointed to the polished handmade Italian shoes on the shelf.

"Actually, that pair's mine. What's the damage?"

Franck lifted the shoes from the counter. "Nice! Eh, they fit you?"

"Should fit even better with the orthotics your boss put in."

René's hip dysplasia made arch adjustments necessary every other month. His hip ached more and more in the damp weather.

"I didn't know . . . well, I mean . . ."

"That I wear regular shoes?" he said, taking a fifty franc note from his wallet and reaching up to set it on the counter. He buttoned his coat. "Even a cashmere coat."

A cheap shot. He wanted to take it back as soon as he'd said it.

A sullen look crossed Franck's face. "Guess you have to, so you feel big."

René saw the worn jacket on the peg and Franck's HLM— Habitation à Loyer Moderée—application for subsidized housing peeking from the pocket. He took the shoes.

"*Merci*," he said and pocketed his change.

He left the shop, glad he hadn't said the owner was an old friend who would have fired Franck on the spot for his comment. Everyone needed a job these days. He, too, after looking at Leduc's finances.

Though he'd encouraged her at the outset, Aimée had jumped into the nun's affair without thinking. As usual. Impulsive, intuitive! It didn't pay the bills.

He paused on the cracked pavement to check his phone messages. The battery was dead. No time to charge his cell phone. As he turned back to buy a phone card at the *tabac* he noticed the man was still reading the newspaper. But he was holding *Le Monde Diplomatique* upside down.

After René bought a card and left, the man folded his

paper. René watched the reflection in the store windows from the corner of his eye. Saw the man keeping a short distance between them. René kept walking. He glanced over his shoulder several times. The man kept in step a few paces behind. Afraid his short legs would give out before he got far, he thought of what Aimée would do, and hailed a taxi.

At the Métro station, he paid the driver, climbed out and ran down the steps. He changed at République, then again in the cavernous Châtelet station. By the time he left, using the Louvre-Rivoli exit, he felt sure no one was following him. Still, he sat in the café below their office and had a snifter of brandy. When he had calmed down, he paid and left a big tip.

On the rain-slicked pavement outside Leduc Detective, a smiling couple asked him directions to the Saint Eustache church. He pointed the way, then hit the digicode. Inside their building, the wire-frame birdcage of an elevator was out of service—out of service more often than in service. He faced a climb of three high floors on the dark, narrow spiral staircase to the office. He paused, wondering how the world would look from two feet higher up.

His hip ached and he dreaded a discussion with Aimée. Right now his cowardly side wanted some way out. He'd ignored the flutter he'd felt deep down the last time she'd hugged him. The hope that soared and flew away as he reminded himself that for her, it was platonic.

At the second flight of stairs, he paused. His leg throbbed and only a hot epsom salt bath would ease the bone-chill in his marrow.

"Monsieur Friant . . . Monsieur René Friant?" a man's voice called from above.

"*Oui.*"

"There's been an accident," he said, footsteps clattered down the stairs. "Mademoiselle Leduc's in Emergency."

"*Nom de Dieu!* What happened?" His pulse raced.

Something to do with her eyes? A car accident? He pumped his legs faster. Had she been trying to call him on his dead cell phone?

He never saw their faces as they blocked the light, only felt the net over his face and arms, hands pinning him down as he struggled.

Wednesday Morning

AIMÉE SAW TWO BLUE and white police cars parked on the pavement of rue de Chazelles in front of Guy's office.

"Not a professional job," the *flic* was saying to Marie, the receptionist.

She saw the broken door lock and overturned chairs. Heard the static of police walkie-talkies.

"I don't understand," Marie said, shaking her head. "The small narcotic supply we keep under lock and key wasn't touched. Dr. Lambert and his partners have just renovated this office. New cabinets, redone the examining rooms . . . *tout!*"

The *flic* nodded, writing in his notebook. "Knocking off a pharmacy makes more sense. There've been several break-ins this month."

"Excuse me, I'm Dr. Lambert's patient and I forgot my bag. I've come for it."

"There's nothing here," Marie said. "We've had a robbery."

Aimée felt guilty. She should have stashed it somewhere else. "May I just check the examining room?"

"We're dusting for fingerprints," the *flic* said. "You'll have to wait."

Just then Guy walked into the office, his coat beaded with rain. His eyes widened in surprise when he saw her.

"Dr. Lambert, I've already called the insurance company," said the receptionist. "The claims adjuster's on the way."

"Good job, Marie," he said, taking in the damage with a glance. "I left at six-thirty. I was on call and had rounds at l'hôpital des Quinzes-Vingts. They must have broken in after that."

"Thank you doctor, I'll talk with you in a moment."

Aimée took Guy aside.

"I feel sick that this happened."

Guy's eyes softened.

"Does your arm hurt?"

Aimée shook her head. "Not much." Only when she breathed. The fingerprinter, carrying his metal case, edged past them into the reception area.

"Didn't you go to the police last night?" he asked.

"Guy, I left something in that room . . ."

"*What?*"

"I have to get in there," she said edging toward the examining room. "Please!"

"You don't mean . . ."

"Just block the door. For one minute."

She slipped past him into the antiseptic white room. A rain of stainless steel instruments and surgical gloves littered the linoleum floor. The cabinets lay open and gaping. She bent down. Under the sink, the bacterial soaps had been pushed aside, the particle board was askew. The backpack with the jade was gone.

She stood up. Stumbled. Guy grabbed her arm. Concern and anger warred in his eyes.

"You owe me an explanation," he said.

"I meant to tell you. It's my fault, I thought it would be safe here."

She looked around the trashed office, sick. Patients arrived and Marie ushered them into the hallway.

"Of course, I'll pay you for all the damage," she said. "Guy, I'm so sorry."

"What hurts, Aimée, is that you *didn't* tell me." He shook his head. "Even after. . . ." He stared at the examining table. "Why didn't you go to the police?"

"Guy, I knew you wouldn't want me to keep it, and I couldn't turn it over to them. . . ."

"Why not?"

Guy had never broken a law in his life. She doubted he'd even gotten a traffic ticket: A rare Frenchman who never parked illegally, drove too fast, or cheated on his taxes. He didn't know the other side, the world outside the law, where things didn't work like that.

"Last night, the RG were waiting outside my apartment," she said. "They threatened me that I'd never work again if I didn't turn the bag over to them. They had ransacked my place, too. There's a lot more behind this than I suspected."

He shook his head. "I thought you had changed, that you wanted a new start, not a job that endangered your eyesight and your life," he said, his gray eyes hard. "But you haven't changed. You never will."

"Please, Guy, it's not like that. Try to understand!"

"Dr. Lambert, we'll take your statement now," the *flic* said, as he entered the examining room. "If you'll come with me, please."

"Of course," he said.

The policeman's back was turned and she put her finger over her lips, then mouthed "Please" to Guy. But she couldn't read his expression.

Out in the reception area, she heard Marie. "Dr. Lambert, the adjuster's here to estimate damages."

Aimée edged past the policemen to Marie's desk. "Please tell Dr. Lambert I'll call him later."

She left the office, emerging into rue de Chazelles. What

had she done? She called the temple, left a message for Linh that she was en route, and took the Métro to the Cao Dai temple.

By the temple's storefront window, Linh came into view, her eyes bright under a hooded burnt orange shawl, her hands placed together in greeting. Aimée's heart sank. There was no way around it; she had to tell Linh the truth. She took a deep breath and even though she wanted to run in the opposite direction, said, "Linh, I'm sorry. There's no other way to say it," she said. "The jade's been stolen."

"What do you mean?" Linh stepped back, shocked.

"Forgive me. I hid the pieces of jade, and someone broke in . . ."

"But Thadée gave them to you, *non?*"

Aimée nodded.

"Everything's gone?"

Aimée reached in her pocket. "Here's the envelope you gave me for him."

"How do I know you're not lying?"

"Someone must have followed me and stolen the jade after I hid it in my doctor's office."

"Why hide it there?"

"I needed stitches. I knew the doctor. I'm sorry, I thought it would be a good hiding place."

"Stitches . . . why?"

"From a bullet's ricochet," she said. "Linh, I'm all right, but Thadée Baret . . . was shot and killed."

Linh closed her eyes, fingering her amber beads.

Aimée felt sick with guilt. "My mistake." Then she remembered. The jade disk! She reached into her coat pocket.

"I do have this."

Hope, then sadness, filled Linh's eyes. "So you did have the jade." She nodded. "You must find the rest and get them back for me."

"Forgive me," Aimée said. "But . . . why didn't you warn me? Why did you entrust such things to me, almost a stranger?"

"I had no choice." Linh's eyelids fluttered in the nervous mannerism Aimée remembered. "The Communists' grip has loosened. Next year or the one after, the country will open up to foreign trade. We should be able to return too. But to legitimize and rebuild our congregation, we must have the jade."

"Legitimize in what way?"

The wind rose and whipped around them. "If we want to return, we must give the jade to the government. It's a national treasure that was in our care. The Cao Dai safeguarded it. Then just before the French left, it was stolen from us. It must be returned to my country."

"This jade was looted during the battle of Dien Bien Phu?"

Linh nodded.

"But how did Baret come to have it in his possession?"

"We've searched for a long time. We don't know how he ended up with the jade. All I know was that he needed money, quickly, and promised to deliver the jade in return."

"We should go somewhere and talk," Aimée said.

Cockleburs fallen from the row of chestnut trees littered the wet pavement. Ahead, steam billowed from the Métro grill vents. Passersby pulled their collars up and fastened their winter coats tighter.

Linh looked behind her. "It's not safe," she said. "Keep walking while I explain. There's a whole culture of jade," Linh told Aimée. "The ancients revered jade's durability and luminous quality. Jade was believed to be a sacred embodiment of essential vital forces; it was used for ritual objects with cosmological and religious meaning."

"Used how?" Aimée asked.

"To channel supernatural powers, to communicate between the mortal and celestial worlds."

Aimée recalled the aura she'd felt radiating from the pieces.

Buses shot past on the wide boulevard. A siren resounded in the distance. In front of them, two women with wheeled shopping carts met and exchanged *bisous* on each cheek.

Linh pulled Aimée closer. "The vital force, the power of jade to channel the spirits of the other world, still exists."

She gave the envelope containing the cashier's check back to Aimée. "You're my only hope. Keep this and the disk you still have. Find the rest for me."

"But I wouldn't know where to start."

"Gassot, a French engineer, saved my father's life at Dien Bien Phu. I never was able to thank him. He knew about the jade."

Gassot . . . that name. He'd written the article she'd found online, about jade looted from the Emperor's Tomb.

"Do you know if he's still alive?"

"I have no idea."

"How did you meet Baret?"

"I didn't," Linh said, pulling her robe's hood closer about her head. "He contacted the temple. He knew we'd been searching. We'd heard a rumor that the jade was in Paris."

"What rumor?"

"Something about an auction catalogue?" Linh asked, shaking her head. "I don't know about these things. I understand your country less and less every day. Bloodshed. . . that's not our way. We don't believe in taking life, not even an animal's."

Yet, Linh came from a country that had been at war almost continuously for the past hundred years. Aimée had to keep her on track. "Linh, what about Baret?"

"He telephoned and said it had to be arranged quickly, but as we were the rightful owners, we could have the jade for a small payment. Somehow, I felt that he had a good heart."

A good heart?

"Bad luck curses those who have evil intentions," Linh said. "You will find the jade. I count on you."

Guilt warred with Aimée's promise to steer clear of this kind of thing.

Linh paused at the temple door. "Follow where this disk leads you."

And Aimée knew she would. Not only to restore the jade to Linh and subvert the RG's agenda, but also because, somehow, the trail might lead back to her father.

AIMÉE STOOD in yet another café-*tabac* in the Clichy *quartier*, drumming her chipped boa-blue nails on the zinc counter. So far, in the six she'd visited, no one had seen or remembered Baret. If she had to drink yet another espresso she'd sprint down Avenue de Clichy and never fall asleep again.

"*Une tisane, s'il vous plaît*," she said, ordering an herbal tea. She caught the owner's eye during a lull between commuters buying Métro passes and Lotto tickets. She pulled out the PMU betting receipt, handed it to him, and he ran it through the machine.

She was about to engage him in conversation when he slapped one hundred francs on the counter. "You won."

Aimée had never won anything in her life. But she took the hundred francs. Thadée didn't need it now.

"Monsieur, it belongs to my friend Thadée Baret. Maybe you remember, I called last evening and you passed him the phone?"

"Not me," he said, ringing up a sale. "Too busy. Me, I work the early shift."

"*Bon*, who would have answered?"

He shrugged and turned to another waiting customer.

"Monsieur, it's important. Do you know who worked last night?" she asked, determined to discover more about Baret.

"Ask Gérard," he said. "He's stocking the beverage shipment."

Aimée wound past the curved zinc and old streaked bubbled mirrors lining the café. Mechanics in jumpsuits, workers in blue smock coats and an old man with his dog at his feet sipped a morning espresso or *un demi de bière blonde*. This was a working class pocket of the old Paris like the one she had known growing up.

"*Pardonnez-moi*, Gérard?" she asked a thirtyish man, buff but bulky, in a T-shirt and stovepipe jeans, lugging a crate of Stella Artois beer.

"Did you work last night?" she asked, her feet crunching sugar cube wrappers littering the floor.

"Why?"

She pulled out the PMU racing receipt and twenty francs. "Maybe you sold my friend Thadée the winning ticket. If so, I owe you a little thank you."

"Congratulations, but I was at the gym," he said.

"So, who should I talk to?" she said.

Gérard jerked his thumb at a middle-aged man, tying an apron around his waist, by the orange juice squeezer.

"*Alors*, Jojo, something to brighten your morning," he shouted.

Aimée smiled at the man. "Did you answer the phone last night when I called for Thadée Baret?"

"Eh? Speak up," Jojo said.

She noticed the calluses on his hands.

She held out the form. "Did you sell this to Thadée?"

"I sell a lot of those," he said, "more than a hundred yesterday."

Great. "Of course, but when I called around 5:30 you passed the phone to Thadée. Remember, a *mec* with glasses, no coat?"

He nodded. "Comes in here almost every day. A nice guy."

Heartened, she grinned. "Here's twenty, he wanted to share his winnings with you."

"So I brought him luck!" Jojo squeezed another orange on the spinning machine. Juice trickled through the thick orange pulp.

Aimée didn't want to inform him just what kind of luck.

"Know where I can find him, now?"

"At work, I'd guess," he said.

"Where's that?"

Jojo's eyes narrowed. "How'd you get his ticket anyway?"

"He gave it to me," she said. "Said he moved. And I've got to give his money to him."

Despite the reluctance in Jojo's eyes, he wiped his hands and pocketed the twenty francs. "He lives above the art gallery on rue des Moines. The *chichi* place."

Elated, she buttoned her coat.

"*Merci,*" she said.

Now she had somewhere to start.

AIMÉE KNOCKED on the closed door of Galerie 591, a renovated warehouse. Rain pattered on the cobblestones. She wound her black wool scarf tighter against the chill, trying to figure out what she'd say. Posters advertised an upcoming British collage exhibition. She peered inside the darkened gallery: framed oils, collages, and metal sculptures filled the space. Upscale, and with prices to match, no doubt.

The gallery lay one street over from where Thadée had been shot. She figured he'd cut through a back courtyard or passage to rue Legendre. Didn't most of these warehouses have rear courtyards?

A wrought iron fence closed off a long courtyard leading to the gallery entrance. Further on stood more warehouses, some converted into lofts. Aimée opened the creaking gate, and used the house phone to call the gallery's number. As she stood under the eaves by a leaf-clogged gutter, she heard the echo of the gallery phone ringing. Her call went unanswered.

A dilapidated tire factory crumbled under a soot-encrusted glass roof at the rear of the couryard, the faded sign bearing the letters PNEUS in blue type. Huddled next to it was what looked like an old car parts warehouse from the thirties.

She crossed the courtyard from the art gallery to a doorway under the sign GRAPHIX. Strains of jazz came from inside. She pushed the door open and saw a space divided into red cubicles, each containing a drawing board.

"Is anyone here?"

"You lost?" asked a man wearing a black ribbed turtleneck sweater. His shaved head glinted in the light focused on his desk. Rain beat a murmur on the dirty glass roof.

"Does Thadée live next door?"

"You mean the gallery owner?" Irritation shone in his eyes. "I imagine he did."

Aimée thought it best to feign ignorance. "Did? What do you mean?"

"Far as I know, he's at the morgue. His ex-wife made a scene this morning when the *flics* came."

So she'd found his home. Now the next step. Try her hunch.

"You mean Sophie?" she asked. If that name didn't ring a bell she'd try the other one.

He nodded, bent over his drawing. An uphill battle, this conversation. He had the personality of wallpaper paste. Lumpy, and sticking in all the wrong places.

"Did Sophie go with the *flics* or . . ." She hesitated to say *to identify the body*.

"The last I heard was her screaming for everyone to leave her alone," he said. "Then I shut the door and went back to work. Look, my firm rents this space and I'm on a deadline."

"Sorry to disturb you," she said, backing out. "You won't mind if I poke around back then?"

But his head was bent over his work as he mumbled a reply.

"I'll take that as a yes," she said, closing the door.

She rang another doorbell. No answer. The rest of the courtyard lay deserted. If Sophie had to identify her ex-husband's body she'd be gone a while. It would make more sense to come back to interview her later.

Aimée left the way she'd come in, avoiding the fluttering

yellow crime scene tape by the *boulangerie*. The busy life of the village-like *quartier* streamed around her. She walked down rue des Moines, her boots wet from the slush, her heart as leaden as the gray sky above.

What else could she check? She remembered what Linh had said about an auction catalogue. But no auction house opened this early.

The only other lead she had was the name Gassot and the Sixth Battalion. She stepped into a phone cabinet, checked the phone book listings. The *anciens combattants* center was nearby. No better place to locate an old soldier like Gassot or someone who knew him. Or knew *something*. She was clutching at straws. But, until she found Sophie she had nothing else.

"C'EST DOMMAGE," said the middle-aged man behind the *anciens combattants* reception desk. He puffed at a cigar hanging from the side of his mouth. "Not my war. But the Dien Bien Phu vets meet on the second Sunday of the month. You just missed it."

Merde!

Regimental plaques and blue, white, and red banners lined the wall of the center. Black and white photos of troops from the first and second World Wars, the Indochinese and Algerian conflicts, accompanied them. She searched the photos, but none showed the Sixth Battalion.

"Monsieur, I'm looking for Hervé Gassot or the number of the group's secretary."

"Let me see," he said. He ran his tobacco-stained finger over a directory. "*Voilà!* Hervé Gassot himself's the secretary now; he saw combat at Dien Bien Phu."

Her hopes rose. "There were rumors that a cache of jade was looted from the Emperor's tomb near Dien Bien Phu. . . ."

"Gassot spent time in Indochina. He knows all the stories,

that's for sure. But he keeps to himself. There's only one number listed for him." He scratched his grizzled head of hair.
"*Non*, here's another one, not sure which is which. Maybe a
contact number. Not all of the members have telephones."

He wrote them both down on paper and passed it to her.

"*Merci.*"

"We've got a symposium tonight," he said, heading toward
a stack of folding chairs. "I need to set up, if you'll excuse me."

She tried one number on her cell phone. After ten rings
she gave up. She tried the second. Again, the phone rang and
rang. Disappointed, she hung up.

She walked toward the Batignolles church and then, under
the brown awning of the *boulangerie*, she saw him: the hawk-
nosed *flic* from the RG visit. The one from the team involved
in the Place Vendôme surveillance where her father had been
killed. She had never known his name or rank. The whole
project had been hush hush. Ministry of the Interior, Ministry
of Defense, they all peed in the same place, as her father used
to say.

Had he been following her or was he nosing around for the
jade on his own?

The man buttoned up his rain jacket and strode past the
crime scene tape. She tailed him down rue Legendre for several blocks to a small two-story café-*tabac*: one of those she'd
already visited this morning. She followed him inside, smiled
at the owner, and bought some cassis-flavored gum at the
cigarette counter as he mounted the back stairs.

A minute later she, too, went upstairs to find a smoke-filled
rectangular room, the restroom beyond. Cracked leather banquette seats lined the wall, mirrors above them. The room was
deserted, except for several tables and chairs. At one, three
men played belote, a card game similar to bridge, a game she'd
never had the patience to learn.

She sat down at the hawk-nosed man's table, nodding to the heavy-lidded owner/waiter taking his order for an espresso.

"You know my name," she said. "What's yours?"

"Did I ask you to sit here?"

She heard more annoyance than surprise in his voice.

"I invited myself," she smiled. "Sometimes I do that. But we already know each other."

"How's that?"

"Last night your group searched my apartment without a warrant, remember?"

He looked away. "You've mistaken me for someone else."

She bit back a remark about short-term memory loss, and got to the heart of the matter. "Think back to five years ago, *Inspecteur. . . ?*"

"Pleyet," he acknowledged, shifting away from her.

In the mirror she saw the belote players look up, then go back to their game, slapping cards on the table. From below came the sound of the *télé* with its replayed horse races.

"I'm in the traffic division, Mademoiselle."

And if she believed that, she'd believe anything. He didn't look like a meter maid. Or act like one.

"Then where's your ticket book?" she asked. "You were with the RG last night."

He shrugged. "They called me."

"You were involved in the Place Vendôme surveillance five years ago."

"Never." His eyes narrowed. "Why do you keep bringing that up? Such persistance is rude."

"Remember one of your old colleagues, Jean-Claude Leduc, my father?"

"Guess he forgot to send you to charm school," he said.

She felt the wooden floor vibrating as his foot began tapping.

"Is the man who works with the RG your evil twin?"

No smile answered her back. "Traffic's my job," he insisted. "Since 1992."

The heavy-lidded owner returned with two steaming espressos and two glasses of water, and set them on the water-ringed table together with a glass carafe. Aimée handed him a ten franc piece. Light from the wall sconce caught and danced on the carafe's thick rim. Around them rose occasional exclamations, then the shuffle of the belote players' cards.

"Looks like you're on duty," she said.

"The traffic bureau closed early," he said, yawning. "Just a quick cup of coffee, then the train home."

She doubted that. "How is the jade tied to the RG, Inspecteur Pleyet?"

Anger flickered in his eyes and he gripped her elbow in a steely hold.

For a moment the card game stopped. The only sounds were the rumble of the milk steamer machine below. She looked up. One of the men said "Fold" and the others threw their cards on the table.

Pleyet relaxed his grip. In one movement, he pulled on his windbreaker jacket and stood.

"You didn't answer my question, Inspecteur. Were you on assignment in postwar Indochina?" she asked, taking a gamble. "You look the type."

"Why do you say that?"

She might as well probe deeper. "After Dien Bien Phu a lot of archeological treasures went missing, didn't they? There were several incidents of looting. Did the Sixth Battalion have anything to do with that?"

"I don't know what you're talking about."

He threw some francs on the table and left.

She gulped her espresso and watched him from the window as he walked down rue des Batignolles. Pleyet was lying. She smelled it. She could understand him not revealing his cover in a café. But would he tell her more somewhere else?

She figured Pleyet was the type to have been airlifted into a pre-dawn Lagos when things got sticky, or infiltrated into an aborted revolution that needed suctioning out. The "gleaners" were what some called them. "Mopping up" was the other term she'd heard. Guess it depended on how big a mess they found.

One of the card players, a man with a silver-white tonsure of hair, brushed past and bumped her table, spilling her glass of water.

"*Pardonnez-moi*, Mademoiselle," he said, his wide grin exposing several gold-capped teeth. "So clumsy. May I buy you a drink?"

She didn't fancy a *tête-à-tête* with this old *mec* or his cronies, but he'd been civil.

"*Pas grave*, don't worry, monsieur," she said and made her way downstairs.

She checked her Tintin watch. The doors of the auction houses would be open now.

Wednesday Morning

Hervé Gassot gazed nervously at his two comrades. Yvon Nemours, stocky, wearing a too small tracksuit that strained around his thick waist, searched the crowd. Picq, standing by the blue-veined rabbit carcasses in the covered Marché de Batignolles, lit a cigarette.

Was this safe enough? Did the crowd of shoppers and market hawkers that surrounded them make them inconspicuous? All around them, women wheeled shopping carts and jockeyed for position at the cheese sellers. Pungent, acrid odors emanated from the stand where a man in a white apron, stained with yellow runny streaks, discussed the merits of a ripe St. Nectaire with a customer.

"Albert had become chummy with Thadée, the gallery owner shot yesterday," Picq said, cupping his cigarette between his forefinger and thumb like a Pigalle mobster.

"We know that, Picq."

"More than chummy. You know Albert's big mouth. Seems he talked about the old days and this *mec's* related to the family."

"Related?"

"They own the buildings, that's why he had his gallery there. That's two blocks from here."

Gassot edged closer. He glanced behind his shoulder. Couldn't help it. "So what are you saying?"

Picq ground out his cigarette with his foot, shook his head.

"Someone was asking around the *anciens combattants* center," Nemours said. "And those two we saw in the café. . . ."

"I don't like it," Gassot said.

He could tell by Nemours's and Picq's faces that they didn't like it either. Had the past resurfaced? Was someone after them for their mistake at Dien Bien Phu?

"I check every fifteen minutes but the gallery's closed. No sign of life."

"We'll break into the gallery tonight," Nemours said, "and ask his ex-wife about the jade. And if she doesn't know anything. . . ."

"We should check with Albert's doctor," Gassot interrupted.

"The coroner's report declares 'Death by unusual circumstances,' " Picq said. "Lucie's convinced Albert was murdered."

Nemours turned to Gassot. "You have to see Tran."

"Tran?"

"If anyone knows what's happening, Tran will."

* * *

GASSOT HURRIED through Parc Monceau under chestnut
trees that shuddered in the wind. A turtledove swooped
down near the pond. He passed the mansions overlooking
the green lawns. The gilt trimmed fence gave it the look of a
private park. Marie-Thérèse had walked Napoleon's heir
here; Proust had loved this little lake. Hadn't he—or someone—waxed poetic about the perfume of a childhood spent
in the Parc Monceau?

Gassot resented the butter and shallot smells emanating
from the kitchens of these mansions, the scurrying hired help,
and the smooth hum of the limousines: the sounds and smells
of the homes of the rich.

Thirty minutes later, beyond Porte de Clichy at the
Cimetière des chiens, he faced Tran. Tran, a smooth-faced man
with thick, paper-white hair, wore navy blue pants and shirt
and soft-soled canvas shoes. He chain-smoked as he weeded
the gravel walkways. Lean and compact, Tran looked as he had
in Indochina, except for the lines around his eyes and his
white hair. The younger son of a Cao Dai priest, Tran had seen
combat with Gassot's regiment until his elder brother died at
Dien Bien Phu. When the government outlawed the Cao Dai
sect, he'd gone into service with French colonials.

That's when it had started, Gassot remembered. The whole
sad mess. The meetings, the whispered asides during humid
Haiphong nights where the corpses of fluorescent jellyfish glittered on the surface of black harbor water. Rumors of jade
treasures amidst the rolling rhythmic slap of the waves. The air
heavy with the scent of rotting mangoes in the compound
guarded by the Montagnard hill tribesmen, with their green
metal bracelets, multicolored loincloths, and carbine clips
slung over their shoulders.

"*Bonjour,* Tran," Gassot greeted him.

"A wonderful treat to see you," Tran said, one hand holding a weed-filled bucket, the other motioning to a marble bench. "Sit down."

A formality. They met here on the first Wednesday of every month on a stone bench overlooking the dog cemetery. But Gassot was three weeks early and he knew Tran must be curious.

Gassot hesitated. He wanted to explain the fear and doubt, the smell of vengeance surrounding Albert's death—explain it in a way so Tran would help, rather than dismiss them as scared old men.

Rows of small blackened stone crosses and suitcase-sized marble slabs stretched before them. Withered white chrysan-themums left from Toussaint, All Saints Day remembrances, defied the wind whipping over the small tombstones. Funny, Gassot thought, dog owners tended their pets' graves better than the families of the military tended theirs.

"Makes you wonder about the world, eh, Tran," he said. "Humans are less remembered than dogs."

Tran smiled and shrugged. "Maybe because dogs are more faithful. Truer," Tran said, offering him a cigarette, a Vinataba brand. "Remember the La Bai we smoked, *camarade?*" Tran asked. State Express 555, Ho Chi-Minhs' favorite brand, had been a black market exclusive, too expensive for him.

"*Merci.*" Gassot accepted one and lit his from Tran's: the way they had in Indochina, where no one had matches to waste.

He remembered the woody tobacco taste of the unfiltered cigarettes and the picture of playing cards on the package. He'd never smoked so much as in Indochina where it was a national pastime. That, and sabotaging the French. Of course, that came later. Much later, it was the Americans' turn.

"Has something happened, *camarade?*" Tran asked. He exhaled smoke that spiraled in a blue-white haze.

And then the Paris sky opened, rain spattering down in furious fits and starts. Unlike the warm Indochina monsoons that descended steadily onto corrugated tin-roofed huts, Gassot remembered, leaving fat beads of water on the curled palm leaves.

Tran tugged his arm and they ran for cover.

"*Ça va?*" Tran said. "Your eyes are far away today."

Gassot could still hear the rustle of the silk worn by the half-Asian mademoiselles, denigrated as *bui doi*, the dust of life. He remembered the acrid odor coming from the opium smokers next door.

"What's the matter, *camarade?*"

In the shed where tools were kept, Gassot straightened his shoulders, realizing Tran was studying him. He forced himself back to the present and took a deep breath.

"Do you ever hear from Bao?" She had been Tran's cousin, Bao of the pale oval face and laughing eyes. He knew that after forced marches and prison camp, the light would have gone out of them.

"Not for several years," said Tran.

"Still in Indochina, is she?"

"Seems we're talking about the old times instead of why you came here, *camarade*. . . ." Tran's voice trailed off in disappointment. His manners were more French than Gassot's and his accent was impeccable. But then he'd lived in France almost as long as Gassot, working for a wealthy old colonial family as an indentured servant until his retirement. Though slave would have described it better.

But he liked to keep busy, so he worked part-time now, here, as groundskeeper.

"You're worried. It's Albert . . . his heart?" Tran said.

Gassot gathered his courage. "Albert died in the hospital. But he was murdered there."

"What makes you think he was murdered?"

"Who else knows, Tran?" Gassot asked.

"*Mais*, you don't mean—"

"Who else knows about the massacre at Lai Chau?"

"The dead know," Tran replied. "And your comrades."

And it had been their regiment's fault. Their bombing coordinates had been off. Off by half a kilometer, sending them into the no-fly zone.

A plain of burning flames, so intense the heat had melted the straps of Gassot's helmet on his neck. The hidden mines planted by the Vietminh in the plain had exploded under the hail of the French bombing attack—an attack that had been meant to destroy the Vietminh forces, not ignite a incendiary vortex claiming thousands of both Indochinese and French lives. The deafening explosions cratered the red earth. Rice paddies were clogged with body parts kilometers away, destroying the ancient drainage system. The peasants starved the next season, refusing to eat a crop nourished by the blood of their ancestors.

No one talked of their mistake; the reports were destroyed, the incident hushed up.

"Only three of us left now," Gassot said. "But someone could have escaped."

"No one escaped from that hell," Tran said.

"A victim in a field hospital? Or an eyewitness?" he said. "Someone who heard the stories and has come for revenge?"

"Go ahead and torment yourself, *camarade*," Tran said. "You're good at that. But it can't bring them back. Nothing will. As they say, it's all termite spit."

"Albert opened his big mouth; he talked about the jade. And then the man he spoke to was shot. Killed."

Tran's hand shook as he lit another cigarette. "*Merde!*"

"Tran, reestablish your connections," Gassot said. "Go back to the house. Talk to the old buzzard about the jade. You're the one who heard the rumor in Haiphong."

Tran bowed his head. "That's so long ago," he said.

"The jade is here. In Paris. We know it. We're not the only ones looking for it, Tran," Gassot said. "Remember that."

"But we're the only true believers."

Gassot turned away. He stooped, tried to control the quiver in his shoulders. "Tran, you have to go back to the house."

No one would suspect Tran. Gassot kept to himself his fear that someone was picking them off, one by one.

Wednesday Midday

AIMÉE NUDGED HER WAY through the throng of patrons at the Drouot auction house counter, to the catalogues. Around her, in the long *salle* hung with paintings celebrating Drouot's history, patrons milled in the display rooms, looking at items in glass showcases or piled in corners. Her *grand-père*, a habitué, had frequented the auction house. More often than not, he'd spot a frayed Savonnerie carpet or a Baccarat chandelier with missing crystals in a heap to be auctioned off as part of a lot. Many of these "finds" furnished her apartment now. "I've got an eye for these things," he'd say, grinning and crossing his eyes, making Aimée laugh. As a young girl, she'd loved the smell of old furniture, the blistered oil paintings, and the sound of the wooden gavel of the auctioneer.

Afterwards they'd walk to the *confiserie*, her hand nestled in his overcoat pocket. Inside, he'd let her choose from the old-fashioned sugared violets and candied almonds. They'd end the day at the *Guignol* puppet theatre in the Jardin du Luxembourg.

Now all Aimée saw were the feral gleams in dealers' eyes and the video surveillance cameras tracking patrons. She doubted her *grand-père* would have been able to discover bargains or "finds" now.

She consulted November's auction catalogue. Nothing. But

in October's issue, on page 114, she found a black and white photo that did little justice to the eleven exquisite jade pieces pictured. Yet even this photo took her breath away.

A short description read: Incomplete set of Chinese jade astrological figures, reputedly of fourth century Chinese origin. Provenance unknown.

This didn't make sense. Who had put the jade figures up for auction, and more importantly, how had Baret ended up with them? Why sell them to Linh for fifty thousand francs when their value was estimated in the hundreds of thousands? Had he been short of money and so, motivated to make a quick sale? Or was he sincerely trying to help Linh?

"Excuse me," she said to the smiling woman behind the counter, "I'd like to find out the result of the sale of lot #8793. What it sold for and to whom, if possible."

The woman beamed at her, looking past people consulting glossy catalogues and smudged typed lists. "Just a moment please," she said and consulted a binder. "According to the current auction log," she said, "this lot was withdrawn from the auction."

"Withdrawn?" Aimée asked in alarm. "You mean it was never auctioned?"

"*Oui*, taken off the list."

Frustrated, Aimée leaned against the counter and thought. Nothing seemed to fit.

"I need to find out who put the pieces up for auction. How do you suggest I proceed?"

"I'm sorry, I can't help you. Queries regarding previously catalogued items must be submitted to Madame Monsour in our archives division."

"*Merci*," Aimée said, and bought the catalogue. She wouldn't give up without trying. By the time she reached Madame Monsour's office, she knew she'd have to improvise. Again.

"What . . . no appointment, Mademoiselle?" said a harried man carrying a thick stack of files.

Aimée gave him a big smile. "Forgive me, I know she's busy. Five minutes of her time, that's all I ask."

"If you'd made an appointment. . . ." he said.

"Marcel, so you finally found the Asian art estimates!" interrupted a slim young woman in a black suit, emerging from the office whose doorway bore the nameplate MADAME MONSOUR.

"But, Madame Monsour, that's what I need to speak with you about," Aimée said, stepping forward. "I need background information on a jade collection."

"Do your homework. Go read some books, Mademoiselle. I suggest—"

"But I have, you see, and they raise more questions."

Madame Monsour was attractive and well put together, with coiffed black hair that almost disguised her small ears: very small, which she hid with her thick shoulder length hair. Except when, with a the nervous motion, she tucked it behind her ears.

Aimée moved closer, toward the office door. "Please, I'm sorry, but just a few minutes."

Madame Monsour said, "The auctioneer needs my assistance and I must prepare."

Aimée showed her the page from the October auction catalogue.

"Please, Madame Monsour."

Madame Monsour pursed her lips and without a word, showed her into a high-ceilinged cramped office piled high with books.

"Make it good," she said.

Aimée gave an edited three-minute explanation to Madame Monsour, leaving out Thadée's murder. Then she showed her PI badge.

"Is this some official inquiry? If so, here at Drouot, we make it a policy to have our lawyer present."

"No, not at all," Aimée said. "Nothing like that."

Madame Monsour wavered.

"Give me a request in writing," said Madame Monsour, "stating the full background and reasons for your inquiry."

Typical bureaucrat. But she didn't have time for that. "Forgive me, but would the consignor's name be in your archives?"

"It's impossible to furnish information about the piece."

"What about online?"

Madame Monsour shook her head. Little of the old fashioned Drouot system had entered the Internet era.

"How long will the data be kept?"

"Not my field, I'm sorry."

And where was it kept?

"You must realize, I can't help you," Madame Monsour said. "Consignors sign a contract with us. Their identity is confidential. By law, we can't reveal their names." She paused and looked at the page. "Such incredible pieces, too. More than their historical interest, it's their mystical quality which make them so highly prized."

Aimée heard a wistfulness in her tone.

"What do you know about these jade astrological pieces?"

Madame Monsour shook her head. "I only came on board this month, sorry," she said. "And old Monsieur Valdeck's passed on. A pity, he would have known a lot."

"The research I did also mentions the mystical quality of jade," Aimée said, venturing to articulate a hunch. "Could these pieces be even older than the catalogue says?"

Madame Monsour seemed to be considering. "Sometimes descriptions are conservative," she said.

What did she mean by that? "Why would someone put these pieces up for sale and then withdraw them?" Aimée asked.

"Pick a reason," she said. "Change of heart, a private collector approaches the seller, or as is often the case, the early bids don't match the consignor's expectations."

"May I ask a favor?" Aimée asked. "Could you contact the owner and ask if he, or she, would speak with me?"

"Only if I want to lose my job," she said. "We've had so much trouble with scandals concerning provenance and authenticity, I'm afraid there's little I could do, even if I wanted to help. The archives are kept on the outskirts of Paris. I've never even been there."

If she could find out where, Aimée thought quickly, could she bribe a guard? "Where's that?"

"On the île de la Jatte, but don't get any ideas," Madame Monsour said. "Even I'm not allowed inside. It's a secured facility."

"Then how can I find out more concerning the mystical attributes of the jade?"

"Where you should have looked in the first place, Mademoiselle," Madame Monsour said, handing the catalogue back to Aimée. "At the Musée Cernuschi. They have a marvelous Chinese art collection. And a well-respected Asian art curator, Professor Dinard."

Madame Monsour's phone rang. "If you'll excuse me."

Aimée thanked her and left the drafty wet-wool smelling rooms of the Drouot. She pulled out her cell phone and made an appointment to meet the curator of the musée Cernuschi.

AIMÉE STOOD outside the Second Empire–style Musée Cernuschi located on the border of the seventeenth. The museum had a mansard roof, and its façade, veneered with white stone, was topped by a frieze of mosaic faces encircled by gold and overlooked chic Parc Monceau. Puddles flooded the street lined with nineteenth-century mansions on which it stood. She hoped Dinard would elucidate the jade's provenance and know who might have put them up for auction.

On the museum's ground floor, a calligraphy exhibition, delicate, wisplike black brush strokes like trailing smoke on thick rice paper, caught her eye. Ethereal and beautiful.

"Everyone calls it 'rice paper,' " a docent was saying to a small group of visitors by the display. "Yet this paper, made from kozo, a plant prized in China and renowned for its strength, is also used by the Japanese for currency. Its appearance of delicacy is misleading."

Monsieur Dinard's assistant, whose name was Tessier according to the nameplate on his desk in the front office, was a tall thirtyish man with small close-set eyes and a prominent nose. He gestured toward a suite of office rooms.

"He's got an appointment soon," Tessier said. "But he'll see you for a few minutes. Go ahead."

Aimée knocked on Professor Dinard's door. A stout middle-aged man, with a flushed complexion, round glasses, black hair—too black to be natural—and sporting a bow tie with his tweed suit, opened the door. The high-ceilinged room beyond displayed a blue silk Chinese rug on the floor. Carved details in the woodwork, picked out in gold and ivory, framed the walls.

"Professor Dinard?" she asked. "I'm Aimée Leduc. Thank you for seeing me."

"*Désolé*, I regret that I can only spare you a few minutes," he said, smiling and glancing at his watch. "But I'm happy to help if I can."

"I'm fascinated by the mystical qualities of jade," she said.

"But Mademoiselle, you don't have to stand here. Come in, please," he said, his smile wider. "Come inside, please sit down." He showed her to a straight-backed provincial cherrywood chair. His round, smiling face was welcoming.

"Professor, you're pressed for time so I'll get to the point. Can you tell me about these pieces?"

She passed the Drouot catalogue across his matching cherrywood desk, bare except for a single white orchid in a Ming vase. He nodded, then looked up at her, his eyes magnified by his glasses.

"What do you want to know? And why?"

He seemed suspicious but she she had to take a chance. "Someone showed me this jade collection, Professor," she said, leaning forward. "If these pieces were looted during the battle of Dien Bien Phu in 1954, why would they turn up now? Who might have consigned them for auction?"

Professor Dinard stared at her. "What magazine do you write for, Mademoiselle?"

"None. I'm a detective," she said. "Here's my card."

He studied it. She saw a slight tremor in his hand.

"Forgive my inquisitiveness, but where did you see this collection?"

So far he'd posed questions and answered none. "I'm not at liberty to say right now."

His fixed stare behind his round glasses disconcerted her.

"Why play cat and mouse, Professor?" she asked. "You're the jade expert. Madame Monsour from Drouot recommended I speak with you. What can you tell me about this jade."

He shook his head.

Didn't her taxes go to pay for this City of Paris supported museum? And his salary? But she didn't say that.

"Fascinating. But I'd have to study these pieces more carefully," he said. "Do research. Say two days. Give me the pieces, and I'll do a thorough investigation."

Before she could reply, she noticed a black Renault pulling up outside. Several men in suits emerged. One was Pleyet. What was he doing here? Was the RG still on the scent of the jade?

Dinard stared at the open catalogue in his hand. "You haven't told me how you obtained these jade pieces."

So he thought she had them. She'd never said that. Had she

implied it? No, she was sure she had not. Yet he seemed to know the pieces had been stolen by someone. And he thought it was her.

"Plundering destroys archeological sites," Professor Dinard said, sadly. "Whatever value looted objects possess diminishes to almost nothing without a provenance, a documented history attached. A terrible shame, of course."

Did he think she was here to unload the jade? "Professor, I need your expertise."

Professor Dinard opened his drawer and pulled out something, a small crocodile-leather glasses case. He took off his glasses and put them inside.

Before he could speak, a woman's voice came over the intercom, "Your appointment's arrived."

"You're in the art world, Professor. Don't you have any idea as to who might have put the jade figures up for auction?"

"I'm a museum director," he said. "Show me the pieces and I can give you my opinion. Otherwise there's no way I can help you."

"Do you think I want to sell them?" she said. "You don't seem to understand—"

"I'll see you out," he said, motioning her to the door.

Confront the RG again? No reason for Pleyet to know her investigations had brought her here.

She scanned the room. Only the window. "Please, isn't there another way out?"

"Why Mademoiselle? Please use the door."

Didn't these old *hôtels particuliers* have water closets cleverly concealed in panels flush with the wood?

Something behind his glasses had changed. Compassion or—

The office door opened. "Your appointment's here, Professor."

She had to find a way to leave without Pleyet seeing her. Maybe Dinard would make a deal.

"*Bon*, Professor, I'll show you," she said, playing for time. "I only carried this piece with me." She put the small jade disk in his hand.

For a moment he held it, his eyes half-closed, and rubbed it. It was almost like a caress. Then holding it between his thumb and forefinger, he lifted it to the light. A luminescent river-green hued orb held their gazes. Amazingly it seemed to change, the color varying each time she looked at it.

Exquisite.

"Mademoiselle, the tiny dragon etched in the jade is a motif. . . . It is part of a larger pattern. Some of the images common to the period would be clouds, or a phoenix. But unless you have all the pieces together, you cannot see the pattern. This is part of a set, but only a part. The whole. . . ."

Now she'd hooked him.

"Do we have a deal, Professor?"

He nodded and pressed a button under a window ledge. A door opened. "This leads to the old kitchen. And the back stairs."

She put her hand out for the disk, sensed his reluctance to give it up, but he handed it over. She slid into the passage and the door clicked shut behind her. Darkness, dust, and the odor of old wood. She heard voices, indistinct, absorbed by the carpet, and what she took for a cell phone conversation near the door about the chauffeur's return instructions. Her phone vibrated, and she answered, moving away from the panel so she couldn't be heard.

"Mademoiselle, Monsieur Verlet wonders when you can discuss the project," said the secretary from Olf.

She looked down at her jeans. She had to change.

"Say two p.m., would that work for him?" she asked.

"See you then," the secretary said.

Once outside on boulevard Malesherbes she caught a taxi to Leduc Detective.

Inside the office, René's desk sat undisturbed since last night. She opened the armoire, pushed aside a streetcleaner's jumpsuit,

Agent Provocateur silk underwear, Italian jeans, and retro boots. In the back she found the black suit, vintage Dior, discovered in a *dépôt-vente* consignment shop without a tear or slipped seam in it. A classic even to the skirt's knee-length hem.

She stepped into black sling back heels threaded with bubble-gum pink ribbon. Clattering down the stairs, she wondered where René was.

She'd try him later. She ran for the bus.

In the Olf foyer, she signed in at the security post and caught her breath.

Upstairs, Aimée smiled at the secretary, a middle-aged woman with a swollen cheek.

"Root canal," the secretary explained. "Monsieur Verlet's in conference but can spare a brief word."

Or at least that's what Aimée thought she said.

"But we had an appointment."

"Some bigwigs appeared—you know how that goes!" she said. "Please, go into the conference room."

A word? The man was vociferous. He hailed from Perigord and liked to talk.

"Monsieur Verlet . . ." she said, peeking in to the room. "Your secretary said to come in."

Several men, sitting around a long walnut table, looked up.

"Aaah, Mademoiselle Leduc, glad you dropped by," he said.

Dropped by? They had an appointment, she wanted to get his signature on a revised contract. And a check.

"Let me introduce you to the board, Mademoiselle Leduc."

Thank God she'd worn the Dior.

Talk about a power enclave. Most of the men wore the uniform: pinstriped suits, blue shirts, red ties. They emitted a *Grandes Ecoles* air. Government and corporate types. Graphs and charts lined the wall and someone was giving a presentation. She looked closer: *Holdings of PetroVietnam*.

PetroVietnam? Might that connect to the Cao Dai?

"Tell us about your work," Verlet said, "if you don't mind. Just a quick summary of how your computer security could work for us. I was impressed with your new ideas for the project."

Why hadn't he prepared her?

"Mademoiselle Leduc, we're ready when you are."

She hesitated, wishing she could have planned a presentation in advance.

"I don't mind telling you," Verlet said, grinning, "I had to nudge our board's thinking toward this new security project but as I told the gentlemen, safeguards and state-of-the art security are demanded today."

He needed her to dazzle them. Sell them. Convince them they'd make a good choice picking Leduc Detective on his recommendation. When she'd spoken with him last week, he'd been cordial and reasonable. Maybe this had happened too fast for Verlet to warn her.

"Of course, Monsieur Verlet, delighted." She smiled, figuring she'd throw technical jargon at them, get Verlet's signature and then beg off on the ground of another appointment. "We're always thrilled when clients want to understand how our system enhances and builds on their own security."

She pulled out the proposal, noted the key points. She began, "Gentleman, the web offers unique advantages and security challenges—"

"Would you be so kind as to cut to the heart of why we need your firm, Mademoiselle?" said a white-haired man looking up through reading glasses perched on his nose. "Specifically regarding computer hackers who could explore our data and create a channel to download it?"

Great. One of the elite with a computer attitude, and a bit of knowledge. The type who took a course and knew it all.

"How technical do you want it, Monsieur . . ."

"*Monsieur le Ministre* Langan," he said. "When our eyes glaze over might be a good place to stop."

Nice. Couldn't Verlet have warned her?

"You posed an excellent question, Monsieur, but if I may back-track and give some historical perspective, you might understand more of why we do what we do and its impact."

A few looks of interest came from the men at the table. Langan sat back in his leather chair and crossed his arms.

"If someone tells you they can put an extra security guard on the server, well, they can't," she said, walking toward him and pouring herself a glass of water from the carafe. "I assume you're referring to that when you mentioned exploring data?"

"Something like that," he said.

A hard sell, this minister in the tailored double-breasted custom made jacket. The others sat and watched.

She smiled and prayed the run on her thigh hadn't traveled further down her black pantyhose.

"Cyberthreats are really the vulnerabilities, potential open doors in software, that hackers trawl for. All a hacker needs in order to shut down your system is a single Web-connected computer without proper security software; a fourteen-year-old's desktop Mac, a university's e-mail server, or a government ministry's laptop. We see it all the time. Using e-mail software or other applications on an unpro-tected computer, hackers can bog down your Internet oper-ations with 'distributed denial of service' attacks that generate more traffic than the network can handle. Meanwhile, they hack into a vulnerable system undetected in the mass confusion."

She paused, took a sip of water. Wondering if she'd scored any points yet. But she was telling the truth. And if they didn't like it, they'd let her know.

Her eyes rested on the PetroVietnam graph of profit and earnings. The connection with the Cao Dai was probably a coincidence; she must be paranoid. Just because there was a Vietnamese connection didn't mean. . . .

"We watch, warn and share information. Not to mention continual updating and monitoring. And your system has not only firewall protection in place but a backup in the event of a Web attack."

"And if the firewall is breached, *and* the back-up?" Langan interrupted.

"Automatic alarms inform us of any attack, monsieur," she said. "I doubt they'd breach our firewall before we discovered and patched or disarmed the attack."

"*Bon*, your firm guarantees this?"

"Of course, that's what we do 24/7, Monsieur."

Verlet stood and smiled. Was that relief on his face?

"Mademoiselle Leduc, we appreciate this and don't want to inconvenience you any more," he said. "*Merci.*"

She took her cue and left. Considering her sweaty palms, it was a good thing she didn't have to shake anyone's hand. She leaned against the wall in the video surveillance room and waited for her heart to slow to a normal beat.

A knock sounded on the door. Verlet with the verdict? So quick? She took a deep breath and opened it.

"*Oui?*"

One of the men from the conference room, all six feet plus of him, stood before her with a copy of Le Monde tucked under his arm. Early forties, brushed back black hair; his pinstriped suit didn't disguise his muscular frame.

"Good job for being put on the spot, Mademoiselle." He winked, smiling. A nice smile. "I felt it necessary to go along but forgive me. I mean, for not rising to your defense. You see, we're part of the consortium insuring this firm and so . . . You handled yourself quite well. Impressive."

"So my firm passed?"

He nodded.

"We like to establish a relationship of confidence with our clients," she said, relief flooding her.

"Exactly." He said, "I've already apologized to Verlet, didn't want him to have an attack of apoplexy in view of his *crise de foie* and high blood pressure."

Crise de foie. Why did every Frenchman connect bad health to a mysterious ailment of the liver?

"I'm curious as to why the minister attended this meeting," she said. She was aware of the rumors that Olf, a state-owned firm, had dealt in backdoor diplomacy since de Gaulle's era. But she wanted to hear his explanation.

"Why, it's common practice for the minister to keep informed about investments in unsettled countries. Here, if you need to contact me," he said, handing her an oversized vellum card engraved with the name Julien de Lussigny.

She handed him hers. "I thought you said you were with the insurance consortium. . . ."

"But I am," he said. "There are a few things for us to discuss. Why don't we have lunch?"

"With pleasure," she said.

Eager to seal the deal, she tried to ignore the pangs of wariness she felt.

"Say tomorrow?" With people like this one had to smile and nod a lot.

"*Bon*, I'll call you to confirm the restaurant tomorrow," he said.

De Lussigny was distinguished and a tad conservative for her but power oozed from him. His footsteps clicked on the marble floor as he joined the others from the conference room who were spilling into the corridor. By the time they reached the reception area, she'd slipped back into the room and was scanning the PetroVietnam charts. There were lots of arrows on the graph, all pointing upward, indicating profit, staggering profit, in the Gulf of Tonkin. Blue, black, and green triangles indicated British, Chinese, and French drilling areas. Her wariness increased.

"Here you are," said the nice receptionist who had entered

the room silently. "Monsieur Verlet's engaged now but he asked me to tell you that he'll sign the addendum and we'll messenger it over with a check."

Aimée turned away to hide her relief and the warm flush that now suffused her cheeks. She couldn't wait to tell René.

Wednesday

RENÉ CHOKED ON THE oily rags filling his mouth. Ropes cut into his tightly bound legs and arms. He could barely move.

If only he'd paid more attenion—not walked into a trap!

His head throbbed from the blows they had inflicted on him. He was in darkness. He could just make out a beeping sound, or was it a muffled honking? But it continued . . . a car alarm? He tried to kick his legs, fighting the terror that flooded him as he lay on a hard surface, trussed like a pheasant. Dull rhythmic flapping echoed near his ear, like the tread of tire on asphalt.

Was he in the trunk of a car? He might be. How long had he been like this?

He worked the tight cord, trying to loosen it, but it only cut harder into his skin. His phone bulged in his jacket pocket, but he couldn't reach it, or talk if he could.

Make a plan, René. Wasn't that what Aimée would say? First things first, he must loosen his bonds and work his hands free. If this were a car trunk wouldn't there be back taillights or a tirejack? Something sharp that might stick out.

And then he remembered his dead phone battery.

But his phone had beeped. He had a message. Was there some life still left in it? He had to reach his phone.

He wiggled his arms, found metal, and rubbed his hands

back and forth. Nothing. Where were the rear taillights? Then his wrists struck a sharp edge. A small gleam of red behind it, the rear brakelights. He moved his wrists back and forth, sawing at the cord. Time after time, he missed, and sliced his skin. When he'd freed his hands, he'd try the phone. When the car stopped he'd be ready to spring out and drop kick his assailants.

Why hadn't he seen the attack coming? All those years of training in martial arts, even a black belt! But hearing Aimée had been hurt, he'd panicked.

Was she? Were the captors taking him to her? Or was that just a ruse?

He'd never let her know. But considering his situation, this was a moot point. His legs hadn't hurt so much since the doctor had broken, then reset them when he was six. They'd been so severely bowed he could hardly walk. Only after a year in casts with a bar between them to straighten the bones had he walked again.

His neck stung from where his carotid artery had been pinched until he passed out. With all the jerks and starts, he figured they were still in Paris traffic, not all that far from the city center.

He tried to ignore the sharp pain and keep sawing away. The rope finally loosened and gave way. With bloody hands he reached for the rope around his legs, tied in a double knot. Now the phone! He pulled it out of his pocket, sticky and mute. He punched the numbers. Nothing.

And then the car stopped. Panic gripped him. Footsteps crunched on gravel. His hands . . . what should he do with his hands?

Don't freeze. Yell, he told himself. But he hadn't yet worked the tape off his mouth.

The trunk opened. Dim light and the sway of branches overhead in the wind. Dark figures huddled; he couldn't see their faces.

"Don't his kind work in carnivals?" asked someone with a

gravelly voice. "Freak shows? With two hundred kilo women and two-headed snakes."

A blanket whipped over him, smothering him, blocking out the light. Arms gripped and carried him, bumping him over the back of the trunk.

"Over here," a voice said.

A blow struck his jaw and he moaned.

"Quick!" Cold air and footsteps echoing on stone. Down, they were going down. A cellar . . . a basement? He was thrown down on something hard. Pain shot up his hip socket. The blanket was removed and a bag slipped over his head. Rough, with the texture of burlap.

"He's been a quick worker," the gravel voice said. "Tape those hands."

"Water every four hours," said a higher pitched voice. "Let him pee. Here's his phone. Anyone got a battery charger?"

René shivered as hands taped up his bloody wrists.

"Does this cord fit?"

"*Bon*," the voice said with a chuckle. "We'll wait and use his own phone for the phone call. Have fun."

"Don't worry, I will," the gravel-voice said.

Wednesday Early Evening

THE RINGING OF THE phone woke Aimée. She must have nodded off at her desk at Leduc Detective while finishing the stats. On the green computer screen her eyes focused on the bright cursor blinking by her face. Familiar and reassuring. She'd promised herself never to take her eyesight for granted again but of course she had, more and more, as she recovered and tried to forget.

"*Oui . . . allô?*"

"We'll give you forty-eight hours," said a hoarse voice.

She rubbed her eyes and sat up. Yellow rays from rue de Louvre's streetlights slanted across her legs. The old station clock above her desk read 6 P.M.

"What? Who's this?"

"Then we start sending you the dwarf. In little pieces."

She froze.

René.

"What do you want?"

"Thadée's backpack."

Aimée stared at the flickering cursor, trying to think fast. They hadn't mentioned jade. Did they know what was inside?

"Who are you?" She glanced at René's untouched desk. "How do I know you have my partner?"

A sound like the muffling of a receiver came over the line. Choking.

"Aimée, don't. I'm OK—" said René.

The line went dead.

She panicked. Stupid, stupid, stupid! Let them have all her money, the jade . . . anything to get René back.

How could this be happening? Thadée shot to death, then the jade stolen, the RG tracking her, and now René, kidnapped! She hit the call back number. It was René's own cell phone. No answer. Smart.

Her head whirling, she had to figure something out and rescue René. She thought of his hip and . . . didn't want to think of what they could do to him.

Calm down. She had to calm down.

They'd call back. And she'd arrange to meet them. Try and convince them to accept the fifty thousand franc check and call it quits.

They'd let her stew before calling to give her the "drop." But what if they never handed René over? Terror clutched her.

Never rely on criminals to do the expected.

She thought of Louis; "Nut," as she and René had nick-named him since he kept bags of nuts in his pockets at all times, saying he was determined to eat healthily in the radar infested world he worked in. They'd met him at an electronics seminar when they'd skipped out of Sorbonne classes.

He worked at France Télécom. He'd know a way to trace the kidnappers, if anyone did. She dialed.

"CPMS division."

"*Bonsoir*, Nut?" she said, pulling on jeans and a worn cashmere sweater from the office armoire.

"Aimée . . . hold on," Nut said. She heard beeping in the background. Clicks. "*Ça va?* I'm the night network supervisor, so I need to monitor transmissions and take calls."

"I'll make it quick," she told him, keeping her voice steady with effort. "Triangulation, can you do it?"

"To a land line or cell phone?"

"René's cell phone. He's been . . . kidnapped."

"You're joking."

"I wish," she said. "Listen, no time to explain but. . . ."

She heard him take a deep breath.

"Only in Paris within the service antenna's or tower's range," Nut said. "No suburbs or outlying districts. Paris maintains multi-antennas. Even so we've had only limited success. Montmartre and the Butte Chaumont hill give us trouble."

"Will you try?" she asked, turning off her computer, switching off the lights.

"Picking through voluminous CDR records and verifying the data from the base stations which pick up calls to reconstruct and pinpoint the whereabouts of phone users, that's worse than dental extraction. And more time-consuming."

"I can give you the number to trace," she said.

"That lessens it a bit but not enough," Nut said.

She heard beeps and clicks in the background.

"Talk to a ham radio operator," he advised. "They monitor cell phone transmissions all the time."

"René needs help, right away. There's no time to lose."

"Go to Club Radio, 11 rue Biot," he said. "Tell Léo I sent you. That's the best I can do, Léo helped another friend last week. And don't forget, Aimée."

"That I owe you?"

"René's a black belt. Give him some credit."

Nut clicked off.

Fear rippled through her as she stepped into her boots and grabbed her knee-length suede shearling coat in the hallway. She ran down the stairs, onto rue du Louvre and found a taxi letting out passengers.

"Eleven rue Biot," she said to the taxi driver.

"Clichy's out of my way." The driver shook his head. "They were my last fare. Sorry, I've been working since six a.m."

Lights glittered on the Seine below. A passing barge churned the black, sluggish water. No other taxis in sight.

She reached for her wallet. "Fifty francs extra for your trouble."

"Must have a hot date."

Little did he know.

The taxi driver hit the meter switch. "Get in."

NUMBER 11 RUE Biot, between the old Café-concert L'Européen, where Charles Trenet had sung in the thirties, and an Indian restaurant, was a cobblestone's throw from Place de Clichy. She pressed the buzzer, the door was buzzed open, and she stepped into a small courtyard. Against the night sky, a row of antennas poked from the rooftop like twigs: a good sign. She passed the old stables, now garages, and mounted the back stairs to the second floor.

The door stood ajar. She walked inside to what she figured had once been two rooms that had been opened up into a large space. Bare putty-colored walls, a wooden farm table, a bag of potting soil on the floor. Instead of the buzzing and static she expected, she saw a plump woman in her forties wearing an apron, sitting at a scanner by several radios. She wore headphones.

"I'm looking for Léo. . . ."

"Short for Léontyne," she said, smiling. "My mother loved opera and Léontyne Price."

"Nut sent me."

"I know," she said. "Can you hurry up? Sorry but I've got to add forty-five megahertz in about seven minutes."

She gestured to a large red clock, and pulled off her headphones.

Aimée nodded. "I don't know if my friend's in Paris, but he's in trouble. I'm desperate. Can you help me find him?"

Léo hit several switches and adjusted a black knob that caused a needle to quiver on the volumeter.

Aimée wrote René's name and cell phone number on a pad of paper by Léo's elbow.

"*Parfait!* Most people don't even have that much. Now we can tap into the ocean of dialogue, ignore the police bandwidth, firefighters, ambulance drivers, paramedics, sanitation workers, and infant monitors and pinpoint it. Like they say, it's an electromagnetic jungle out there."

Aimée was out of her depth. "How does it work?"

"I set up a system for this phone's ESN and MIN code, its serial number and identification number. So each time," she paused, rubbing her neck, "René . . . that's his name, René?"

Aimée nodded.

"So when René makes a phone call, my scanner picks up his ESN and MIN numbers, my computer, hooked up to my scanner, recognizes his cell phone, and tunes in to his conversation and records it."

"Sounds easy. But I'm sure it's not."

"So far there's no encryption in the radio spectrum," she grinned. "When it happens, we'll figure something else out."

"And if the phone's not on?"

"I can only monitor what's out there."

Aimée paused looking around the room filled with radios. She clenched her fists, trying to keep her hands still, to keep her nervousness in check.

"His kidnappers used his phone once. To call me on my cell phone."

Léo's smile vanished. "Kidnappers?"

"How closely can you track, Léo?"

"Well, during the Occupation the Nazis found hidden British crystal radios transmitting from cellars. This operates on the same basic principal. But the Nazis had roving trucks with tracking equipment to follow the signals and triangulate. Primitive, but it did the job. Stationary antennas have limitations; it depends on the signal and relay time. Keep them talking."

"What if I can't?"

"You must. If he's in Paris—and we don't have an electrical storm—the longer the phone call, the closer I can pinpoint. If the gods smile, not only the street but the building."

"*Merci*, Léo," she said. "I'll owe you."

"Don't thank me yet," Léo said.

On her way out, Aimée noticed the wheelchair folded by the door, and end of a metal hospital bed peeking from behind a draperied alcove. Aimée wondered when Léo'd last been out of this apartment. But then, she traveled through Paris every night. Riding the airwaves.

EARLY EVENING quiet had descended over the shadowy, intimate, crescent-shaped square near Clichy. Strains of an accordion mingling with a guitar wafted from somewhere above her. Familiar, an old working-class song her grandmother had played. Aimée looked up to see the silhouette of a couple dancing behind a lighted window.

And for a moment, she forgot the drizzle on the pavement and it could have been the countryside. Low stone buildings, a cat slinking around the corner, the church clock pealing the hour. But she couldn't get away from the awful sound in her head of the bullets' ricocheting by the phone cabinet where Thadée had been shot. The sickening scene replayed over and over.

Why kill Thadée?

If she couldn't meet the kidnappers' demand, René would be next. She looked at her watch . . . already an hour had passed! She willed her fear down; it wouldn't help her find René.

She remembered the door closing yesterday in the Olf office foyer, her *frisson* of fear. If she'd been the target and escaped, and now they'd gone for René, it was her fault.

Darkness blanketed the narrow street, the furred glow of dim streetlights the only illumination.

She had to find Sophie, the woman Thadée had named with almost his last breath, his ex-wife. She had to try to figure out where Thadée had gotten the jade—and who might have it now.

She walked past the glass awning to the rear of the courtyard. Under the stone lintel, by an ancient water spigot, a nicked metal sign in old formal French forbade children to play in the courtyard. She wondered when was the last time any children had lived here.

She passed the back stairs, wrapped her scarf around her head, belted her shearling coat tighter, and thanked God she'd worn her good boots. Only a three-inch heel.

Adjoining the old tire factory, beyond the fence, she saw an eighteenth-century limestone townhouse. Preserved, with an air of neglect at the edges. Was this where Thadée had lived? She hit the two buzzers. No answer. Only darkened windows.

Galerie 591 was locked. But a dim light shone through the mottled glass. She called the gallery telephone number. The phone rang and rang.

Aimée knocked on the service door. No answer. Looking in the window, she saw a dimly lit office with state of the art computers on several desks. Beyond lay a room with metal sculptures and paintings strewn across the floor. Curtains blew from an open hall window. Glass shards sparkled on the floor.

Someone had broken in.

She turned the knob of the door. Locked. She pulled out her lock-picking kit, inserted a thin metal skewer into the bronze cylinder-like Fichet lock. A few turns and she heard the tumble of the chamber and the lock snapped open.

Inside, a 1920s-style lamp with beaded fringe cast a reddish glow over the gallery.

". . . *Ohé*, someone here?"

She caught a faint whiff of classic Arpège emanating from a damp sweater flung over a chair.

Glancing out the open window overlooking the adjoining townhouse, Aimée saw a woman going out the door. In the glare of the streetlight, this woman, a pint-size Venus, was applying lipstick as she crossed the desolate square, her heels clicking on the cobbles. She wore a vintage mini-dress over beat-up jeans. A chic, downplayed look.

A chainsmoking, Vespa-riding thirty-something man puttered by, idled the engine, and stopped. Aimée noted the woman's black hair with purple braids. Could she be Asian? But her face was turned and it was too far away to tell. After exchanging a few words, she swung her leg over the man's Vespa and they rode away.

Aimée chewed her lip and listened. She pulled out her penlight and shone the beam on the wood floor.

"Sophie Baret?" she called out.

The only response was the rushing of water and creakings of the old warehouse mingling with the flushing of pipes and the sound of water from the roof gutters hitting the street.

Flushing? Or something else? The sound of water in the background continued.

She crouched, grabbing what seemed to be a shovel leaning

against the showcase. She realized it was an artwork inlaid with a mosaic of blue glass and ceramic tile tesserae. A fairy dust-like glitter sparkled as she carried it. Making hard contact was all she cared about. The floorboards creaked. Dampness permeated her bones and she shivered.

As she kept walking, the sound of gushing water grew louder. Inside a dank hallway lined by old showcases from thirties millinery stores, lay more *objets d'art*: sculptures and installation pieces. Aimée recognized several of the artists from the current art scene. An older Jean Basquiat painting hung on the wall.

The dim, gray streetlight worked its way through the grime-encrusted windows. Aimée heard a tapping noise.

By the time she reached the rear bathroom, her boots were soaked. She raised the shovel as a weapon and opened the door. A rush of water streamed over her feet.

She gasped. A woman, tied by her scarf to the snaking water pipes of the Turkish style squat toilet, her body oddly twisted, writhed and kicked. Her brown knee-high leather boots beat a pattern on the dirty tiled floor. Only the whites of her eyes showed. Her eyes had rolled up in her head.

Aimée rushed to lift her up, loosening the scarf from her neck and shoulders. Had she been tied up, tried twisting to free herself, but enmeshed herself further?

As the handle was released, the water slowed to a trickle. But the woman's flailing arms knocked Aimée into the mirror. It shattered, splintering. Bits of glass studded Aimée's coat.

"Killer!" the woman screamed.

"Wait a minute," Aimée said. "I'm trying to help you! You're Sophie? Thadée's . . . ?"

Aimée ducked as the woman swung a fist at her, then slipped, her head hitting the tiles with a loud crack. Her body slackened and went limp.

Filled with panic, Aimée listened for the woman's shallow, irregular breaths. She moaned and struggled against Aimée.

Somehow Aimée dragged her out of the bathroom and propped her against an old counter top. Thuds and noises came from the floor above them, then there was a clatter on the stairway. Her heart skipped. Was someone coming back to finish Sophie off?

Wednesday Night

NADÈGE PULLED DOWN HER sleeves, took a breath, and entered her father's mansion facing the Parc Monceau. She had to explain to him about Thadée; she needed his help. She could hear her father's reply 'He's always in trouble . . . like you.' True. But Thadée was still his brother-in-law, wasn't he? Her tante Pascale's ex, it's true, yet part of the family. And there was a lot more to it.

The uniformed butler stood aside, letting her ascend the marble staircase lined with hanging tapestries. She grabbed the handrail to steady herself. Her spike heels clattered above the noise of the reception; conversations, tinkling of glasses and the strains of a baroque chamber music ensemble.

The usual.

Her petite great-grandmother, tottering on her bound feet in their tiny embroidered shoes, had told her when she was small, "You are of the Lang-shun princess blood line. There's royal blood in your veins." Right now there was a lot more than that in them.

With Chinese and Vietnamese heritage on her mother Phuong's side, French on her father's, Nadège had been termed *l'asiatique* behind her back at school. Her mother had died when she was four. Nadège had been raised by her grandmother, the first in her generation not to have bound feet.

She found her little boy, Michel, asleep in the black lacquer bed, *grand-mère's* marriage bed. A tart odor of incense surrounded him and the faint, suffused red light from the small altar in the corner gave a blush to his cheeks. Against the wall, a Chinese chest held linens and his tumbled treasures of Legos and wooden blocks.

She planted a kiss on his warm forehead, leaving a fuchsia imprint, then headed next door. Passing through a long parlor, she entered a small, darkened sitting room. 1950s Chinese movies flickered in scratchy black and white on a large screen. *Grand-mère* lay snoring, her thin jet-black hair combed into a bun. Her head rested on a stone pillow.

Nadège saw the Longchamp racing forms, the betting stubs under the chaise. Everything neat and arranged. *Grand-mère* played the horses, winning more often than not. And she liked modern gadgets like the newest cell phone.

For a moment, Nadège wanted to lie down next to *grand-mère*, to nestle in her arms like she had as a small child. But the craving wouldn't go away. No good wishing it would.

Nadège rooted in her makeup bag. Found her small pipe, rolled the gummy black-brown pellet between her thumb and forefinger, lit the pipe and inhaled. The heavy, sickly sweet smoke hit her lungs. Took her away.

When she came to, she found herself sprawled on the wood floor, her nose running, her sweater ripped, its feathers and beads stuck in the parquetry crevices. The TV screen still flickered. Her *grand-mère's* eyes were open, watching her.

"No good girl!"

Guilt flooded her. As it always had throughout her childhood.

Her *grand-mère* lapsed into a harsh mixture of Vietnamese interspersed with Chinese.

"I don't understand when you talk like that," Nadège said.

"Where is your *hiêú*? Your greeting for your elders?"

Nadège knew she meant filial respect. *"Tiens, grand-mère!"*

"Little Michel doesn't need you around. A bad example," she said. "Don't come back. *Méchante . . .* like your *mère!* No good!"

But you raised us, Nadège wanted to answer. "I'm hungry," she said, instead.

"Too much food downstairs. Too much drink. Fancy French like your papa. *Gweilo,"* she spat. "You like them."

As if every person outside her *grand-mère's* enclave was a white-faced devil.

"Papa won't talk to me," she said. "You know that. I need your help, *grand-mère.*"

She had no place to stay now. Nowhere safe.

"Thadée's dead."

Grand-mère shook her head. "Sad. Sorry. He your uncle by marriage but mix with bad people. Like you. You too *lo fan,* all foreigner," she said. "Don't listen nobody. Too much this," she said, pulling Nadège's sleeve up.

Only old bluish marks.

Nadège chased the dragon now, inhaling the wispy trail of smoke from a pellet burning on tin foil. Quitting, she was quitting.

"The horses running good, *grand-mère?*"

"Don't change subject. I try but no good breeding." She sat up, readjusted the jade hairpiece in her bun. "But I take care, Michel. So smart, that boy."

Just as she'd raised Nadège. After her mother's death, Nadège's papa had shunted her off to these rooms in the back wing. *Grand-mère* kept her own servant, her own entrance, even her own little kitchen filled with the special smells of Saigon. And every Friday night, under the watchful eyes of Victor Hugo and Buddha, both revered as saints by her *grand-mère's* Cao Dai sect, her mah-jong pals could be found clicking the mah-jong tiles atop the black lacquer table.

"Thadée was killed," Nadège said. "Shot."

Grand-mère shook her head. Was there something else in those sharp eyes?

"Sad, like I say. But bad people, bad business. Bad aura, all *gweilo*," she said. "He no relation to me, no business of mine."

Her *grand-mère's* ringed hand put a fistful of francs in Nadège's hand. "Go now."

"Where's papa?"

But her *grand-mère* had already turned up the volume on the TV set.

Nadège cleaned up her nose, applied more makeup, and found her way through the kitchen. The cooks, busy stuffing squabs, ignored her and the hired servers, with full trays, elbowed her out of the way.

She slipped into the main room and took a glass of kir royal from a waiter. Her former stepmother, a year older than Nadège, whose blonde hair hit her waist, was holding court by one of the Rodin statues.

Nadège made her way to the high-ceilinged glass solarium. Often her father hid in there; he hated this kind of party, just as she did. And there he stood, under the Belle Epoque iron-and-glass framed roof. Her father, black hair graying at the temples, glinting in the candlelight, tapped his cigar ash into the base of a palm tree.

As she moved closer, she saw he was speaking with two men. One wore a blue police uniform. And from the tense look on her father's face she realized he now knew about Thadée. Nadège edged out of the solarium, through the kitchen, and into the night.

Wednesday Midnight

AIMÉE POUNDED ON HER godfather's door. She saw Morbier's sleepy-eyed surprise as she half-carried a stumbling Sophie across his doorway.

"*Tiens*, Leduc," he said, pulling his flannel shirt around him, consulting his worn watch, and sniffing. "It's late. Don't bring your drunken friends here, eh . . . especially one who looks like trouble."

"She needs babysitting and she's not drunk."

"Nice of you to extend my hospitality, but I don't have room for guests. Like I said—"

"Round the clock until I discover who has kidnapped René."

Startled, Morbier pushed his socialist newspaper aside, kicked his wool *charentaise* slippers away, and spread a blanket on his couch. She laid Sophie down, pulled off the wet, brown boots, and covered her.

Sophie, who'd passed out again in the taxi, blinked, barely conscious. Aimée poured her a glass of water and helped her to sit up and, painfully, drink it.

"Sophie, did you see who attacked you?"

"Where am I?" She rubbed her eyes, sniffed. "Smells like the warehouse."

Morbier's housekeeping skills left a lot to be desired, but a warehouse? Then Sophie stiffened.

"I was tied up, hung from. . . ." She stiffened. "You're kidnapping me!"

"I found you and helped free you," Aimée said. "This man's my godfather, he's a *Commissaire de Police*. Show her your badge, Morbier."

"À *vôtre service*, mademoiselle, you're safe here." He winked, finding his wallet and opening it to show his ID.

"Poor Thadée." Sophie burst into tears, her shoulders heaving.

"Listen to me, Sophie, someone on a motorcycle shot him, then came after me," Aimée said, leaning closer. "I pulled him into the phone cabinet, where he died in my arms."

"We were divorced," Sophie said, wiping her blue eyes with her sleeve. "But we remained friends. I became his partner at the gallery. We were always better at that anyway."

Sophie's eyes were pools of hurt. Did she still love Thadée?

"Can you remember what happened?" Morbier asked.

Sophie blinked several times. "They took me to the morgue to see Thadée's body this morning. It was horrible," she said, her wide eyes filling with tears again. Her light brown hair was matted to her cheeks.

"Did you talk to him before he was shot, Sophie?"

"I only arrived from London this morning to prepare for the exhibition," she said, rubbing her head.

"But you must have talked, *non?*"

"He hadn't even hung all the artwork for the show!"

"Sophie, did he speak about jade?"

She shook her head and winced. "The only time I saw him was in the morgue." Tears rolled down her cheeks. "Tonight, after I checked the gallery for the shipment, I turned the light off in the bathroom. Someone grabbed me. Next thing I knew, I was hanging from the overhead water tank."

"Shall I call a doctor?"

"Give me a Doliprane, eh? Let me sleep."

Aimée reached into her pocket for the aspirin packet she carried. "Here. Do you know who Thadée owed money to? Had he mentioned—?"

"*Merde* . . . aches like a. . . ." Sophie swallowed the pill, leaned back, her eyes closing. "*Une catastrophe*. The gallery exhibition's supposed to be hung, but nothing. . . ."

"I think he wanted me to give you something. A check?"

"I don't know what you're talking about," Sophie said, pulling her stained silk blouse around her. "A check for what?"

"Do you know how he came into possession of . . . ?

Sophie yawned. "I don't know what you're going on about." She curled up on her side and within a minute she was snoring.

Morbier shook his head. "I can't take care of her, Leduc," he said. "I work, remember. And this trouble's not my business. My retirement's around the corner."

"You always say that," she said. He was the busiest *commissaire* on the verge of retirement she knew.

He shrugged and motioned her to a dark wood table by his window overlooking a dilapidated ironmonger's courtyard in the Bastille district. The dark building's corners were burnished by the moonlight.

"Marc's staying with me this weekend," Morbier said. "I don't have room for her."

His grandson Marc stayed with him more and more despite his Algerian grandparents' frequent requests for visitation rights. They kept insisting Morbier's choice of a Catholic boarding school was no proper education for a good Muslim.

She pulled out a bottle of *vin du Vaucluse* from her bag, shoved a dirty plate aside, and reached for wine glasses above his cracked porcelain sink.

She needed a drink. He looked like he needed one, too.

"Open this and I'll tell you about it," she said, giving him no choice.

"You know how long it takes to get old, Leduc?" he said, pulling out the cork and pouring. "Like this . . . *pfft*. Overnight. You wake up and . . ."

"*Santé,*" she said, clinking her glass against his.

She felt Morbier's eyes on her. Studying her like the RG had.

"How do you know René's been kidnapped, Leduc?"

She looked at her watch. "Morbier, it's six hours since their phone call and I'm no closer to finding what they want." She took a long sip, sat back on a wooden chair missing one of its three rungs, and told him what had happened.

Morbier shook his head. "A hollow threat."

How could he say that? "Didn't you hear about the shooting in the 17th?"

"Not my *quartier*, you know that." Morbier rolled his eyes.

"Morbier, what should I do?"

"Why ask me? Leave it to the professionals, Leduc."

"And what are *you*? It stinks, Morbier." She hid her trembling hands under the table. "I'm scared," she said, hating to admit it.

Morbier looked away. He never liked dealing with emotions.

"Call the RG man, Regnier," he said. "Tell him. He seemed to like you so much."

"Like me?" She shook her head. "Regnier wants the jade. René's life wouldn't matter."

"Do you have a choice? Can you come up with the jade?"

"I don't trust Regnier and the RG as far as I can spit. They were responsible for papa. . . . The ministry never acknowledged our involvement or their responsibility. Papa had a dishonorable record until I made them clean it up. And it took two years. They still won't acknowledge it was their mission. You think I'd believe them?"

No flowers at the funeral, but a bill for her father's autopsy.

"Leduc, you don't do that kind of work anymore, remember? If anything happened to René, could you live with that?"

His words stung. She'd never forgive herself if René was hurt.

But what he really meant was that she wasn't up to it. The damage to her optic nerve made her useless. A liability.

"I worked all through my hospital stay," she said. "I don't intend to stop now. The medication and meditation control it."

At least she hoped so.

"Hostage negotiation's a fine art," he said. "How did they find you, and trace René?"

"They must have followed me," she said.

Weariness had settled in her cold, damp legs. She noticed Morbier's thinning salt-and-pepper hair, more salt than pepper now. When he was tired, his jowls sagged, reminding her of a basset hound.

Morbier poured them each another glass.

"What if you were the target, Leduc? Victim of a setup?"

Her chest tightened. "I wondered about that, too," she said. "But why, Morbier? Then there's the *flic* I saw with the RG. He was involved in the Place Vendôme surveillance."

Morbier raised his hands to ward off her words. "Not this again. Get a life, Leduc."

"When the secret service or their lackeys are involved, everything stinks."

Morbier pulled out a box of cigarillos and another of wooden kitchen matches from near his black phone. A relic, with a rotary dial. He scratched one of the matches and lit up a Montecristo.

"I thought you quit," she said.

"These little cigarillos from Havana?" he said, tossing the empty yellow box into the trash. "They don't count."

Like hell they didn't. And what she wouldn't give for one right now! She leaned over the table wishing she didn't want a puff so much. Wasn't that stop smoking patch working anymore? She rolled down her jeans waist. *Merde!* The patch was gone. She pulled out one from her bag, unpeeled it, and stuck it on her hip.

"Like one, Morbier?"

"After I finish this coffin nail," he said, taking a deep drag.

"Plant a word, I need to see the file on Thadée Baret. The kidnapper said forty-eight hours, Morbier," she said. "Look into it, please."

Morbier shook his head.

"After all, what's a godfather with an ear at Brigade Criminelle for?"

"That's rich, Leduc. I'm only there one day a week," he said, rubbing his jaw.

"It's for René. Morbier, please," she said. "I swear I won't ask for any more help."

"You'll deal with the RG?"

She looked down. Noticed the peeling brown linoleum, his thin ankles and worn brown wool slippers, like those her grandfather used to wear.

"Consider it," Morbier said. "Otherwise I won't stick my neck out. And I'm not even promising that. Lots of the old boys have retired."

She nodded.

"How do I know you mean it, Leduc?"

"You want a pinky promise?" she said, remembering when she was ten years old and making a pinky promise put the world in order. Too bad it didn't do that anymore.

"What about her?" Morbier gestured to the sleeping Sophie. "Just one night."

She held up the jade disk. It glowed with a pear-hued translucence in the dim light of Morbier's galley kitchen.

"And what's that supposed to mean, Leduc?"

"I don't know," she said. "But I'm going to find out. Meanwhile, I'll sleep on your floor and monitor Sophie to make sure she doesn't have a concussion."

Morbier went to bed. She tucked the blanket around Sophie's shoulders and tried René's number again. Three rings and then a click.

"*Allô . . . allô?*"

She heard breathing. Her pulse raced.

"René!"

"The dwarf's tied up at the moment. . . ." She heard snickering.

"Please meet me. I have what. . . ."

In the background, she heard scuffling. The sounds of splintering wood.

"Not now," a voice said.

Then a cry. René's cry. And the line went dead.

Nervous, she tried Léo.

"*Allô*, Léo?" she said. "Could you locate it?"

"In five seconds?" Léo said, her voice sleepy. "The Northeastern sector antenna responded; he's in Paris. Keep him on longer next time."

"*Merci*," Aimée said, pacing the worn wood floor.

Thursday Morning

AIMÉE WOKE AT 6 A.M. to darkness, her shoulders and legs stiff.

Twelve hours had passed since the first kidnappers' call. She had to get to work. Morbier snored in his back bedroom. Sophie lay asleep, after a night of twisting and turning on the couch. But she had no fever, hadn't thrown up.

Aimée wrote "Call me when you wake up" on a graph-lined piece of paper and put it on Morbier's kitchen table.

She swallowed her pills with an espresso at the corner café on Morbier's street and made it to her apartment, changed into a black leather skirt and long pullover. She walked an eager Miles Davis on the fog-lined quai, then dropped him at the groomers' for a much-needed trim.

Aimée tried Gassot's number again but it rang and rang. Frustrated, she wanted to beat her head against the stone wall. So far, she was spinning her wheels in the sand.

On her calendar the day was circled in red . . . payday. Time for

René's paycheck. All over France, veterans and retirees collected their pensions. Most banked at their post office accounts.

That's where Gassot would be! Too bad her bike had been stolen. She jumped on the Number 74 bus to Clichy, passing old ladies walking their *chichiteux* dogs in front of bourgeois gray Haussmann buildings.

Aimée knew the Clichy area, boasting bigger apartments, was about to become the next "in" place. It was becoming sprinkled with avant-garde boutiques whose back windows overlooked the trainyard, with newcomers who could ignore that water wasn't connected to the main around the clock, and the fact the *quartier* had been "in" once before, then out. Far, far out.

Here Degas and Zola had argued at Café Guerbois, over Zola's infamous article on the Salon that had refused Manet's painting of Nana, a courtesan. Now the café was a Bata shoe store.

The rail lines, a symbol of modernity and access to the lush countryside for the Impressionists, were now grimy and soot-encrusted and the countryside better known for cinderblock *HLM* low-rent council housing. Place de Clichy's former 1930s showcase Gaumont cinema had become the 1970s do-it-yourself Castorama hardware store.

Aimée left the bus. Her shoulders slumped when she saw the line at the post office trailing out the door. How could she find one particular veteran in a sea of old faces?

She took a black marker and on an envelope wrote "Hervé GASSOT, *anciens combattants*," as she'd seen done at the airport.

On her third trip walking the line, an old woman tugged at her sleeve. "What's he done?" she asked.

Aimée noted the sixtyish woman's white hair held in place by a hairband, the tailored winter-white wool coat with dirty, too short sleeves, scuffed 70s Courrèges patent leather ankle boots.

"Nothing yet," Aimée said. "Can you help me?"

The woman shrugged and looked away.

"Feel like a coffee?" Aimée asked.

"*Un demi's* more my style," she said.

"*Bon*," said Aimée. "Let's go. My treat."

They ended up across the street in a working class café facing Avenue de Saint Ouen. Aimée tapped her chipped nails on the zinc counter as the old woman knocked back a beer and then another.

"*Alors*, Madame, have you seen Hervé Gassot?"

The green jockeys' jerseys flashed on the mounted *télé* above the bar. Besides them, the espresso machine whined as it steamed milk and a line of drab raincoated commuters waited to purchase the November Carte Orange pass or a phone card. Aimée could use both.

"I see him around. Plays cards."

"So you know Gassot well?"

"Who knows anyone well? That's relative, *n'est-ce pas?*" she said. A slight white froth edged her lip. "The Existentialists would argue that we can never know anyone, really."

"*D'accord*," Aimée agreed.

But it was her franc and she didn't care to discuss philosophy. She wanted to know about Gassot. On top of it, this lady in white didn't smell all that fragrant.

"So you've seen him around?" Aimée said. "What about today in line at the poste?"

"I'm still thirsty."

Aimée nodded to the barman to give her another.

"He came early."

She pushed the holder with boiled eggs toward the woman. "Try one, tastes good with a *demi*," she said, noticing the tremor in the woman's hands. Her thin legs.

The woman cracked the egg. With effort, she peeled the

eggshell. Bits of white shell sprinkled on the floor. She took small bites and chewed slowly, each bite measured.

Aimée had a sinking feeling that this was the woman's meal for the day. A loud ringing sounded in the woman's pocket. She pulled out an alarm clock, white and oblong, with large numerals on it.

"Time for my scrub," she said. "Wonderful hot showers at the municipal pool."

"So where does Gassot play cards?"

"He cheats, you know."

Aimée hid her smile. "*Alors*, Madame," she said. "Can't you help me?"

"I've seen him in the square," she said, shrugging.

"What does he look like?"

She pointed to an older man leaning against the counter, drinking a *verre*; white haired, stocky. Like a lot of older men in the *quartier*. The woman shrugged.

Aimée figured the old woman was hungry and needed a drink, that's all. But Aimée didn't begrudge her the food. She put some francs on the counter, stood, and hitched her bag onto her shoulder.

"But Gassot's peg-leg gave him trouble today," the woman told her.

At last! Aimée paused and leaned closer to the old woman, hoping gentle prodding would elicit more information.

"You mean he has an artifical limb?"

"He limped more than usual," she said. "Might get a new one, since he cashed his pension today."

"An injury from the Indochinese war?" she asked.

"Wouldn't surprise me."

"He was an engineer, wasn't he?"

She raised her eyebrows. "Talked about oil drilling. How he couldn't do that anymore with his pegleg. Worked with drawings."

"*Merci*, Madame . . . ?"

"Madame Lorette," she said. Her eyes changed. "Sorry, I haven't helped you much."

Did she notice the pity in Aimée's gaze?

"Look at my hands. You wouldn't know it, but once I was a concert pianist. Schubert was my forte. I even played at the Châtelet concert hall."

Did this woman have someone to help her? "Do you have family?"

"I wasn't a very good mother," she said. "Some women shouldn't have children. And my daughter knew that."

"Maybe so, Madame Lorette," Aimée said. "But children eventually get on with their life."

Aimée felt a pang of sorrow. Had her own mother felt that way? For a moment she wished her mother was sitting in some faraway café thinking about her, knowing guilt like this woman. Whenever she'd asked her *grand-père* about her mother, he'd sigh and shake his head. "*Ma petite*, some women aren't meant to be understood. Just to be loved."

And in an odd way, she did understand, had no choice but to accept it. But deep down, a part of her waited for the mother who'd left one day without explanation. A woman who'd gone to fight revolutions and change the world, but left a little part of it incomplete.

After finding that old letter from her mother in the Sentier district, Aimée had known it was time to move on.

"You know my mother left us," she said. "Like you, I guess she did better without children. It doesn't mean she didn't love me or that you didn't love your daughter in your own way."

She slipped Madame Lorette fifty francs and hoped it wouldn't be spent all at once. But she'd found something out from the old woman. Now she knew where to search for Gassot.

AIMÉE DISCOVERED six *orthopédistes* in the 17th arrondissement. Two had retired, one specialized in sports injuries and the other two, in mastectomy fittings.

The last, near Clichy, didn't pick up the phone. But her father's words rang in her ears: "Check each lead or you'll regret it later when it smacks you in the face." So she bundled her shearling coat around her and trudged down rue Legendre to the last address.

The Centre Orthopédique was a small taffy-colored storefront nestled in an ancient building. Wooden legs and old corsets filled the shop window. She pulled a pair of heavy brown-framed glasses from her bag. A sleepy-faced middle-aged man answered Aimée's knock.

"No more appointments this morning, sorry," he said.

"Pardon, I'll get to the point. Did Monsieur Gassot have a fitting this morning?" she said. "Or was it later this afternoon?"

"What's it to you?" His eyes narrowed and he scratched his chin.

She rooted through her bag and opened her cryptography notebook. She took a moment, pretending to consult it. "We're doing you a service," she said smiling. "Our social worker teams now visit in the field. We coordinate directly with the service providers, such as yourself, to expedite the clients' prosthesis delivery and make less paperwork for you."

She thought he'd like the last part.

"They never did this before. Sounds new to me."

"But it is!" she said, eager to keep talking and throw him off balance. "You know we may have made a mistake. Perhaps Monsieur Gassot's obtaining his prosthesis from someone else, but I've checked with all the concerns like yours in this arrondissement, so I assumed he dealt with you."

A wonderful scent of rosemary came from inside the shop. The man's eyes darted away.

"Look, I don't want to hold up your lunch," she said. "Can you just tell me if he's getting a new prosthesis today?"

The man shook his head. "No new prosthesis appointments today."

A dead end.

"*Merci,*" she said.

She had a bad feeling. Was Gassot so scared that he had run away with his *pension* check? She turned to go.

"But the old goat came for an adjustment," he said. "Won't get a new leg, always tells me he likes this one, but today he admitted he's considering a modern one."

What did that mean? She kept her excitement in check. "I'll have to look into our coverage," she said.

"He's been too cheap to admit he needs a new one. Maybe some relative died and he got a windfall."

A windfall? Or the jade?

Or was the *orthopédiste* trying to drum up business?

"*Aah,* so that's it," she said nodding, thinking quickly and looking at the number the man at the *anciens combattants* had written down. "I'd like to follow up with him. Is his number still 01 38 65 02?"

"Doesn't have a phone. Doesn't like them, he says."

Whose number had she been given?

"Well, Monsieur, you've nailed the problem for us. Now we know why we haven't been able to reach him. I suppose he's still at the same address." She flipped through her cryptography notebook. "I must have left that on my desk, can you give me his address?"

"No clue."

Did Gassot move around, stay with friends? "Do you treat others from the Sixth Battalion?"

He shrugged. "You name it, I treat everyone. Few of the old ones talk much. One of them just died, Albert, a crusty old bird. The kind who thinks the world owes him a living since he saw a few bullets in Indochina. He'd gone to the clinic for a routine checkup. Rumor says he got offed."

"What do you mean?"

The man shook his head. "That's all I heard. These old vets imagine things. Who'd go for an old coot like him anyway?"

"I'll check into it," she said, writing on her pad. "What's his name?"

"Albert Daudet. Sorry, but my lunch is waiting."

Now she had an idea. "We're pushing for added benefits for the Sixth to make restitution for limited services."

"You mean, so they won't take you to court?"

The man wasn't so sleepy after all. And he probably knew all of them. Or at least more than he let on.

"Did I say that?" she smiled. "But your cooperation would be appreciated. It's the men of the Dien Bien Phu Sixth Battalion we're hoping to contact. I'm meeting with a few, informally, not at my office, but at a café. Of course, I'd help with the forms and expedite your insurance claims if you could help me."

Short of an out-and-out bribe, that should entice him. At least make him consider it. She pulled out a card from her card file, one with just her name on it. "Here's my number." She wrote it down.

SHE FOUND a phone booth downstairs at a café, nestled between the Sexodrome and the soup kitchen run by priests, where boulevard de Clichy bled into Place Pigalle. Garish life-size faded photos of 1985 big-haired strippers stared back at her in the hall by the phones. Her first call was to Serge, her pathologist friend at the Morgue, to inquire about Albert Daudet's autopsy.

"Sorry Aimée, Serge is testifying at the Tribunal in Nantes," said his secretary. "He took the kids."

Serge turned his work trips into a holiday for his twins to

give his wife a break. Like two balls of mercury, the twins never stood still.

"Will he check in?" she asked, disappointed.

"Last I heard, one of the twins had a fever," she was told. "But I'll tell him you called."

Serge was the only pathologist she trusted at the Institut médico-légal. She'd wait until he returned and, if she wangled it right, he'd read her the autopsy results over the phone.

Then she called Division 17 at *le Préfecture de Police*. If they traced the call, this café was perfect. She waited while the receptionist connected her to the landline search office.

Why hadn't she thought of it before? The man must be lying low because of what happened to Thadée Baret. Baret looked old for his age, a hazard of drug use, but he was a generation younger than Gassot. What possible connection between Baret and Gassot existed? So far all she knew was Gassot had written the article about the jade and Thadée had paid for it with his life.

"*Bonjour,*" she said, consulting the number the man at the *anciens combattants* had written down for Gassot. "I'm on detail with Commissaire Morbier. We need a land location for a phone line, 01 38 65 02."

"Your authorization code?" a disembodied voice asked.

She prayed Morbier hadn't changed his code.

"Alfa Romeo280," she said. His favorite car.

Pause.

"Checking authorization."

Perspiration dampened her collar.

"Authorization code confirmed. Checking."

Morbier would be mad as hell when he found out. And he'd change it right away.

"Twenty-seven, rue des Moines," the voice said.

Encouraged, fifteen minutes later she stood in front of the shuttered townhouse with a wild, unkempt garden at its side.

The townhouse, separated only by a wall, stood behind the art gallery. At one time, she figured, the buildings had been joined, like a compound.

Maybe they still did?

What if Thadée let old vets live there, or rented them rooms? That could be the connection!

No one answered the door, and the place looked deserted. She tried René's number as she had all night. No answer. Then her cell phone rang.

René's kidnappers? Her heart leaped and she looked at her Tintin watch. If she told Léo the time, it might help her track the call.

"Mademoiselle Leduc," said a clipped voice. "Commissaire Ronsard would like to speak with you."

Her heart sank. Ronsard from the *Brigade Criminelle* quartered in the *Préfecture De Police* at Quai des Orfévres. How had he found her?

"Concerning?"

"He'll expect you within half an hour, Mademoiselle Leduc."

AIMÉE STOOD in the Brigade Criminelle outer office by a scuffed mustard-colored door. Wet wool, unemptied ashtrays and the sad smell of fear kept her company. She shivered, staring at the ancient brown-tiled floor and the yellowing announcements on the faded green walls. Thick, webbed skylights let in gray diffused light.

A NO SMOKING sign hung above the metal desk and a scratched billy club lay next to binders of the staff shift schedules and a log labelled SICK DAYS.

A bored *zigzag*, a low-ranking officer with three stripes, passed by.

She tapped her high-heeled boot, smoothed down her leather skirt. The chilly waiting room felt like the polar ice cap. And the frigid glare of the young uniformed receptionist, who insisted she empty her pockets and bag twice before passing through the metal detector, didn't help.

"Mademoiselle Leduc," she said, at long last, "go in."

Aimée passed a vaulted window in the long corridor. Below, the Seine snaked, pewter and dark khaki, under the overcast sky.

"You wanted to see me, Commissaire Ronsard?" she said, entering his office.

Commissaire Ronsard nodded. "*Un moment,*" he asked, handing a uniformed *flic* a red labeled file: evidence complete and ready for *la Proc'*, the Prosecutor.

The Brigade Criminelle boasted of their 72 percent solved-case rate. That didn't include the *banlieue*, suburbs with high-rise concrete projects that the brigade didn't police—or care to. Even the Paris *flics* avoided them.

She noted the wooden desk with stacked folders, two folding metal chairs, and photos of former department chiefs lining the mustard colored walls—one very familiar to her. Bound manuals of the Code Civil sat on a window ledge.

"Tell me about your relationship with Thadée Baret," Ronsard said, indicating a wooden chair.

"Relationship?"

"Were you *l'autre femme?*"

Quaint, the old expression for the other woman.

"Not at all." She stuffed her anger. "Why ask me?"

"But Mademoiselle, you lured him to the phone cabinet," he said, as if she hadn't spoken. "Accosted him. Bystanders heard you shouting. Said he seemed desperate."

"Thadée was desperate, Commissaire," she said, keeping her voice patient. "How did you get my name?"

"Bystanders heard you identify yourself," he said.

"Of course, I stood—"

"Right here," he interrupted, pulling down a screen with a diagram of rue des Moines. The half-moon-shaped square, the *boulangerie* and the phone cabinet were outlined in blue. Polaroid photos of Thadée's body from various angles were tacked up beside the diagram. She winced. Thadée resembled a twisted broken doll.

"Commissaire," she said, "he told me someone was following him. And I know he waited for my call in a café. Perhaps his phone was tapped. On top of that, my partner René Friant has been kidnapped."

"Mademoiselle Leduc, that's the first I've heard about it."

"The kidnapper wants this." She showed him the fifty-thousand franc check. "They said Thadée owed them. If I didn't pay, they'd dismember my partner."

"Did Thadée Baret say something to anger you?"

Why was he obsessed with that?

She shook her head. From the walls dampness emanated through the rectangular office. Goosebumps went up her arms.

"You yourself admit you pushed him into the line of fire."

"Don't you understand?" she stood up, paced closer to the diagram. "I'd never even met him. If I planned on killing Thadée, I wouldn't lure him into a crowd to be the target, too. But if someone wanted to stop him talking, it was the perfect way to eliminate him and throw the blame on me." She stared at the commissaire. "You know that as well as I do."

She watched his face. Did a flicker of understanding cross it? She figured right now he had no other leads so he'd jumped on her.

"*Au contraire*," he said. "A witness heard you threatening him. Saw you push him."

How convenient. She wondered if they'd find this witness again. She was glad she kept the information about the jade to herself.

"Like I said, I told him to duck, but too late. What can you do about my partner, René Friant? Commissaire, I'm not a civilian." She walked to the wall, pointed to the photo of a tall man, with a gray mustache and sharp eyes. "That's my *grand-père*. He left the Deuxième Bureau, as they used to call this section, and started Leduc Detective."

Commissaire Ronsard would listen to her now, wouldn't he? He pulled at a loose thread from his jacket, then looked away.

"Mademoiselle, how do you explain Baret's ex-wife Sophie's disappearance?"

"Disappearance?" Aimée asked. "That's a question for you to answer, Commissaire," she said. "She had been assaulted in her home and tied up. I cut her down from the toilet pipe, otherwise—"

"*Attendez.*" He opened a folder, took out more Polaroids. "A courtyard resident called last night and said he saw you carry a struggling Sophie to a taxi."

The graphic artist.

"But I was helping her."

"Then where is she?"

Should she tell him? But he didn't seem to believe anything else she said. And she worried for Sophie's safety.

"Sophie checked into a clinic to rest, she seemed distraught." A small fib.

"We need to question her."

Sleet silvered his office window, sheeting the barges in the Seine in a gray mist. The office temperature matched the dampness outside.

"Commissaire, that's for you to arrange."

"I can keep you in *garde à vue* until you cooperate," he said. A *garde à vue* would smell of unwashed socks, vomit, and urine, on a good day.

"Clinique Parc Monceau," she said. "At least I dropped her off there."

She knew someone would check. That's why she'd made a reservation there on her cell phone from the taxi the previous night.

"Why didn't you help her register at the clinic?"

"Commissaire, she didn't want my help," she said.

"We found this in the gallery," he said, slapping it on his desk. "Does this look familiar?"

Aimée's black wool scarf.

Great.

"*Merci*, this must have fallen when I helped her," she said.

"But Sophie Baret never checked in. We consulted all the registers at clinics and hopitals. Standard procedure. Found a reservation but Sophie Baret didn't check into the clinic. Matter of fact, her name appears on an Orly flight manifest to London."

"London?"

"On an Air France flight. How do you explain that, Mademoiselle?"

Wasn't she still at Morbier's? "That's news to me."

"So you took her to the airport," he continued, "or made it appear that way."

"Commissaire, I had no idea—"

"Did you silence *her*, too?" he interrupted.

Aimée didn't like the look in the commissaire's eye. Or his attitude. She thought fast. "This is the first I heard she went to London. All I know is what I've told you. Commissaire, I could have been a victim, too. What if I was the target? Aren't you pursuing that line of inquiry?"

"So tell me about your enemies, anyone who would shoot at you," he said. "Work related issues?"

"My partner and I do computer security," she said. "As I told you, I got a call. He has been kidnapped."

"So you say." Ronsard stared at her.

"You think I'm making this up? Have you investigated Baret's drug connections?"

"You sound quite familiar with him," he said. "I feel you're holding something back, Mademoiselle Leduc."

What good would it to do to tell him about the jade; he wouldn't believe a word she said.

"Aren't you going to write this down? René Friant, 19 rue de la Reynie, missing since Wednesday evening."

"How did these alleged kidnappers make contact?" He pulled out a notebook.

"They called me on my cell phone from René's." She punched in René's number now but the only response was his voice mail message.

"How many times have they called you?"

"Just the once," she said.

"They're waiting for somebody."

She agreed.

"Or *something*. What do you think that would be?"

She shook her head.

"I'll alert the *Groupe d'intervention de la Gendarmie Nationale* unit," he said.

The supposedly elite group that dealt with terrorism? Léo's help was more promising.

A look crossed Commissaire Ronsard's face that she couldn't decipher.

"If Sophie Baret gets in touch, we expect to be informed," he said, his tone dismissive. "You can go."

That seemed quick. Too quick. Was he letting her go so they could follow her, see if Sophie got in touch? Or, Aimée shuddered, if she'd lead them to Sophie's body?

She walked to the door.

"Mademoiselle Leduc?"

She turned.

"I'm sure you're aware we have the right to keep you in *garde à vue*," he said. His small eyes never left her face. "We can hold you for forty-eight hours. Think of it this way; it's secure, no enemies could shoot at you."

"I'm aware of the law and the legal system, Commissaire," she said, buttoning her coat. "Matter of fact, I took an oath when I obtained my detective license. Like you, we're sworn to uphold the law. But thanks for refreshing my memory. I thought it was seventy-two hours."

She wrapped the scarf around her neck, hitched her bag onto her shoulder.

"If there's nothing more Commissaire?" she said, looking again at the Polaroids, the sad crumpled body of Thadée Baret.

All the way down the Préfecture's staircase, she wondered how hard they would try to find René. And why the hell had Sophie fled to London? Why hadn't Morbier called her?

Thursday Afternoon

MORBIER, WEARING A SUIT and tie and carrying a briefcase, locked the door of his Bastille district apartment. The briefcase was one her father had given him long ago. She'd only seen him in a suit once before.

"Why didn't you let me know Sophie'd left?"

Startled, Morbier turned around.

"Leduc, don't sneak up on me like that. We'll talk later, I'm late for the Tribunal," he said. "Turns out Marc's other grandparents have called for a mediation to extend their visitation rights."

"Morbier, you were supposed to call me!"

"*Et alors*, Sophie said she'd told you!"

She clenched her hands. The bile rose in her stomach.

"You believed her, Morbier?"

He glanced at his watch, an old one with a frayed leather band. "She's in London by now."

Incredulous, she stared at Morbier. "Why did you let her go?"

"*You*. You didn't tell me to cuff her to the chair, did you?" he said. "I would have. Sophie said there was nothing you could do." He shrugged. "No one can babysit her if she doesn't want it."

True. A scared Sophie might be safer in England, but it left Aimée in the dark.

"Didn't you ask her about Thadée, question her about the jade?"

"Stubbornness runs in your veins and those of your 'friends,' too!" Morbier said. "She said she didn't know anything. And you know what, I believed her. Then she made coffee, complimented me on my taste in Havana cigarillos, and left."

Aimée wanted to steady her shaking hands. Couldn't. Not since Thadée Baret had landed in her arms. But she wouldn't let Morbier see them. Couldn't let him know the stress had gotten to her.

"Morbier, do you think I can't handle this now because of . . . my eyes?"

"Leduc, I recommend you stick to what you do best. Computers."

"But René. . . ."

"Have they called back?"

She shook her head. "I told Commissaire Ronsard."

"Good," Morbier said.

"But he thinks I lured Thadée into the street so he could be killed."

"The kidnappers will call. Ronsard knows his stuff. He'll get them."

She had to convince Morbier. Persuade him now. Like milk, he soured quickly.

"Morbier, you have to speak with Ronsard. Persuade him I had nothing to do with shooting Baret or abducting Sophie. And that René's in great danger."

"I'll try."

And with that, he locked his door and ushered her out.

AIMÉE WOVE her way among the bicycles and buses stalled on rue de Rivoli. The stench of exhaust and beeping of horns wore on her nerves.

She tried René's number again, then listened to her messages. Nothing.

The faint hope she'd nursed with respect to Guy died. Guy hadn't been one to burn up the phone lines. But he'd written her letters from Geneva, putting into words his impressions and feelings about life, and for her. A sketch in the corner, a line of poetry here and there . . . she'd read them over and over. An old-fashioned part of her loved the words he'd penned and even the crisp paper he'd touched.

She missed him. She hesitated, but she knew she had to explain. She called his office. "Doctor Lambert, please," she said. "It's Aimée Leduc."

"He's with patients," Marie said, her voice clipped and frosty. "I'll relay the message."

Was Guy refusing to take her calls?

With a heavy heart she mounted the spiral staircase and opened the door of Leduc Detective. Startled, she saw a young man in his early twenties, with light brown dreadlocks to his waist, eating tandoori chicken next to an open laptop. Turmeric and curry smells filled the office.

"Mind telling me how you got into my office and what you're doing here?" she said.

"Sorry, I'm Saj de Rosnay," he said with a sheepish grin, wiping the corners of his mouth. "René gave me a key, I thought you wouldn't mind."

René's encryption genius certainly knew how to make himself at home. Saj sat crosslegged in her chair, his laptop and files strewn over her desk. He wore beige cotton Indian pants, vest, and flowing tunic. Tibetan turquoise hung from his neck. But with his pale complexion and amber eyes he looked all French.

"René asked me to prepare some data for you," Saj said, pointing to the spreadsheets all over the *recamier*. "Sorry, but I'm not quite there."

René trusted him. And right now she needed his help to keep the business running. She'd reserve judgment until she saw what he could do.

"I'm Aimée," she said, biting back her comments about his work habits. She hung up her coat and shook his hand. Her stomach growled; she hadn't eaten this morning.

"No problem," she said. "Let's see what you've got so far."

"Try a pakora," he said, gesturing to the open cartons. He pulled an Indian shawl around his shoulders, recrossed his legs as he sat on her chair. "I found something interesting when I factored large numbers and then . . . look!"

Threads of numbers stretched over the laptop screen. Impressive.

She nodded and grabbed a warm, crisp, potato-filled pakora.

"I'm curious about you, Saj." She figured he was a hacker, like most of them, who enjoyed the thrill of penetrating a system, leaving a calling card, but not destroying it.

"Fire away," he said, stretching his arms and doing neck rolls.

"You're on loan from the Ministry, *n'est-ce pas?*" she said. "One of the hackers they train for use in the computer division, instead of sending them to prison."

Something in his eyes shifted. Had she gone up a notch in his estimation?

"Rehabilitation, they call it," he smiled.

She opened her laptop at René's desk, booted up.

"What makes you so important to them, Saj?"

"Things I can do make it too scary to have me as an opponent," Saj said. "They didn't know what to do with me so they sent me to the hacker academy to keep tabs on me. But

I'm into meditation for the world good. And I refuse to crack Swiss bank databases any more."

She grinned, rubbing her eyes. Meditation! That's what had gotten her into this mess.

"Should we wait for René?" he asked.

Her stomach clenched. Would he want to work, to get involved, after he heard about René? "Can I speak in confidence?" she asked.

He nodded, his dreadlocks hitting his elbows.

"He's been kidnapped. I'm waiting for a phone call from men who took him."

"For real?" Saj's eyes widened.

She gave Saj a brief account, leaving out the part concerning the jade.

"A ham radio operator's ready to triangulate the call," she said, connecting her phone to the charger. "I'll understand if you don't want to get involved since the Ministry's on your tail. But I need help, and so does René."

Saj shook his head, his brow furrowed. "René's an *artiste*, deft and intuitive. I respect him, he's taught me so much in the short time I've known him."

Aimée turned away, fighting back tears. Saj painted René perfectly. Even if he had taken over her desk.

"René would want us to work, not stew. I deal better with tension by working."

"Me, too," he said.

Three hours later, they'd finished the statistics, drafted a security proposal, and consumed the entire contents of the cartons of Indian takeout.

"Nice work," she said.

She'd deliberately limited her comments to work. Saj was good. Very good. And he'd seemed to take to heart the news about René.

Every time the office phone rang she jumped and looked at the clock. Eighteen hours had passed and still no phone call.

"I'd like to help you," Saj said. "Especially since René . . . well, he's helped me."

"I'll take you up on that," she said. "Give me your number, we'll have more to do tomorrow."

He handed her a card. "*Namaste*," he said, putting his hands together in a gesture of peace. He gathered his laptop and left.

If she took the medication and used screen reading software, she'd avoid straining her eyes. Then she thought about the rent, her renovation contractor, Miles Davis's grooming bill, René's salary, and new equipment.

The phone/fax line rang. Her fingers tensed on the keyboard. She took a deep breath. She couldn't blow it with the kidnappers this time.

Thursday

NADÈGE GATHERED HER VELVET skirt and slid through the hole in the slat fence. She followed the weed-choked rail line to the old train tunnel, now blackened and dark. Moisture oozed from the moss-filled cracks in the stone. Beyond the tunnel lay the thieves' market in the closed down rail yards.

Brick red, peeling rail cars were hooked up to cylindrical ones labeled liquid petroleum gas. She knew the homeless, the *clochards* who were fond of the bottle, slept in them between the periodic raids by the railway police. And weasels scavenged on the old tracks.

Nadège tried not to grimace as she passed the display of

used Prada bags, Vuitton totes, and Christian Louboutin red-soled shoes spread on a blanket.

"Ça va, ma belle?" said Hortense. Her toothless grin and hollowed out face shocked Nadège. Once a model, Hortense had graced *Elle* magazine covers before the drug ravaged her. "Take your pick. Worn once, most of them."

Nadège's stomach cramped and her eyes watered. Withdrawal, never dramatic like in the movies, was more like an aching flu, so bad her bones hurt, laced by nausea and sweating. Now she used the drug just to become "normal," forget getting high. And she hated it.

"Where's Mr. Know-it-all?"

But Hortense had nodded out, slumped against the lichen-covered stone tunnel. Nadège passed the young hustlers warming their hands by a fire of burning railroad ties. An aging *clochard* sold cartons of Dunhill cigarettes, and a man stood by a pile of copper pipe with a sign saying "TEN FRANCS EACH." He rubbed his hands in the cold and shook his head when Nadège asked him if he'd seen her connection. The sky darkened with rain.

Desperate, she asked a thin man taking water from the old rusted faucet, ignoring his leer.

"Looking for candy, eh. Know-it-all's a no show today."

Merde! "*C'est vrai?*" she asked.

"What's it worth to you?"

His eyes were like brown stones. He smelled of earth and the decay around him.

"Take a hike," she said.

"Name the time and place."

Not even in your next life, she thought.

She hurried over the rail lines. Her hands shook. She needed some courage to meet her father. *Juste un peu . . .* she'd cut back. Would cut back even more, if only she could get through the next hour.

Old covered yards led to abandoned, decayed buildings. Nadège had avoided this area after Thadée cautioned her against the heavy-duty types controlling it.

She climbed a rusted-out staircase. Dampness clung to the graffitied walls pockmarked with age. Inside, water dripped and a terse conversation echoed. She bent down and picked her way over the metal rods, avoided the broken glass and randomly strewn bricks to get closer. ". . . *Flics* can't find her, how can we?" She recognized two of the men huddled in a group. One had threatened Thadée last week, the one who had a van.

Did they mean *her*?

Her hands shook so much, she couldn't hold onto the railing. She backed out, step by step. Right into the arm of the leering man from the faucet, his hands still damp.

"*What's your hurry?*"

She pushed his hands away, took off running, and didn't stop until she'd reached the fence.

SHE RUBBED her nose and tottered into her father's home-office on her highest heels. Her feet were sore, brutal *mecs* were looking for her, and she had nowhere else to go. The flu-like symptoms of withdrawal slammed hard: every part of her ached, feverish and sweating.

"*Bonjour*, Papa."

Her father sat by a roaring fire talking on the phone, frowning. Her stepmother's room had been vacant.

"I told you never to come here," he said, after finally hanging up.

"But it's about Thadée—"

"*Oui*, the funeral," he said, rubbing his tired eyes. "Behave this time. If you make a scene at the church service I'll have all your contact with Michel cut off."

She shook her head. "Why won't you ever listen to me, Papa?"

"Because when I do, it's what's running in your veins that

talks, not my Nadège." His eyes moistened. "I blamed Thadée. And now drugs killed him."

"*Non*, Papa," she said. "Not drugs. . . ."

"Nadège, wake up," he said. "Try the clinic. . . ."

She shriveled in fear. He meant St. Anne's, the psychiatric hospital. The dank looney bin on the site of a medieval convalescent house for those with contagious diseases. The place where he'd committed her mother after she'd been thrown out of the last private clinic.

Her mother had never come out.

She had to make him understand.

"You're not listening," she said, pacing back and forth. "Thadée owed—"

"His dealers," he interrupted. "What can I do? A scandal will erupt unless I cooperate."

"Who cares what people think? He's dead, they killed him."

His eyes narrowed. "What was the last thing Thadée said to you?"

What did he mean?

" 'Meet me at my place.' Please, Papa." Why was he so stubborn; she needed a place to stay. Somewhere safe. "So his dealers threatened you," she said, "and you're more worried about that than about me?"

The phone rang. She knew he wanted to answer it, yet his eyes caught on her torn shoes. Pain and hurt softened his look.

"Did he ever mention your *grand-père's* art collection?"

She could never confide in him. Not now.

She slammed the door on her way out.

Thursday

TIGHT DUCT TAPE BIT into René's ankles, cutting off his circulation. His wrists, tied behind his back, stung. He chewed the kerosene-smelling rag in his mouth. He couldn't stop panting nervously, his nostrils working hard under his small, flat nose. The cartilage had never developed properly due to the diminished volume of pituitary secretion, a common problem for those of his size. But he doubted these *mecs* would notice.

Every so often the gravel-voiced man kicked him. He heard murmured conversations somewhere. Waiting; they were waiting for someone, or for instructions.

Musky, mildewed odors surrounded him. His nose itched and ran. They'd taken off the burlap bag. Old timbered beams held up the damp wall, part brick, earth, stone, and flaking stucco that he faced: as if someone had once meant to resurface the old cellar and had given up, abandoning piles of cobwebbed bricks and worm-holed planks.

The light from a sputtering kerosene lantern flickered with a low hiss. He watched a trail of black ants mounting a brick by the sweating moisture-laden wall, moving a large crumb. It looked impossible. He watched them to keep his mind sharp, alert. And to avoid dwelling on the ache in his hip.

He could just make out numbers and letters written on the stone: 5/3/1942, Renault factory bombing, and the name Etienne M. He tried to peer closer. More names on the wall in a faded, old-fashioned script. Now he knew, he was in an old bomb shelter, an *abri*, one of 22,000 shelters used during the war.

He remembered his mother's tales of running to the shelters or sometimes to the Métro. More often she'd gone to underground cellars and caves. Most Allied attacks had focused on outlying train depots and factories that had been taken over by the Germans.

Fat lot of good this information did him; he could be anywhere. If only he could locate his phone, reach it, and call Aimée.

"Get some beer while you're there," the gravelly voice said somewhere behind him.

"Where?"

"Next to Bata."

"No names, shut up!"

Bata . . . the shoe store? René closed his eyes.

"He's asleep."

How many Batas were in Paris? They were usually in low-rent *quartiers*. Places like la Goutte d'Or, the African section, or Belleville or Clichy.

They'd left the rags in a wet pile on his raincoat. Even that he could live with. He disliked more the fact that he could see them. A bad omen for kidnap victims. It meant the kidnappers didn't care if they could be identified; the victim wouldn't be around long enough to identify them.

Forty-eight hours. Then dismemberment and death.

Thursday

AIMÉE HEARD THE HUM of the fax machine. Apprehensive, she stood up to read the fax. Was it René's captors, with a meeting place?

"Meet me downstairs at the Musée Henner. Dinard."

Dinard, the jade expert!

Twenty minutes later she stood in front of Musée Henner, a weathered, sand-colored stone museum that displayed the blue, white and red French flag. Rain pelted the cobbles. She doubted if Dinard had had time to research the jade. But he wanted it.

She needed to string him along, glean information from him. His present interest must stem from the RG's visit.

Aimée entered and saw a wooden staircase mounting to the upper floors of the eighteenth-century townhouse left to the state by the owner, a mediocre German painter. A fresh-faced young woman at the reception met her.

"You're here to see the curator?"

Aimée nodded, not knowing what else to do, and followed the young woman's directions to the bowels of the museum. Too bad; she would have liked to see the view from the top.

The sign on the door read CURATOR. She knocked and Dinard's assistant, Tessier, opened it. He motioned her inside to a room with a computer on a desk next to piles of papers. Oversized art books filled the bookshelves; a large oval window overlooked the back courtyard

She stayed by the door, prepared to back out. "Where's Dinard?"

"Monsieur Dinard asked me to collect the jade pieces," he informed her, his forehead beaded with perspiration.

She played for time. "Why the fax, and the mystery?"

"He's had to leave for the hospital for a hypertension screening."

"No offense, but I'd rather give him the pieces myself," she said. "My understanding is that he's investigating their origin and provenance."

She noted the perspiration on his brow and how he kept smoothing back his brown hair. A nervous habit she remembered from their previous brief meeting at Dinard's office.

"They're holding something over you, aren't they?" Aimée asked.

A flash of anger lit his eyes and she knew. That's what the RG did. Intimidation, threats of blackmail, wiretaps. Sickening. Regnier was probably overseeing the campaign.

"Look, you're not my business," she said. "All I want to know about is the jade."

"They know about you," he said, his anger replaced by a cunning look.

"Pleyet and the RG? Tell me something new."

The phone rang. Was this a signal?

"I have to leave," he said to her. "I don't have much time. To do the research properly we need the jade pieces."

"Like I said, I prefer to give them to Professor Dinard myself. When can I meet him?"

"In Dinard's position, he can't be seen dealing with you."

"So that's why you wanted to meet here?"

He nodded, turning toward the window. The parquet floor creaked as he shifted his stance.

Aimée said, "I have a question. Since the pieces have such a high value and the art world is so small, Professor Dinard must know the identity of the last owner."

"We work in a museum."

"But you deal with collectors, n'est-ce pas? You would know those with jade collections."

"I thought you wanted help, Mademoiselle."

But not the help he wanted to give her. "Who's interested in the jade?" she asked.

"Do you have it with you?"

She shook her head. "I don't think you're a jade expert. You're just full of hot air and questions."

From his expression, she'd struck a nerve. He froze.

There was a pause. She heard a clock ticking, saw the shadows in the courtyard. Felt the chill in the room which had no working heater.

"I assist and help curate exhibitions," Tessier said, his voice lowered. His eyes darted around the room. "But you're wrong. The study of jade is my passion."

Unease filled her. "Did Dinard mention the jade to you the other day after I left?"

Tessier shook his head.

"Or his conversation with the RG?"

"I'm not privy to Professor Dinard's conversations."

Shadows lengthened from the trees casting a dim light in the room. Tessier wiped his brow.

"Tessier, you're wasting my time," she said, heading for the door.

"Wait." He took a deep breath. "Dinard's on the way out," he said. "Museum politics. They offered me his post, but only if I perform like a seal." He wiped his brow. "My life's devoted to art. Why should my education and expertise be wasted?"

"I had the collection, then it was stolen. But I still have this." She held up the jade disk.

Tessier's eyes widened. He took a magnifying glass from the desk. "May I examine this, please?"

"Tell me about the jade," she said. "Then I won't bother you. Tell them anything you want. I'll leave you in peace."

His eyes shone. "The first Emperor of China waged war for some jade beads. We call them disks. They symbolize the sky and the earth, hence the round shape. Jade's more than a stone, it's an integral part of an ancient system of worship, essential in the ritual propitiation of the gods and in the performance of homage. There's a cultural parallel with our discipline of philosophy; it had both a political meaning and a practical function."

He studied the disk, then shrugged. "But I don't know if this small disk decorated jade astrological figures or belonged to another, older piece," Tessier said. "The original disks were small. And sacred. It's so hard to tell."

"You're saying these disks could be older than the zodiac animals they were attached to like halos."

"I'm speculating," he said. "The original meaning of the Chinese word for "ritual" was "to serve the gods with jade.""

Tessier pulled a small book from his pocket and translated from Chinese:

> Shamans, represented by the earliest Chinese character 巫 (wu), used tools to draw circles superimposed at right angles. From this we may deduce that shamans monopolized the technology for making circular 璧 bi disks or beads, and thus had the exclusive power to present sacrifices to the gods and ancestral spirits. The round shape of the bi is said to derive from the circular path that the sun follows in the sky. According to accounts from 283 B.C. we know an unblemished 璧 bi disk was not only worth the price of several cities but that a king would ceremoniously feast for many days upon receiving the disk.

Aimée gasped. Was this disk such a rare ancient ritual object?

She pulled out the creased page from the auction catalogue and looked closer at the photo illustration. She hadn't been able to understand why a Vietnamese emperor would have entrusted the jade figures to the Cao Dai for safekeeping. She'd assumed the emperor would only have Buddhist objects. But how clever it would have been to disguise the ancient disks by using them as part of later figurines—using one treasure to mask a much more valuable one.

Footsteps on the creaking wood came from the hallway.

"You still haven't explained why Dinard's being so secretive," she said. "Why did the RG visit him?"

"They're not CNN, they don't broadcast continuous updates," he said. "I don't know."

The footsteps stopped. Fear shone in his eyes and he put a finger to his lips. What was he afraid of?

She went to the peephole in the massive door and peered out. All she could see in the dim hall was the spherical body of a dark suited man.

"He's shadowed me from the museum," he said.

"Is he from the RG?"

"Who knows?"

If she left now she'd be recognized. It would be better to have Tessier owe her. Or think he did.

She opened the oval window and set a chair under it. "You've seen this disk, now find out who the jade belonged to, Tessier, and who would want to steal it," she said. "Otherwise, your new job's in jeopardy. Call me from a public phone, later."

She swung her leg over the windowsill and climbed outside into the chill air.

AIMÉE PUNCHED in Leduc Detective's number on her cell phone and listened for messages. One. The reception wavered and cut out as she passed the high voltage lines by the railway.

"I thought we might have a late lunch."

Guy? Had he reconsidered and forgiven her? But his voice sounded different.

"Place des Ternes. I'm in the bistro across from Villa Nouvelle." She recognized him now. It was de Lussigny, from the Olf meeting. "I know you were going to call me, but I hoped you could fit it in today. Forgive me for not confirming with you beforehand."

Merde! She should have checked her messages earlier. Olf was a big account. She looked at her Tintin watch, and called the bistro.

"Please tell Monsieur de Lussigny that I'm en route for our lunch appointment," she said.

Aimée hailed a taxi and jumped in behind the driver. "Count on a nice tip if I make my lunch date."

He grinned, ground into first gear, and took off.

She tried René's number. Again no answer. Why hadn't the kidnappers called back? What was happening to René? If only she knew what to do. But what else could she do but wait?

In the taxi mirror, she slicked down her spiky hair with gel, reapplied mascara, and touched up her traffic-stopping red lipstick. She pinched her cheeks for color, dotted them with lipstick, and rubbed it in. Thank God she wore a black leather skirt and silk top underneath her sweater. She pulled out a gray silk scarf, knotted it several times and looped it around her shoulders, then found a hip-hugging thin silver chain belt in the bottom of her bag and hooked it on.

Seven minutes later and thirty francs poorer, she was seated in a dark wood-paneled bistro amidst gleaming mirrors, vases of flowers, and the hum of discreet conversation.

De Lussigny, in a black suit, his hair carelessly brushed back, looked younger than she remembered. *Soigné*, with an effortless air. The small bistro was understated yet the attentive waiters who hovered made her self-conscious. People like nearby resident Jeanne Moreau and cabinet ministers ate here.

"Smells wonderful," she said.

"And with a wonderful wine list from Languedoc," he told her. He ordered for them both and requested a demi-bottle from the reserve cellar.

"First, let me apologize again for not helping you when the minister put you on the spot, Mademoiselle Leduc."

"Please call me Aimée," she said.

Better watch out, she told herself, lest she run off at the mouth. A man with his corporate power didn't need to wine and dine her. What was the real purpose of this lunch?

The wine arrived. He sipped and complimented the sommelier

who poured the dark red liquid into Aimée's glass. A Cabernet, full-bodied, tart and a bit pebbly. Nice.

"I realize, after checking with your other accounts, that this Olf project is routine for you," he said. "Of course, it didn't hurt for the board to hear it, too."

"I understood you were testing our firm."

She placed the napkin on her lap, took a piece of bread from the basket and tore off the crust. "Forgive my directness, but I get the feeling this meeting concerns something else, Monsieur . . ."

"Julien, please. The consortium has an agenda that you should be aware of."

"I don't understand. Which hat are you wearing right now?"

He smiled. His large eyes were reddened with fatigue.

"Everyone wants the inside track. I've attended so many meetings in the past few days, I can't keep my head straight."

What did he mean? "But how does that concern me? Our firm does computer security. What agenda are you referring to?"

"We'd like you to keep your eyes open. And *I'd* like to have copies of your reports sent to me."

Industrial espionage? What was that saying about no free lunches?

"But Olf is paying me; I don't understand."

"Look, to insure this venture overseas will be an immense risk."

"But the financial rewards would be astronomical, wouldn't they?"

She was guessing but from the way he drummed on the table with his knife, it looked like her question had hit home. The charts and graphs she'd seen in the conference room indicated the project involved PetroVietnam.

"So Olf's negotiating, or vying, for oil rights and you want to know about the competition."

"Under your sweet and innocent exterior," he said, sitting back, "you're sophisticated and complex."

Sweet and innocent? But she had obviously guessed right.

"We know who our competition is. The British and Chinese. We'd like you to monitor the engineering department's e-mail."

"I run a detective agency specializing in computer security, not in industrial espionage. Now you don't have to buy me lunch. I can just leave, no hard feelings."

A waiter appeared at her elbow with an appetizer of smoked salmon dotted with caviar.

"And you, Aimée, what's the expression, 'pack a punch.' We'll pay you accordingly. I've mentioned this to Verlet, so you're not going behind his back. But you're welcome to confirm my request. Why don't you call him right now?"

"I take your word for it," she said. But suspicion nagged at her.

What was it about de Lussigny that made her wary? The smile in his tired eyes, the languid way he commanded attention from the waiter, his aura of power, the way he had brushed her hand with his as he reached for the bread?

A slow throb mounted in her head. Centered in her right temple. Fractals of light fused into a bluish fog.

She rubbed her eyes . . . *non* . . . but it didn't go away. Fear clutched her. Where were her pills? She reached in her bag, felt for them, and downed two with wine.

"Our consortium finds it prudent to monitor this activity. It's just a slight extension of your job."

A blurred fuzz bordered her vision. The sideboard with assorted tarts and pastries tilted, the walls unfolded. Panic overtook her and she felt sick to her stomach.

"As I suggested, confer with Verlet," he said, taking a forkful of salmon. "The salmon's Norwegian, why don't you taste it?"

Guy had warned her that stress would affect her optic nerve. She took a deep breath. Tried to relax.

But she couldn't.

She wanted to leave the resto before her eyesight blurred even further; before she saw two of everything. She had to get away from this man who had just asked her to spy on the Brits and Chinese. But one didn't say no to a client. At least not to his face. What if he put pressure on her, or Verlet, threatening to withdraw their contract? Would René think it best to cooperate?

"I'd appreciate your help," he said, his voice pleasant. "Just copy me on your reports."

Her peripheral vision was fading. She gripped the napkin, felt the crumbs on the table.

"That's all?" she asked.

He made it sound easy. But she sensed there was more to it. "I don't foresee a problem but I need to let my partner know; he's the one who'd coordinate our other jobs while I did this."

She had to get away and think: the oil rights, PetroVietnam, the Chinese. Did the jade link up to any of this?

"So, it's a workload issue?" de Lussigny asked. "Of course, I understand."

The fog began to recede to the edges of her vision. She prayed it would stay there. She pulled on her dark glasses.

"I need to check with him. Now."

She put her napkin on the table.

"But your food!"

"Please, excuse me."

She stumbled, gathered her bag and left. Outside, in the chill wind, she had to grab the stair railing to orient herself. If she could just get back to the office. If only she could talk to René and figure out what to do. If only she could be sure René was safe. She had to put an ice pack on her eyes.

Someone familiar approached. She recognized that gait, the roll forward on the balls of his feet, even if she couldn't see him clearly. It was Guy. His office was a few blocks away. Now she felt guilty for having lunch with de Lussigny. She was about to run and hug Guy, apologize again. Explain about René. Somehow convince him . . . and then she realized he was engrossed in conversation. *Non*, kissing someone. His arm was around a petite blonde.

A sharp pain pierced her. She stumbled and turned away. Afraid to believe what she thought she saw. She looked again as they walked right past, too busy to notice her, and studied the resto menu.

Aimée took a few steps, trying to blend with passersby and reach the Métro entrance. Could she have mistaken someone else for him?

And then she heard laughter, a woman saying "Stop teasing, Guy."

Ahead, the green metal around the red Métro plaque glinted. The pills were taking effect. Her vision was clearing. She kept walking: telling herself to concentrate, to make it to the Métro steps, then to the platform. Trying to ignore the recollection of Guy's invitation to move in together. How quickly he'd forgotten. Only a few stops and then she'd reach Leduc Detective and could collapse. She had to keep going while she could.

The womanizing traitor! A wave of dizziness overcame her and she reached for the side of the magazine kiosk. Missed. Caught herself on the newspaper rack.

"*Ça va?* You look green," Julien de Lussigny said, catching her arm.

Startled, she froze. "Please, I feel terrible if you left your meal on my account—"

"Just got a call and have to rush off to a meeting," he interrupted, buttoning his coat. "The investors have questions. As always!"

No aura of power or mystique surrounded him now as he gave her a tired grin. Or maybe it was the concern in his eyes. He looked more human. Light drizzle misted the gray pavement.

He unfurled an umbrella and held it over them.

"*Merci,* but I'm headed to the Métro," she said.

"Look, my driver's here, let me give you a ride."

Right now it sounded wonderful. Gratefully, she entered the black Citroën idling at the curb. She slumped in the back seat and kept from turning to look out the back window for Guy and the blonde.

"*Ça va?*" he asked. "Should we stop at a pharmacy?"

"*Non, merci,*" she said. "My office on rue du Louvre, if you don't mind."

He was strangely quiet in the few minutes it took them to get there.

Aimée thanked him and mounted the steps to Leduc Detective, feeling her way up by clutching the cold banister. Crystalline streaks webbed her vision, like the *fleur de sel* salt crystals she'd seen harvested in the Mediterranean, floating sheetlike to the water's surface.

She opened the frost-paned office door, now fractaled with light. Inside the office, she dropped her bag, her hands shaking. Would her vision clear?

René was in danger, the RG threatened her and she still hadn't found the jade. And Guy. . . .

She rooted in her desk drawer for more pills, found two and a bottle of Vichy water. When her hands steadied she downed them, sat, and took deep breaths. Think, she had to think. To calm her mind. She tried to visualize a river, flowing and smooth, with a current like a dark ribbon.

A loud knock on the door startled her. "Who's there?"

"Linh," the voice said.

"Come in please," Aimée replied, and opened her eyes to see a blurred Linh, her hands upheld in a gesture of greeting.

"I'm sorry Linh . . . my vision."

"Chaos fights your spirit," Linh interrupted.

"We call it inflammation of the optic nerve," Aimée said. "Please, do sit down." She indicated the Louis XV chair, then reached for an ice pack from the first aid kit.

"*Non*," Linh said. "Cold chills the channels." She reached into her bag for an embroidered pouch and pulled out a small packet. "Try the Eastern way. Herbs. Let me take your pulse."

Long deft fingers pressed Aimée's wrist in several places.

"Open your mouth."

"What?"

"Like this." She stuck out her tongue and Aimée did the same.

"Abnormality of the liver is evidenced by a tense, pounding pulse and red tipped tongue indicating post-traumatic stress," Linh said. "For this we build the fever, let the heat burn out the infection, unlike doctors in the West."

Aimée smelled mint. To each his own, Aimée thought. It was worth a try.

"You're an herbalist, too?" she asked.

Linh shook her head as she applied mint oil to Aimée's temples and brow. "Everyone in my country treats it this way. From when we're little babies."

So they carried herbs instead of aspirin?

"Close your eyes. Take deep breaths," Linh said, massaging Aimée's hands. "Let the mint oil take effect."

Aimée felt a warmth and slight tingling on her brow. The curious warmth traveled to the top of her skull and down her neck.

"René's been kidnapped," she told Linh. "The kidnappers want the jade. I found no clues at the auction house. And Gassot's proving elusive."

"*Mon Dieu!*" Linh leaned forward, worrying her beads. "I will pray for him tonight."

"Linh, an RG agent is seeking the jade, too," Aimée said. "What do they have to do with it?"

"Who?"

"The RG's a secret service, affiliated with the Préfecture and National Police." And under the watchful eyes of the Ministry, she added silently.

Aimée felt a cold ruffle of wind by her knee, the musk of incense, and Linh's hand on her shoulder.

"I'm being watched," Linh said. "By whom, I'm not sure. One of the meditators gave me a ride here. She let me off around the block. But I may have been followed."

Aimée opened her eyes. Linh had gone to the window. Shadows from the trees on rue du Louvre bruised the office walls. Aimée couldn't read Linh's expression.

"The pieces were disguised—" Linh began.

"Don't you mean they *were used* to disguise twelve much older jade disks?" Aimée interrupted. "To hide them in plain sight, so to speak?"

Silence, except for the buses shuddering in diesel agony and the klaxons heralding a traffic jam below. A cobweb clotted the edge of her vision. Linh made no reply.

"And they've been stolen. Tell me, what do they have to do with—"

"*Reste tranquille.* Let the herbs work," Linh said, soothingly. She rubbed more mint oil on Aimée's temples.

"The Vietnamese secret police are watching me. I told you that," Linh said. Her eyelids batted in the nervous mannerism Aimée remembered. "My mother gave me a jade bracelet when I was five. She called it a fortune teller. Good quality jade changes color after its been worn. If the jade fades, it indicates bad luck. But if it grows more vibrant, a lush green, life energy is flowing well and this predicts good luck, good health, wealth, and many offspring."

"And your bracelet?"

There was another long pause. Now warmth ringed the crown

of Aimée's head, her palms felt moist and she noticed a tingling sensation coursing down her arms.

"That's personal," Linh finally said.

Was that why Linh became a nun? Now, Aimée felt a deep sadness emanating from her.

"You Westerners don't understand. Jade means much more to us than a trinket in a jewelry store window. The only way to win our people is through our beliefs, our souls."

"Does this have to do with PetroVietnam and oil rights?" Aimée asked bluntly.

"The only politics I'm concerned with is obtaining my brother's release," Linh said. "Please, you're the only one I can trust. Find the jade, before someone else does."

Then Aimée's vision gave out.

AIMÉE BLINKED several times. Afraid to try to focus. Light reflected and prismed from the decanter on her office desk. Her silk sleeve smelled of mint and her head felt curiously clear. No cobwebs or blurriness. Just a curious tingling at the base of her skull. And clear vision.

The herbs? A combination of pills and herbs? Linh had left a small vial of mint oil on her keyboard.

She reached into her pocket for the jade disk. Felt the cold comforting roundness.

Her pills were finished. She picked up the phone to call Guy. But he had had a blonde in his arms on the street.

She debated. But a minute later she punched in his number, determined to sound businesslike.

"Guy?"

"I'm in the middle of rounds right now," he said, curtly.

"Sorry, I just ran out of pills," she said.

"I'll call a prescription in."

Coward. She wished she could tell him she missed him.

How it hurt her to see him with another woman. Did he hear the false bravado in her voice?

"Right away," he said.

She heard someone say 'Doctor, what about the intravenous line?' and the pinging of bells in the hospital ward.

"If that's all . . ." he said.

Silence.

"Can we talk later?"

"What's there to talk about, Aimée?"

"I guess nothing." The words caught in her throat and she hung up. She'd blown it again.

She forced herself to stand up, get her bag. Not to call him back and accuse him of being with another woman. What would be the point? He'd made his choice and moved on fast. Seems he'd had someone else waiting in the wings. Better to end it now.

She'd ignore the hollowness she felt. Sooner or later she'd get over it. What if she'd agreed to move to the suburbs? He'd have expected her to have his dinner waiting. She couldn't even whip up an omelet! Forget Guy. She had to focus on finding René. Somehow the disks were the key; Linh had as good as confirmed it. Why had de Lussigny tried to enlist her to spy?

She pulled out Regnier's card and called him. She hated to deal with the devil, but perhaps he could help find René, as Morbier insisted.

His phone rang. No answer. Great! Waiting stretched her patience. The little reserve she had, as René often told her. She had to *do* something.

She locked the office and pushed the button for the elevator, a temperamental, grunting wire-framed affair from the last century. She stepped inside and rode it down to the second level. The glass elevator door slid open. She came face to face with Regnier. His freshly shaven scalp gleamed in the chrome yellow light. He stepped inside the elevator car and stood a few centimeters from her.

Fear was the worst thing to show with someone like him. She was afraid he could smell it on her.

"Any reason you don't answer your phone, Regnier?"

"Did you call with good news for me?" Regnier's aftershave bothered her. It smelled cheap and metallic. The accordion pleated gate closed and the elevator juddered upward.

"My partner's been kidnapped. The captor's threatening to dismember him. Believe me, if I knew where the jade was—"

"I'd be the first to know, Mademoiselle Leduc?" he said. "I hope that's what you were going to say."

Had he kidnapped René? She watched his dull black eyes, saw no quiver of response.

"I'm sure you want to help me now." He hit the out of service button. The elevator halted with a jerk. Her spine tingled. Up close she saw the threads in his overcoat.

Then he leaned closer, and whispered in her ear, "You're under surveillance."

First Tessier and now Regnier, but it didn't make sense for him to warn her. He'd ransacked her apartment.

"By who?"

"We're not all what we seem," he said.

"What do you mean?" Was she a pawn in someone else's power play?

He lifted her chin with his cold hands, so he could see her face.

Only then did she realize that she'd lowered her head and remembered how he'd stared at her on the quai. And that she had seen the butterscotch-colored button in his ear.

"How long have you been deaf?" Aimée asked.

His mouth twisted in a sad grin. "Long enough. Mine is only a tonal deafness at low range decibels."

Was this a crack in his tough-guy façade? Aimée heard a buzzing sound and his finger shot up, adjusting the clip behind his ear.

"So the RG uses you, like they used my father, Regnier," she said. *Could she play on his sympathy?* "I can help you," she said. "If you help me find my partner."

He stared at her. In the small elevator with him and his aftershave, she felt claustrophobic. But she knew she should play along with him.

"You have more resources than I do, Regnier," she continued.

Then his hands circled her neck. Terrified, she stepped back, tried to loosen his thick fingers. How could she have misread him like that?

"Let go!" His grasp tightened. Nowhere to move. It was like before, when she had been attacked. All she knew were those hands squeezing her neck. Choking her. No air.

She kneed him hard in the groin. Hit the elevator service switch with her elbow, then the button. The elevator shuddered and descended, throwing him off balance. He cried out in pain, let go of her neck and knelt on the floor.

She pried the elevator door open.

"*Eh bien!* I've been waiting a long time," said a disgruntled man, on the ground floor.

"It's all yours." She squeezed past him and ran into the street. She didn't stop until she stood on the quai de la Mégisserie, several blocks away. No Regnier in sight. She leaned on the stone bridge, her shoulders shaking and her breath fanning into the air in frosted puffs. How were Regnier and Pleyet involved?

She caught her breath. Lars would know, or he could find out. She walked to the Préfecture de Police, glad she'd kept her fake police ID updated, and entered the Statistics Bureau. The wide door stood ajar, pieces of plaster sprinkled everywhere.

Her footsteps crunched across the floor. A man with a mask gestured toward a penciled sign.

Due to pipe refitting, Statistics temporarily in Bâtiment B, second floor cellar.

Several stairways later she found it. And her friend Lars Sorensen, who headed the Préfecture's statistics department. Statistics, a broad term, provided Lars interdepartmental and interministerial access.

The makeshift office, once a vaulted medieval cellar, consisted of rows of metal file cabinets and several vacant desks. The burnt odor of metal soldering pervaded the office. A green beanbag pillow sat forgotten in the corner.

Lars, wearing army fatigues, leaned back on his chair and drank Orangina. She figured he'd come from the special training he did midweek outside Paris. His prominent jaw and punched in nose made him look like a prize fighter. "Do me a favor, Lars, check what these *mecs des RG*, Regnier and Pleyet, are working on," Aimée said. "Like you, they could be in reserve special ops."

"*Moi?*" Lars grinned. "Let me see. Every month each commissariat turns in a report, some big patron's idea so we classify and subclassify them. Like we've got nothing else to do, eh? Besides get manicures, trim the commissaire's ear hairs, and play *skat!*"

Her father had put up with Lars, pointing out not many could ferret the devil out of a hole like him. But she actively liked him. Lars was half Danish. But to hear him talk you'd think he'd been born and bred in Copenhagen, not lived in the working class district of Batignolles since infancy, now with a French wife and three children.

Lars searched in his files. The whine of a sander came from the hallway.

"You didn't see this, okay?"

She nodded.

Lars opened a creaking file cabinet, pulled a state-of-the-art Titanium laptop from inside, and powered it up.

"How old is Pleyet?" he asked, typing in his password.

She noted the last four digits Lars entered.

"Fifties, in good shape, with deep-set gray eyes that take everything in, like a hawk."

"But that describes a lot of them."

She remembered something. "Keloid scars on his right wrist."

He scanned the report. "Did he tell you he was RG?" He rolled his eyes. "More like Surveillance Circle Line."

"Circle Line?" she asked. "What's that? Regnier, too?"

"Regnier's RG," Lars said. "But, according to this, he's under suspension."

Her mouth dropped.

"Suspension? For what and since when?"

"Let's see. . . ." Lars hit some keys. "Pretty generic, misappropriation of operating funds last June. The chief discovered it in September." He clicked more keys, "On the ball, eh, your government *fonctionnaires!*"

So Regnier had gone rogue, but felt bold enough to threaten her. He had sniffed the jade. But how? And that didn't explain Pleyet.

Aimée leaned over Lars' desk. "What does Circle Line mean, Lars? How's Pleyet involved, eh?"

For the first time she saw hesitation in his eyes. He shifted in his chair and the springs squeaked.

"Don't ask me, Aimée, I can't tell you."

"Please, Lars." She ran her hand through her damp hair.

"I can't tell you because I don't know," he said. "Just rumors."

"Hinting at what?"

Lars didn't meet her gaze. A plume of sawdust shot up in the hallway.

"Lars, your papa and mine were friends. Why hold back? Pleyet was on the Place Vendôme surveillance. He looked familiar but I never knew his name. Any of their names. They made sure of that. I want to know his background, at least."

Lars looked away.

"It's important to me, Lars."

"Nothing in here concerns the past," Lars said. "This comes from Special Branch. They don't data entry old, failed missions. You know that."

But she'd figured one thing out. "So this Special Branch Circle Line's new?"

He nodded.

Wiretapping? But the RG had been doing that for years.

"It's not all governmental, that's what I heard," Lars said.

"Meaning industrial espionage?" she asked.

Two men in suits walked in and gave Lars the eye.

"Of course, mademoiselle," Lars said, his tone businesslike now, as he closed the folder and shut down the laptop, "when I tally the figures we'll report the amounts to your father's insurance agent. The Commissariat will have that information on file."

"Merci, monsieur," she said, playing along.

The men kept walking and passed them. She heard their footsteps echoing on the metal stairs leading to winding corridors and, eventually, to the holding pens under the Tribunal. She could imagine the sweating stone walls, and the prisoners awaiting sentencing in cells little changed since the Reign of Terror.

"Can't you do a quick search to see if there's a report filed on missing Asian jade?"

"You're looking for missing oriental art?" asked Lars. "You want me to check the list, you mean?"

She nodded.

He sat up, pulled at a drawer that stuck, then slammed it hard and it opened.

"A stolen Rodin sculpture in the 14th from narrow Impasse Nansouty near Parc Montsouris."

"Try the 17th arrondissement."

He thumbed through the file. The crinkling paper competed with the low whine of the saw in the background.

"What about missing jade?"

"Hmmm . . . a dope racket and bordello, but that's as close as it gets in the 17th."

Frustrated, she pulled out her map, studied it.

"My brother-in-law delivers meat to a *boucherie* in the 17th," Lars said. "He always bitches that he can't unload. One time he had to walk with a whole side of a cow through the narrow passage and an old lady fainted right on her poodle."

She read the map, half listening to Lars, thinking of the threadlike streets of this village within a village, still beating with a provincial life of its own.

"Sorry, that's it," Lars concluded.

She exhaled with disgust, leaning against Lars's grease-stained metal filing cabinet. If the jade was "hot," no one would report it stolen.

"*Merci*, Lars," she said, and left his office.

SHE TRIED to make sense of what she'd learned. Regnier, under suspension, had gone rogue, which made him more dangerous. Pleyet, still a cipher, worked for the "Circle Line." All along the quai, as brown leaves rustled past her on the gravel, she thought about Lars's change of attitude after he had spoken those two words. She pulled off her leather glove and wrote down the last four digits of Lars's password on her palm. She'd play with the numbers later.

Time was running out for René. She tried Commissaire Ronsard on her cell phone.

"The Commissaire's in a meeting," said a bored voice.

She tried Léo.

"Club Radio," Léo answered.

"It's Aimée, any luck with René's phone, Léo?"

"*Désolée*, so far the antenna's picked up nothing."

Aimée's heart sank to her feet.

"They could have trashed it, or just not turned it on," Léo said. "Keep your cell phone calls to a minimum, in case they try you."

"*Merci*, I'll check with you later."

She was stymied. The only person she knew of connected to Thadée was Sophie. Sophie *had* to know a detail, a name. Even if she didn't realize she knew it. But she was in London. Aimée had to reach her. Besides the art gallery, watched by the police, the best place to look was in Sophie's house.

Thursday Afternoon

AIMÉE MADE HER WAY toward the address, near Clichy, she'd found for Sophie. She passed small Indian shops selling suitcases out on the pavement as well as everything from manicure sets to bootleg tapes. Nestled in between them were Vietnamese florists, and discount clothing stores with jackets on racks bearing signs that read EVERYTHING UNDER 100 FRANCS, as they whipped in the rising wind.

Mothers wearing stylish black suits, or Muslim headscarves over dark robes, hurried little children to the *école primaire*, and a motor scooter putt-putted on the cobblestones waiting before a café doubling as a takeout for Turkish *kebab frites* sandwiches. She ordered a *kebab frites*, paid, and ate the steaming spiced lamb sandwich as she walked down the street.

Aimée found Sophie Baret's stained-glass-paned front door in tree-lined Cité des Fleurs. The cobbled lane of nineteenth-century houses, each with its front garden, felt like another world: ornate pink brick façades with statuary carved over the lintels of two-story houses. A spill of sunlight illuminated the trellis-covered walkway to Sophie's house.

Aimée knocked on the open door. "*Bonjour?*"

Something hissed, then crashed.

In the hall, Aimée saw a pink and orange-haired woman, wearing chunky black boots, and a tight, red rhinestone-trimmed dress under a faux fur orange jacket, lugging a snare drum and cymbals.

"*Pardon*, Sophie lives here, right?"

"Some of the time," said the woman, bumping into her. "I'm Mado, her sister. I housesit when she's away." The woman's face was quite pretty despite the black kohl-lined eyes and red eyeshadow that matched her outfit.

Sisters? Two bookends that didn't quite match. Mado looked the type who didn't trust anyone not wearing eyeliner.

"I'd appreciate if you could give me her number in London, something came up."

The cymbal crashed, causing the dog next door to bark.

"London . . . again?"

"She rushed there after the attack."

Mado's mouth widened. "Attack? My sister, the drama queen, does it again! She overeacts to everything," Mado said. Then paused. "She's not hurt or anything?"

"Someone broke into the gallery," Aimée said. "But I'm worried that she fled to London."

"Then she's fine," Mado said.

"But her ex, Thadée—"

"That scum! Sorry, we've got a rehearsal right now! There's a chance a scout for the label will drop by," she said. "The bass player's waiting for me."

A small Mini-Cooper with METALLOMIX spraypainted on it idled at the curb. The long-haired driver tooted the horn.

"Do you have her number in London?"

Mado shook her head as she edged down the walkway. "Shut the door for me, will you?"

Aimée closed it, leaving the thumb of her glove in the lock. Worried that Mado would notice, she blocked Mado's view and handed her a card. But Mado gripped the drum case and shook her head.

"Put it in my jacket pocket, eh?"

"It's important that I speak with her."

Mado nodded, shoving the drum through the opened car door.

"Sophie's in danger," Aimée said,

"Danger? According to her, that's the only way to live."

"You don't understand," Aimée said. But she was speaking to a closed car door.

The Mini roared down the lane.

Aimée knocked on the door of the neighboring house to ask about Sophie. No answer. She tried the small house on the other side. A smiling woman wearing an apron, holding a mop, opened the door.

"*Bonjour*, I'm. . . ."

"*Non fala française . . . Portugais!*" the woman said, retreating.

Aimée returned to Sophie's front door, pulled out her glove, and in ten seconds was inside. A pile of mail sat on a stool in the hallway. Water bills, gas notices, British *Vogue*, and postcards of upcoming exhibitions.

The angles and colors of the walls reminded her of a child's drawing of a house. Mauve walls, terracotta tiles, and antique and 1960s retro furniture jumbled together. Marabou feathered scarves smelling of cigarettes, and an electric keyboard littered the couch in the small living area, indicating Mado's presence. Aimée figured she slept there. A jam jar of wilted roses, whose pink petals were strewn over an old rattan table, gave her the impression little time was spent on housekeeping. Something she could relate to.

She identified Sophie's room by its faint Arpège scent. A Vuitton suitcase, partially unpacked, sat on her rose silk duvet, with a bulging cosmetic bag inside. Sophie didn't seem the type to run off without her makeup remover.

Aimée searched for an address book, a daytimer, anything with an address in London. But all she found was a selection of Clarins eye lift and skin serum cosmetics in the modern bathroom that Aimée wished she could afford.

In the pantry-sized kitchen, a glass coffee *pression* with its tin plunger screwed tight for coffee to drip through was still warm. She found Surgelé *croque-monsieur* frozen food boxes in the trash.

Aimée turned the garbage can over, its contents spilling onto the turn of the century mosaic tiled floor. Among the receipts, she found an airplane boarding pass and a crumpled piece of paper. She spread it open on the counter. A postcard, with a picture of Big Ben, written but never sent. Sprawling black script, crossed out words, and blotched letters. Tears?

She read the fragment:

> 'You *bastard!* Promises broken again and again. How can I believe you, Thadée? I sold the paintings, all of them and the exhibition here's a success. Don't deal with that scum Blondel. The last shipment passed customs. Yours, Sophie.

The rest was torn off. Shipment . . . art . . . that made sense, but who was Blondel?

Now she had a name, something to check.

And then a footstep sounded behind her. Before she could dive behind the kitchen cabinet something hard was stuck into her ribs.

"Hands up!" Mado said. "You *salope!* Trashing our place."

"Wait, let me explain . . ."

"Explain to the *flics*," she said. "Turn around slowly, eh!" Mado was another one who had watched too many movies.

Aimée spun and knocked the gun to the floor. Mado slipped on the frozen food box and fell, as Aimée grabbed for it. "What's this? A cheap party favor?" She pulled the trigger and a small plastic sheet with the word BANG! on it, dropped from the snout of the gun. Aimée pointed it at her, stuffing the postcard into her pocket.

"The *flics* are on the way," said Mado, her lip quivering.

"Nice try," Aimée said. "Listen, as I tried to tell you before, Thadée was murdered. Your sister's in danger. Real trouble. Start talking to me about this Blondel."

"Who?"

"The one who strung your sister up to a Turkish toilet because he figures she knows where some stolen jade is. If she knows, she's in trouble. And she's in deeper trouble if she doesn't, because they think she does."

"What's that to you?" Mado scowled.

"They're after me, too! And it's my job."

"Who hired you?"

Sirens blared from in front of the house.

Merde . . . Mado *had* called the flics!

No time to explain to them. She doubted they'd listen to her. For the second time one of the Baret sisters was blaming *her*. That's all Commissaire Ronsard needed to put her in *garde à vue*.

"You're as stubborn as your sister, Mado," Aimée said. "I have to find out about Thadée. They won't give up, and she's next."

Mado said, biting her lip, "An old man was asking questions. A pain in the derrière. I told him to get lost. Like I want you to."

Old man . . . Gassot?

"What did he look like?"

"Gray hair," Mado said. "With a wooden leg."

Gassot!

"You're in cahoots with him, aren't you?"

"When you realize I want to help Sophie, let me know."

Aimée kicked the back door open and ran. The small yard, enclosed by a rusted wire fence, was filled with wet leaves and tufts of crabgrass. The Portuguese cleaning lady next door was shaking out a carpet and beating it with a stick. A vacuum cleaner roared behind her.

Aimée waved. "I'm locked out," she said and mimicked trying to turn a key.

But the cleaning lady bent over and whacked harder. She wore headphones and was beating in a rhythm. Aimée pulled an old wheelbarrow over to the fence, gathered her leather coat, and climbed over, ripping her stockings. The spindle-branched thorn bushes offered little protection from observation as she ran behind them. Sirens wailed from the small lane.

Beyond lay the schoolyard containing a climbing structure and a sand box. Perspiration beaded her lip despite the cold air. The *flics* would talk to Mado and, any second, they would come after her. At the next fence, she shoved old clay flower pots together, stepped on them, and heaved herself over. She landed on a tricycle, the handlebars bruising the arm that had needed stitches, but cushioning her fall. And then she stumbled into the sandbox.

"That's mine," said a serious-faced child wearing ladybug rainboots. "It's not your turn."

"Sorry, of course," she stood, brushing the sand off her coat and scanning the playground. "Go ahead, take your turn."

"Big people aren't supposed to ride tricycles," the child said. "I'm telling the teacher."

Aimée didn't like the flash of blue uniforms she glimpsed through the fence. She thought fast.

"I made a mistake, I'm here to pick up my daughter," she said.

"You're in the wrong place. Parents wait over there," the little girl said.

"Of course, you're right."

Aimée edged toward the throng of teachers and laughing students lining up at the school gate.

"What are you doing here?" said a teacher with a clipboard. "You must wait outside, it's the law. Who let you in?"

"Forgive me, but I had to run to *le cabinet*, Madame," she said, patting her stomach. Aimée wiped the perspiration from her brow. "It's morning sickness, but with this second one it happens all day long."

The teacher's eyes softened as Aimée joined the waiting parents on the curb. Aimée melted into the crowd, careful to avoid the police cars.

Thursday

RENÉ SQUIRMED ON THE dirt floor and thumped his feet. The dank chill, and the diffused light from the kerosene lantern, reminded him of the ancient cave in the Loire Valley he and his mother had camped in one August holiday. With its thick walls it stayed cool despite the heat of summer. But he hadn't had his ankles taped up then.

"Time for *pipi?*" asked the gravel-voiced man.

He nodded and tried to talk but the tape over his mouth garbled his voice.

"Water?"

He nodded harder. The *mec* came into view, blocking the pile of bricks, and the ants still pushing their crumb. He had to get out of here.

"Let's see, it's been a while," said the *mec*.

A while . . . more like six hours!

The *mec* was wearing denim overalls, snakeskin boots and his brown hair was pulled back in a stringy ponytail. He slit the duct tape binding René's ankles with a knife and pulled René to his feet. Were they going to kill him?

"Little guys like you have an interesting sex life, eh?"

René snorted.

"What's that?" he grinned. "Oh I forgot, you can't speak."

René's cheeks burned with a searing pain as the *mec* ripped the duct tape off his mouth. He groaned.

"Quiet!"

"Sick. I'm going to be sick," René whispered, his voice hoarse.

"Watch the boots," the *mec* said, pushing René toward a rusted iron bucket by a pile of old newspapers. "Over there."

René gagged. "I'm dizzy," he gasped, heaving. "Help me."

"Hold the wall," said the *mec*, a look of disgust on his face.

"Can't." He gagged, spitting near the man's boots.

"Not on the boots, dwarf, or I kick you with them."

René heard the slow rip of duct tape and felt his wrists being freed. Numbed, tingly, but *free*. He leaned on the wall for support, pushed off and shot out his left leg, kicking the surprised *mec* in the kidney. The man doubled over. René's next powerful straight kick landed under the *mec*'s chin and whipped his head back.

If his hip hadn't throbbed so much he'd have broken the *mec*'s fourth and fifth rib, too. Still, he would need a hospital visit.

René flexed his short, swollen fingers, grabbed the duct tape and wound it around the *mec*'s mouth, hands, and feet. Then, huffing, he pulled the limp body behind the high cobwebbed pile of bricks.

Phone, where was his phone? Not on the dirt floor where there were only men's magazines and a small notebook. He grabbed the notebook with his numbed fingers and stuck it in his pocket. He took the kerosene lantern, the fumes making his nose itch, and searched the moaning *mec's* pockets. Only a pack of Gitanes. His fingers didn't obey well, but he ran them over the packed dirt, back and forth. And near the corner they found his cell phone. With his thumb he turned it on as he stumbled toward the stairs. He punched in Aimée's number.

He heard several clicks, then ringing. But there were footsteps on the stairs. *Merde!*

"I'm underground in an *abri* near a Bata shoe store," he whispered and clicked the phone to silent mode.

"Hey, the beer's cold," said the second of his captors. "Wake up! Where are you?"

René ducked behind a rotting wood chair and felt something long, like a pole. He grabbed the end, slid it across the third to bottom step, and raised it. The chair blocked his view but he heard the whoosh of air and a loud *ouf!* as the man tripped and fell. Bottles crashed, spraying beer. There was a smell of malt everywhere.

Stunned, the heavy-set red-haired man sprawled on the dirt floor. René reached for his thick neck, pinched the carotid artery, and gave it a twist. The man's head sagged. René shone the lantern on him, took the roll of duct tape, and covered his mouth with tape.

Sweat dripped between René's shoulderblades. After binding those thick wrists he had run out of tape. He undid the man's belt, shifting and moving the inert body until it finally came free of the man's waist. Then he looped the belt and knotted it several times around the man's ankles.

René tried to ignore his throbbing hip as he hobbled upstairs. He felt along the pebbled wall in the dark, ran into a rough wooden door and tried the handle. Locked.

So close.

He had to think fast. The third man was bound to arrive at any moment.

He called Aimée.

"René . . . don't hang up," she said. "Are you all right?"

"Aimée, I'm in Paris, underground someplace."

"I know. Stay on the line," she said, breathless. "Whatever you do keep the phone on. We're triangulating your position."

"Hold on. Don't talk," René said.

He kept the phone in his pants pocket and inched his way back down the steps, fighting for breath. The key had to be on the big red-haired man. He felt around in the pocket of his down-filled jacket and pulled out a cheap pocket calculator. It took him two tries to turn the unconscious man over so he could examine his shirt pockets and his pants pockets. A wallet. Then a ring of keys jingled, and he pulled them out.

René made his way up the stairs again, in the dark. He took one of the long-handled old-fashioned keys, reached up, and slid it toward the keyhole, but the bunch of keys fell from his still swollen fingers and vanished in the darkness.

Below, René heard one of the men stir and groan. René ran his fingers over the stone step. Nothing. He panicked.

If only he could see!

Then his fingers grazed the top of the keys. He tried to grasp them but his fingers just pushed them down into a narrow crack. He needed something with which to pull them up to him.

He slid down the steps once more, saving his legs for the climb back, and with the knife cut some excess duct tape from the man's wrists. He climbed back, his legs and hip protesting. He lowered the tape into the crack, tamped it carefully around the bit of key sticking up and prayed the tape would hold. Slowly, centimeter by centimeter, he lifted the keys. By the time he had them in his hand, perspiration was running down his forehead in rivulets and dripping into his eyes.

More noises came from the big man, a knocking and rustling as he struggled against his bonds. Then there was a metallic clang.

The kerosene lantern!

A crackle and *thupt* of something igniting. René's hands shook. Despite the cellar's dampness, with so much old wood and paper, the flames would catch, then suck up oxygen for fuel and create an inferno!

He reached up, aimed for the keyhole, and willed his hand to be steady. He missed. He tried again, leaning his short arm against the door. The key didn't fit. Smoke and kerosene fumes rose, choking him.

René tried the next three keys. The fourth was the right one. He turned it, but the key stuck. With all his might, he pressed and turned. And tried again. The old-fashioned lock clicked and he rammed the door open with his shoulder.

He fell on a wet floor by bags of cement, striking a small cement mixer. A worker, wearing overalls and a bandanna around his head, jumped back in surprise.

"Where is this place?" René said.

"*Señor, no habla Français,*" he said, alarm in his eyes.

René crawled across the floor to pull himself up by the wall. Black smoke billowed up from the staircase. The worker yelled and grabbed a bucket of water.

René made his legs move. Step by step, past an open door and into a garden courtyard. Birds sang by a low ivy-covered wall. He'd never noticed the sweetness of the tang of wet leaves or realized how beautiful a gray sky could look.

Keep going, he had to keep going, follow the narrow lane past the parked vans, and get to the street. Get away. The arched *porte cochère* lay just before him and he heard a car slow down, shifting into first. He ducked behind a van as the car turned in. A black Peugeot.

Hurry, he had to hurry. Despite the searing ache in his thigh, he had to keep walking. The car pulled behind him, a door opened and shut. He panicked, knowing it would only be a few minutes before they discovered he'd escaped. He heard someone yelling to call the *sapeurs-pompiers*, the firemen.

He edged past the van, keeping close to the walls, and made it through the arch. Saw a narrow cobbled street lined with parked cars.

He looked up, wiped his brow and saw the street sign: rue Lemercier, a one-way street. He reached into his pants pocket for his cell phone.

"Aimée?" he said. "I'm on rue Lemercier, wherever the hell that is."

"Near Clichy. Go to your right René. Walk."

He heard honking. And there she was, jumping out of a taxi and running toward him.

For once in his life the earth and stars aligned: He'd done something he never thought he could do, and with arms opened wide she was running to him.

Somehow he walked, he didn't know how.

"René!" Tears spilled from her eyes as she grabbed him.

"What took you so long, Aimée?" he said.

Thursday Afternoon

GASSOT, PICQ, AND PORTLY Nemours sat in the back of the Laboratoire de Prothèse Dentaire in Passage Geffroy-Didelot, Picq's nephew's denture-making shop. Acrid adhesive smells and sounds of running water came from the front.

"We've taken the matter into our own hands," Picq said.

Gassot hoped his comrades hadn't done anything stupid yet, but it sounded like they already had.

"That doesn't make sense," Gassot said. "Let's wait and see."

"We didn't discover anything in the art gallery," Picq interrupted.

"What do you mean?" Gassot asked, alarmed

"Too cautious, as always, Gassot," Picq said. "And considering your softness toward natives, dogs, and small children, well, we took care of business."

Fools. "You broke into the gallery? Thank your stars you weren't caught. Did the woman tell you anything?"

Gassot couldn't fathom Picq's steel-blue gaze.

"We'd have told you," Picq said.

They hadn't told him about anything else.

"What about Tran?"

"He's going to the *maison*," Gassot said.

"It's time for action!"

Gassot expelled a breath of disgust and shook his head. "Always the hothead, aren't you? It's folly."

The telephone rang.

Picq leaned over the counter next to a sealing machine. His frizzy white hair poked out from his cap. He was there to answer the telephone for his nephew, who'd gone to lunch.

"*Oui, allô?*" he said. "The dentures are ready for you, monsieur."

He hung up and turned back to them. "The Castorama store off Passage de Clichy had everything we needed," Picq said. "Fertilizer, plastic plumbers' pipe," he said, tapping the counter. "All under here. No one suspects *us*, even though it's what they watch for now. Don't you read the papers?"

Gassot read the PMU racing forms when he got his monthly pension, but that was it. He shrugged, "*Et après?*"

"We now have everything we need to make a simple pipe bomb," Picq said.

"I don't like it. *C'est fou*. We want the jade in one piece!" Gassot said.

His comrades had always preferred action to planning. Nothing had changed since Indochina.

"We have to open the safe in the house," Picq said. "I was in the demolition unit, remember? I can do this with my eyes closed."

"Never." Gassot stood up. "If the jade's in there, you'll ruin it. I won't have anything to do with this crazy scheme."

A buzzer went off.

"Calm down," Picq said, "I can coax a newborn from a ton of steel. Tran's in place, right? He lets us into the house and then—"

"But we don't know the jade's in there," Gassot interrupted.

Nemours waved Gassot's remark aside. "Where else, eh?"

Picq switched on an industrial dryer for enamelware and slid in a small tray of gleaming teeth. An even heat emanated from it, warming the back of the lab. Comfortable and safe.

But Gassot shuddered. It reminded him of the false teeth of an old Vietnamese woman at Dien Bien Phu. Her grandson had been caught in a tunnel with French rations. The fire bombing had left her burnt and naked. "Ivory," she'd said pulling the teeth out and offering them, since she'd had nothing else to barter.

The corporal had shot the old woman and her grandson anyway. The next day the elite Parachute troops found out they'd been innocent. Years later he'd seen the photo of the Vietnamese girl burnt with napalm with the same expression on her face.

Gassot knew he had to reason them out of this.

"Listen, Picq, it's just a feeling but I think they stashed the jade in a safe place, somewhere. After the old man died, Thadée must have discovered it."

"Stands to reason," Nemours said. "According to Albert, he talked big, but he didn't deliver."

"You think he was killed because he didn't hand over the

jade?" Gassot said. "But that makes no sense. He was the key, the connection."

"You don't kill a connection," Picq said. "You kill a failure."

So why did this ring false, Gassot wondered.

"Instead of blowing up the man's safe, we should be searching for Albert's killer, and the jade."

"And you think we're not? At least, you concede Albert was murdered?"

Gassot pulled the folded napkin out of his pocket. Showed them the threat scribbled on it: "We're going to roll your pants leg up, too."

Nemours's face paled. "It's all connected. Ever since we found out the jade's in France—"

"Since it's in the wrong hands, bad luck has followed it," Gassot said.

Picq and Nemours exchanged a look.

"You're not going native on us again, eh?"

Gassot's eyes flashed. "Remember the officers, they ate the best . . ."

"And we ate the rest," finished Picq.

Gassot walked toward the glassed-in front of the shop, wondering what more he could say to persuade his comrades to hold back. If they lay low they would be led right to it—and avoid whoever meant to kill them.

He pushed away the thoughts of Bao that crowded his mind. More and more he wondered about Bao. The idealist with soft rounded cheeks, who pared the skin off a mango in deft strokes. Bao, whose laugh had sounded like warm rain.

Gassot stiffened as a uniformed policeman and plainclothes *flic* entered the shop. "We're looking for Monsieur Picq. We have some questions," said a *flic* in a windbreaker, pulling out a search warrant. "Concerning some recent purchases he made at Castorama."

Gassot shivered. "I'm just a customer," he said, trying to control the shaking in his voice. "Monsieur Picq's back there."

And with that, Gassot opened the door and slid into the narrow passage.

Thursday Early Evening

"WE'RE STAYING IN A hotel," Aimée said as she cleaned René's bloodied hands with disinfectant. The taxi pulled up on rue Sauffroy in front of Kinshasa Coiffure, its windows covered with pictures of women with braided corn-rows and Afros. HÔTEL BONHEUR read an old sign by a window of the second-story building. Smells of fish and coconut mingled in the dusk.

"Here?" René asked.

She tipped the taxi driver.

"Always four star with you, Aimée," he said.

"There's an elevator and plenty of electrical outlets. I'll get your car and park it in back, if you want."

"Don't you think we'll stick out?" he said, observing the African women in bright scarves on the street.

"No one will think of looking for us in the African music center of Paris," she said. "And the owner owes my cousin Sebastian a favor."

"But we're still in Clichy."

"That's why it's perfect. Did you see the faces of the men who were holding you? Could you recognize them?"

He nodded. "One heavy-set with red hair, the other lean with a ponytail."

Like the RG men who had been on the quai outside her apartment.

"What happened, René?"

He rubbed his neck. "They threw a net over me on the office stairs, then put a choke hold on my throat. A carotid sleeper special!"

René reached in his pocket and winced. "Does this help?" he said, pulling out the notebook.

"I'm proud of you, partner," she said, scanning the pages.

One had writing on it, with a phone number. Regnier's number.

"This confirms it," she said. "Regnier, the suspended RG *mec*, kidnapped you to make sure I handed over the jade. How's your hip?"

"I've felt worse." Though he couldn't remember when. With an effort, he tried not to limp.

The hotel room's furniture—two beds, an angular leopard-skin couch and 1960s Formica end tables—seemed out of place under the tall ceilings and ornate nineteenth-century scrollwork moldings. Lemon verbena scents came from the bathroom. She took out her laptop and hooked it up.

"Saj will bring laptops from the office and we'll work from here. That's if the doctor gives you the OK."

"I don't need a doctor," he said. "I just need to lie down, and to bandage my wrists. What about Miles Davis?"

"He's on holiday at the groomer's. Loves it, according to the groomer."

"Is Guy coming?"

She turned away.

"What's the matter, Aimée?"

"Time to talk about that later. There's something more important."

René's brow furrowed. She reached for the box of gauze bandages. She wasn't very good at this but she had to say it. "I know I'm not the easiest person to work with René. But I can't see myself anywhere but Leduc Detective. And you're part of that. I do know that with your skills, you could go anywhere. Maybe you've received other offers. Was that what you meant the other day?"

An odd look crossed René's face.

"Are you in pain?" she asked. Or was he afraid to tell her he was leaving?

"You're my family, René, but I don't want to stand in your way. I'll try and talk you out of it, because I'm selfish. But I will respect whatever . . ."

"Did I say anything like that?" René asked.

She shook her head. "But I thought. . . ."

"I'd appreciate a raise when we're solvent again," he said, as Aimée bandaged his wrists.

"Consider it done," she grinned. She took a deep breath. "At this rate I'm going to have to put your name on the door."

He looked away but not before she saw a small smile on his face.

"In the meantime, what I can't figure out is why didn't they call you again," René said, "or make more demands."

Was he trying to change the subject? But he'd made a good point. "True, Regnier was waiting for me to find the jade, or else Gassot." She stood up. "And I haven't found either. Not yet."

She looked out the window to the wet street below. No sign of Regnier or anyone tailing her. The orange-pink neon of Kinshasa Coiffure reflected on the windows opposite. From the resto below, came the beat of the music of Papa Wemba, the King of Congolese Rhumba Rock.

"I have to find out why Olf wants me to monitor the Chinese and British oil bids," she said. "You'll have to help me."

"Oil bids?

René put his feet up on the bed, laid back. His eyes looked heavy.

"And how the jade's involved with oil. This smelled from the beginning and it's reeking now."

But she spoke to a sleeping René.

Friday Morning

"FIND ANYTHING INTERESTING, LARS?" Aimée asked over the phone. She hoped he'd thaw out and pass on more concrete details about the so-called Circle Line.

"That's some pudding you're looking into," he said, then placed his hand over the phone to muffle some background noise.

"Count on me to stir the lumps in the pudding," she said.

The sounds of furniture scraping on the floor, then a loud squeak came over the line. "Sorry, we're moving out the file cabinets. Rumor has it our office has its new coat of paint and they're shoveling us upstairs. Room 20."

It was an old signal he used when other ears were listening in. Good thing she hadn't mentioned Pleyet's name.

"Can you make some time to have a coffee with me?"

"We're worked off our feet. Call me next week; we'll meet at the nice place under the horse chestnuts."

He rang off.

If she hurried she'd make it to the café on Place Dauphine by the roasted chestnut stand in twenty minutes.

She crossed rue de Rivoli, passed the Louvre's imposing Cour Carrée, raced down the small street behind the Art Deco Samaritaine department store, and hurried across the Pont Neuf. The wind whipped at her coat but her vision was crystal clear.

Figures in overcoats, bent against the wind, formed a dark stream across the bridge. The words of Hubert Juin's poem about the Pont Neuf came to her:

> I remember those I had no chance to know, the pavement still mumbles . . . the river Seine swirling near the Pont Neuf, Baudelaire slowly goes by, and Verlaine is smiling. Through the sleeping city, passes history.

Shaped like a ship, the back end of île de la Cité held the Jewish Memorial to the Deported. Aimée turned left into place Dauphine, a triangular-shaped tree-lined oasis. Once the orchard of the king, it was surrounded by the two arms of the Seine. Sixteenth century construction of the Pont Neuf had joined the island and several small *îlots* to the city.

Now, the place Dauphine backed up to the king's old palace, the present site of the courts of the Palais de Justice and the Conciergerie prison, now a museum, with Marie Antoinette's cell as stark and damp as she'd left it.

Aimée pushed past the rattan café chairs. She was startled to see Morbier, wearing an old raincoat, under the canvas awning against the wall. He was reading a newspaper. She sucked in her lower lip. Coincidence? She doubted it.

Flics didn't patronize this place; it attracted residents—such as Simone Signoret and Yves Montand who had lived in the neighborhood and other patrons who could afford the pricey menu. An occasional judge or prosecutor perhaps. But her godfather?

"Right on time," Morbier said, setting down the paper, keeping the rainhat's brim lowered over his face. "Another fine mess you've got me into."

"What brings you here, Morbier?" she asked, keeping her tone steady.

"Ask me no questions and I'll tell you no lies."

"Mademoiselle?" a waiter asked.

She turned. "An espresso, s'il vous plaît."

Morbier puffed on a short, fat cigarillo. Clouds of acrid smoke rose.

"Where's Lars?" she asked him.

"Grow up, Leduc. Time to get out of the sandbox."

Did he know she'd fallen into one yesterday? Why was he here in place of Lars? A ring of intrigue surrounded her and she still knew nothing.

"You're old enough to know better," Morbier went on.

"And young enough to still do it," she said. "So you're in league with the Ministry now, Morbier?" She shook her head in disgust. "And you call yourself a socialist?" He might as well take off the socialist party pin in his lapel and grind it in the gravel.

"Leduc, in case you forgot, we have a socialist government. First you drop off this charming woman for me to guard, then use my code to find an address from a phone number," he said, with irritation. "Now you're badgering Lars to access security clearance files. Of course, it tripped off an inquiry. Forced us both into some pretty lies."

This was deep. She felt it in her bones.

"Lars knows the muddy Ministry waters. He navigates well, always has," she said, reaching for a tissue and wiping beads of rain from her bag. "Inquiry into what?"

"Files requiring special clearance," he said. "And you know that could mean anything—from the chief's girlfriend's flat rental, to his expense account for a lost weekend in Bordeaux."

Morbier seemed intent on passing this inquiry off as trivial. Was it?

"Since when do you cozy up to Lars?"

Morbier leaned forward. "His old man, your father, and I, were colleagues. Or did you forget that, too?"

Of course she hadn't; she remembered his famous Sunday

pot-au-feu lunches. "It bothers me that a man was shot next to me, died in my arms, and *you* let his ex-wife leave the country."

"Murder and thugs near Place de Clichy, druggies disposing of each other! It illustrates the law of natural selection. Those aren't my problems! Or yours."

"I remember the thirteen-year-old with tracks on her arm who washed up in your part of the Seine: Then it was your business! You wouldn't let go of that case."

"Still can't," Morbier said. "Key point, Leduc, *my part of the Seine.* Clichy's landlocked. They can keep their trash there. Plenty to go round."

Compartmentalize. Good *flics* did that. Kept their minds on the business at hand. Yet, she felt there was a lot he wasn't saying.

"You got here fast."

"Group R's office is next to Lars's"

"You've never told me what your group handles."

"Need to know basis, Leduc."

"*Bon.*" She smoothed down her black pencil skirt. Rain pattered on the cobbles. "Pleyet's name came up as part of the Circle Line surveillance and I saw him at the jade museum. How does it tie together? Well, I'm all ears."

Silence. Except for the rain pattering on the café awning and the bark of a dog.

"Morbier, I know Pleyet's not in the traffic division."

"Leduc, people like him, you don't want to know," he said.

True. His hawklike eyes and Special Ops aura were chilling.

"I'm not looking for a date," she said. "Just the truth."

Morbier stood, shuffled in his pocket, then threw some francs on the round table just as Aimée's espresso arrived.

"Article 4 of *Code de la Police*," he said. " '*By the procedural code, police missions are placed under the authority of the Ministry of Interior.*' "

Morbier quoting police procedure?

"So you're saying Pleyet's with the Ministry of Interior? Tell me something I don't know."

"You don't know anything." Morbier bent over and clutched the table. Was that a grimace of pain as he pulled his rainhat down?

"*Ça va*, Morbier?" she asked, alarmed. She stood, took his arm, and rubbed his back.

But when he straightened up, she saw a lopsided grin on his face. "Didn't want to make eye contact with *la Proc'*. She's a ball-breaker that one. Always on my case."

True? Or a way for a wily fox to get out of answering? She turned around and saw the back of *La Proc'* Edith Mesnard's tailored Rodier suit. And then doubt nagged her. Was this a glimpse of real pain after all?

"Give me something to go on, Morbier," she said. "Don't make me beg. That's if you want flowers at the hospital."

Morbier frowned. "Drink your espresso. I'm not going to warn you off any more, Leduc. Wise up, get married, make babies, change diapers."

Babies . . . diapers, where did that come from? And with whom was she supposed to do this? Guy was no longer a possibility.

"Miles Davis was potty trained in a week, and he's more than enough for me to handle," she replied.

He looked away. She noticed the liver spots on his hands, the lined skin around his eyes. He'd aged.

"Leduc?"

She looked up.

"For once, listen to me. Promise to leave it alone and I'll sniff around," he said. "But I mean it. You promise?"

She nodded. "I found out Regnier's on suspension. As far as I can tell, he's gone rogue."

"What do you mean?"

"Just what I said," she said. "And *he* kidnapped René. I've got the proof in this little notebook."

Morbier didn't look surprised often. But now was one of those times.

"He knows about the jade and thinks he can claim it but . . ."

"And René?"

"He sent some scum to the hospital and caused a three-alarm fire," she said. "All by himself. But thanks for asking."

Morbier's eyes widened and he shook his head with a little smile. "I'm getting too old, *vraiment?*"

She nodded. "Soon, I'm going to have to put his name on the door."

"Leduc, I meant to help," he told her.

His chin sagged and he looked lost. Morbier? Now she was worried.

"Morbier, what happened with your grandson Marc?"

His eyes followed the sparrows pecking for food on the crackling brown leaves. "I don't want to talk about it."

Had Marc's other grandparents received custody?

"If there's some way I can help?"

"Not now, Leduc."

Morbier stood, took his newspaper, and walked away. His shoes crunched the gravel as he crossed in the square. Could she still count on him?

As her father had said, If only the *flics'* left hand knew what their right hand was doing, they wouldn't try wiping their arses with both hands at the same time.

Gray mist hovered over the rooftops. She took a deep breath. She would have to flush out the scum herself.

LATER THAT afternoon, Aimée sipped wine at a pre-war *bar à vin* on rue de Clichy. The decor featured white-globe sconces, a stamped-tin ceiling, and enough tobacco in the air to stain her teeth just by inhaling. She wished she could open the window. The smell of wet wool, the sputtering heater, and the stale smoke was suffocating. Even the raw damp wind outside would be preferable. And she wished she could see better through the fogged-up windows.

She watched men enter Académie de Billard, Blondel's haunt across the rue de Clichy. Most were of a certain type. She figured a lot would be named Jacky, would be on the dole, and would have the hots for Arielle Dombasle whose film career had peaked in the 80s. And all were wearing leather bomber jackets.

She was an outsider. She doubted they'd be forthcoming about Blondel, the man mentioned in Sophie's postcard, even if they knew him. Maybe this could work to her advantage. Stir things up. Count on *merde* to float to the top, as the saying went. Instead of going in undercover, she'd play it straight. Try to draw him out.

She punched in the Académie de Billard number. It rang four times. Someone picked up; cleared his throat.

"*Oui?*"

"Blondel, he there yet?"

"*Et alors*, who'd like to know?"

She heard the click of billiard balls in the background.

"Tell him Sophie's gone," she said, not pausing for breath. "But I'll help him. We'll work out the details. Fifteen minutes?"

"What do you mean?"

Was he stalling, unsure of who she meant or—

"Give me your number," he said. "In case he checks in."

Which meant he'd pass her message on. Like in the old days, before cell phones, when few apartments had private phone lines and the café was a central message clearing house. Blondel would call her if he wanted to talk.

Nice, old fashioned, and secure for Blondel.

She gave her number and hung up.

There had to be a back door to the billiard hall, maybe more than one. If she met Blondel there, she wanted to be sure of a way out. She crossed the street to rue de Bruxelles, passing the house where Zola died of asphyxiation and walked the short block to Square Berlioz. Elegant and calm, it held a *vert-de-grisé*-covered statue of the composer Berlioz, and a playground. Seven narrow streets intersected at the square, a few sloped toward Gare Saint Lazare, others up to Montmartre. Hard to imagine that the sex shops of Pigalle flashed their neon only a few streets away.

Haussmann-era apartment buildings lined the street, with their grilled balconies, deep courtyards, and back apartments with service exits. Then she found a cobbled driveway leading to a mansion on the square.

Perfect.

Back on rue de Clichy, she ducked into an entrance beside the greengrocers which bordered the Académie de Billard. It led to a courtyard with shuttered windows, past trashbins, and to the rear door of the Académie's bar. Crates of empty bottles marked the rear entrance.

Inside, she put her phone on vibrate, slid past the side of the bar, and headed toward the restrooms. A few men were shooting pool on dark wooden tables that filled the period brown mosaic-tiled floor. The high ceilings, beveled gilt-edged mirrors, giant Roman numeral clock over the coat room, and stained-glass skylights reminded her of an early train station.

The phone vibrated in her pocket.

"*Allô?*"

"You want to see me?" said a deep voice.

That was quick. He sounded interested.

"I can help you," she said.

"You sound pretty sure of yourself."

"Sophie cut out on me, but we can be useful to each other."

"Who knows?"

Nice and oblique, in case anyone was tapping the phone.

"Meet me in Académie de Billard."

"I'm already there," he said.

In the mirror, she saw a man wearing a leather bomber jacket hunched over the bar, talking on the phone.

She hung up and kept walking, glad she'd entered from the side and had identified him first.

"But I'm here, too," she said to him as she sidled onto the stool next to his.

"I'm impressed."

But she didn't think he was. Like a cat ready to spring, he gripped the beer bottle with white clenched knuckles. His wide forehead took up much of his face, whose features consisted of a zipperlike mouth and dark deepset eyes. Slickbacked hair and broad shoulders completed the picture. But the scar on the side of his neck, the kind *mecs* got in prison from awls used in the shoe factory, put her on high alert.

"You're Blondel?"

"I represent him."

She pushed off from the zinc bar, shaking her head. A *mec* rested his billiard cue on the green baize and moved closer. A set up?

And here she thought she'd been clever.

"Let me know when he wants to talk," she said.

"What's the problem?" he said, a deep chuckle. "I thought you wanted to help me. Jacky wants to talk, too."

He gestured to the other *mec* now chalking his cue with the blue cube in his hand, and blocking her escape.

Of course, a Jacky! Buff body, tight black leather pants and a pompadour. He smiled. Gold incisors. Her throat tightened.

"Maybe I changed my mind," she said, eyeing the restroom door. "If Blondel wants to talk, let me know."

"Where's Sophie?"

"She owes me, Thadée, too," Aimée said, "So I'd like to know, as well. I figured we could work together."

"I'm Blondel," he said.

"And you're going to sell me the Pont Neuf," she said.

"Did Nadège mention a defaulted candy bill?"

Nadège?

"Who's that?"

And then she remembered Thadée saying "Nadège, Sophie," before he was shot.

"Who are you, Mademoiselle?" he asked, a sneer in his voice. His eyes hardened. "Let's go somewhere and get to know each other."

This wasn't going the way she'd hoped it would.

She edged toward the exit, but Jacky barred her way with his cue.

"Give me a moment, I need to use the restroom," she said, in a loud voice. "Excuse me." She smiled as she edged past Jacky.

And then it hit her . . . Thadée's defaulted candy bill?

What had she jumped into? A dope deal that Morbier had warned her against? Was Sophie responsible for it now that Thadée was dead? Or this Nadège? Had this *mec* done him in? But that didn't make sense, why kill him if he owed money? Or might pay his debt with valuable jade in lieu of cash?

Several sweating men shouldering a massive pool table were blocking the back door by the counter. And another delivery loomed behind them.

"Mademoiselle, we're unloading a truck of new tables. Go the other way."

"Blondel" and Jacky stood, feet planted and arms crossed over them, barring the front door. The bulge in Jacky's coat pocket spelled trouble. There had to be another way out.

Passing the door to the bathrooms, she climbed a narrow

staircase that led to game rooms and more billiard tables. No way out up there.

Downstairs, in the restroom, she entered cubicle after cubicle. Odors of evergreen disinfectant came from the stalls. But there was neither door nor window.

Back in the hall, she found a light-well concealed by draperies next to the cloakroom. But it was nailed shut, top and bottom.

The only thing left was the garbage chute. Ripe and pungent. No way would she go down that. Then she heard footsteps. Her phone vibrated in her pocket.

"*Oui?*"

"I'm waiting," the man who had called himself Blondel said. "There's a car out front, we'll take a drive so we can talk somewhere quiet."

Like hell they would.

She lifted the lid of the dirty metal garbage chute, tried not to breathe, and put her legs over the edge. Rank odors swelled from below. She belted her coat tight, grabbed the rim, and lowered herself down a sticky, greasy metal slide. Her toes found a small foothold. Thank God.

Before she could close the chute lid, Jacky's head appeared silhoutted against the light. And then she slipped.

Her arms bumped against the sides and she put them in front of her face.

She landed in darkness on something wet. Scratching came from somewhere. Rodents. Jacky shouted from above. No way would she let him catch her after going through this.

She pulled herself up, then sank. Putrid smells of decaying food and oil surrounded her. Flies buzzed. Then the container she'd landed in tipped over. Her elbows hit concrete. Loud squeals came from the corner, and her heart pounded.

She got to her feet, fell, scrambled for the wall, but her hands came back clutching half eaten melon rinds. Something scurried over her boots. Big, fat, with a long greasy tail. She ran, heading for a patch of light, praying she'd find a way out.

By the time she reached the end of the cavelike opening her stockings were in shreds and she'd lost part of a high heel. Glass crashed and broke behind her. Instead of veering into the courtyard, she spied a green-metal fence and began to climb. She remembered the mansion facing the square and the driveway leading to it.

She jumped, landed in mud, and tiptoed through bushes. Footsteps kept coming. *Merde!* She had to keep moving.

She saw the back door of the mansion's frosted glass conservatory, wedged open with a cane. She stepped inside, closed the door and locked it.

"Mathilde!" said an old man in a wheelchair before an easel painting. A faded woollen shawl, pinned around his shoulders, held flecks of paint. The brush, Aimée realized, was tied to his wrist.

"I'm sorry, monsieur."

"Where's Mathilde? My tea?" he said in a quavering voice. "I want my biscuits. Always have my tea with biscuits."

"*Bien sûr,*" she said, keeping to the shadow. "I'll check."

He sniffed. "Mathilde forgot to take the garbage out again, eh? Lazy one. Twenty years in service and she needs reminding of everything."

"*Tiens,* your tea's here," said Mathilde, an older woman, with short gray hair, wearing a housecoat and rubber boots. She saw Aimée and surprise showed on her face. "Running late, eh? Weren't you supposed to mix the paints, get everything set up for him?"

Aimée heard crashing in the bushes outside. Her cell phone vibrated but she ignored it.

"*Désolée.*"

The older woman shook her head. "You art students are more trouble than you're worth. He'll complain now for days.

Simple, *non*, just mix the pigments with thinner. His hands shake so much he can't manage it."

"But it's beautiful," Aimée said, looking at the oil painting on the easel, "reminds me of Renoir."

The old man spit on the floor. "That old fool. Never paid his rent on time my *grand-mère* used to say. Brought his whole brood to live with him, too."

"Don't get him started," the woman said, setting down the tea tray and rolling her eyes.

"Degas, how the laundresses hated him! They called him a dirty old man. But Manet, eh, he created Impressionism. His atelier was a few blocks from here. The Academy called them upstarts, the school of Batignolles, at first. Manet, Cézanne, Toulouse-Lautrec. . . ." His voice trailed off and his rheumy eyes grew wistful. "Sometimes when the fog hovers over Place de Clichy, the lights mist, like the old gas lamps when I was young. . . it's how he painted it."

Mathilde sniffed. "Never changes. *Zut!* Artists don't bathe, do they?"

"May I wash up?" Aimée asked, reminded of her state.

Mathilde pointed to a small laundry area. "Be quick about it, he pays the art students' league by the hour."

In the closet-sized space, she took off her coat and boots, ran hot water and scrubbed them down, and washed her face. She pulled out her cell phone and called a taxi, then listened to her messages.

"Since you doubt I'm Blondel," the man said, "you'll receive proof when I find you, Mademoiselle Leduc."

Merde. He'd gotten her name from her voice mail message!

Friday Evening

NADÈGE HUDDLED IN THE dark doorway, pulled her jean jacket collar over her pearls, and wrapped her scarf around her feet. She tried to still her hands. Chills and feverish jitters wracked her. She was sweating; she couldn't stop sweating. The searing pain in her spine! The familiar, awful ache of withdrawal.

Globed lights threw a yellow haze on the wet cobbles and illuminated the infrequent evening buses that rumbled past. Quiet reigned, the school crush over, as the post-work apéritif hour settled upon the Clichy back streets.

The gnawing craving filled her. How many hours had it been? She wasn't counting, but it had been all day. She was doing better, cutting back. She'd stopped before, she could stop again.

Waves of guilt rocked her. Leaving her little Michel. *Non*, she'd been right, that had been a good move, she couldn't keep him with her, he was better off, so much better off with *grandmère*. Clean sheets, a full rice bowl, and she would make sure he arrived at school on time.

And now she'd do what had to be done to clean up Thadée's mess . . . and hers. Thadée had regretted introducing her to his supplier when she, in turn, became indebted to him. She struggled against a surge of irritability and nausea.

But which role to play? The indignant, well-bred French girl or the pliant Asian? All her life she'd acted the part that was called for, never sure which fit. Lately, she hadn't cared much.

Mealtimes in Paris with her father or her friends' families had been full of discussion and debate, alive with conversation in between multiple courses. Yet as a small girl her *grand-mère* admonished her if more than the click of her chopstick was heard on the rice bowl; it showed bad manners. "Show reverence for food, with silence," she'd said.

And always, "Show respect for elders, never argue, express self only in harmonious way."

Her *grand-mère* would pull herself to her five foot height, stare at Nadège, and say "Gweilo stole Vietnam, push us out our country, *your* country but, it still is inside us; we never leave it, it never leaves us. Someday we return to tend our ancestors' shrine once more."

Growing up, Nadège had wondered when that would be as her *grand-mère* cursed the régime and her mah-jong cronies moaned about how Vietnam was changed. Later, she'd realized her *grand-mère* would never leave France. She didn't even have a passport.

And "harmony" would get Nadège nowhere unless she found Thadée's stash. It wasn't in the apartment, but she hadn't checked out Thadée's old townhouse, whose rear faced the shadowy gallery courtyard. She clutched her beaded bag, pulled her denim jacket tighter, and took advantage of the mid-evening lull to slip across the narrow street and press 75AB on the digicode buttons. The massive dark blue door opened and she stepped inside.

Thadée had told her once, if anything happened, to go find his cache and she'd be safe. And then distracted by a phone call, he'd forgotten to give her its location. *So typical of Thadée*, she thought, and a pang of remembrance lanced through her. But she had found the key, if only it was the right one.

The dank foyer, lined with old mailboxes, held a green garbage container and puddles. The plaster ceiling leaked and dripped on the spiral staircase. Occasional acquaintances of Thadée had used it as a shooting gallery until he'd cleaned himself up and thrown them out. He'd never used drugs after that. She doubted that Sophie, who disliked her, had ever graced the crumbling place.

There was a ghost in every house. One had to make peace with it or get out. Would Thadée's ghost cooperate?

She reached into her bag for incense sticks, the votive candle and the silk flowers, now crushed and bedraggled, that she carried. She set them on the dry first step as a makeshift shrine. A half-empty bottle of Evian would have to do for an offering, in place of Thadée's favorite drink, Pernod. Her hands shook as she lit the candle, then she put them together in a silent prayer.

May his spirit and all the spirits wander in peace.

The votive candle caught and flickered, casting Nadège's oblong shadow onto the peeling wallpaper. She gripped the wobbling banister and mounted the steps. She'd locate the stash, but not do anything with it, of course. Then she'd go to the station, take a train, and lay low in the countryside. *Non*, better first to take care of business.

But as she went through the rooms, she heard a shuffling sound and saw a flickering of light.

She wasn't alone. Her stomach clenched in fear.

"May I help you?" said an older woman, stroking a purring cat that was nestled in her arms.

Nadège noticed the woman's slender, graceful body and chiseled cheekbones. She must have been a stunner in her day. The woman set down the cat and unfurled an umbrella she picked up from the floor. A good thing, too, as the soggy plaster leaked with a steady *drip, drip*, from the coved ceiling. Nadège worried that Thadée's stash would already have become moldy.

"Gotten chilly, hasn't it?" the woman said, chatting as if they were meeting at a garden party.

"You're Thadée's friend? Do you live here?"

"Sometimes." The woman gave her a wide smile. "*Un vrai Monsieur!* So generous."

Nadège's eyes welled and she nodded. "Do you know . . . ?"

"Terrible," she said, reaching for Nadège's arm. Her hands were ice cold but sympathy radiated from her. "You're too beautiful to be so sad! Come, take a seat."

In the adjoining room stood a bed and an upright harpsi-

chord, whose legs tilted, its wooden frame warped, keys missing. Once, though, it must have been exquisite. Several water-
stained boxes blocked an antique armoire. Nadège fingered the
large old-fashioned key in her pocket. Sniffled, and wiped her
nose.

"Call me Neda," the woman said, sitting down on the
mitered herringbone pattern parquet floor as if they were at a
picnic. "You have such beautiful pearls. You're an *artiste*, I
can tell."

"*Moi?* Just a year in École des Beaux-arts, but. . . ."
Nadège felt shy.

"*Voilà*," Neda said, smiling. "See, I knew right away."

"It doesn't count, really," said Nadège, biting back a smile.

But those months had been unlike any others. She'd taken
stage and set design courses and planned on apprenticing at the
Opéra Garnier. Life had held rose-framed sunsets in the student
quartier. Then she met Michel's father, a costume designer with
a habit. Just after Michel was born, he'd left and everything had
fallen apart.

"Thadée confided in you, *n'est-ce pas?*"

"A little," Nadège said.

"What about that chest he found and the things inside?"

Nadège shrugged her shoulders, trying still to ignore the
pains in her back.

"So, *ma chère*," Neda said as she pulled off her gloves and
shot up between her fingers. Now Nadège understood.
Aristocratic addicts had to hide like everyone else.

Neda leaned back with closed eyes and sighed. "How can I
be your friend? A little *poudre*? Opium? Or liquid morphine?"

Nadège nodded. *Juste un peu*. To help tide her over. That's all.

Friday Evening

AIMÉE'S BREATH TURNED TO fog, then vanished in the chill night air. The taxi had never showed. Her wet leather coat still stank, but at least she'd cleaned up her shoes.

On Square Berlioz cardboard boxes with old clothes and kitchen appliances stood waiting for the morning charity pickup. She took off her coat, rooted through the boxes, and found a jacket. A button was missing, the satin lining torn, but she didn't need to see a label to know it was *haute couture*. Balenciaga. Worth thousands of francs, if you could even find one, at a vintage shop.

She slipped it on, left her coat in its place, walked a block, and mingled with the crowds streaming out of the cinéma in Place de Clichy. Earnest discussions of Godard's symbolism and Bertolucci's directing style buzzed around her.

The *mec* Jacky from nearby Académie de Billard couldn't be far behind. She had to act fast. She grabbed the free alternative paper piled in the cinema lobby and bought a ticket for the next film, *Elevator to the Gallows*, the black and white Louis Malle classic with Jeanne Moreau decked out in pointy pumps and heavy eyeliner, smoking endless cigarettes and beelining for the bad boy.

Pretty much like Aimée, except for the cigarettes and heavy eyeliner.

During the opening credits, Aimée sank down in her seat with her pen flashlight and scanned the club listings in the alternative newspaper. Under HEAVY METAL she found one club in the 17th featuring a Goth band. But searching under FUSION she found the listing she wanted.

Metallomix, Mado's band, was playing at Lush, a former electric power station, a few streets away. Aimée looked at her watch. Metallomix's set began in an hour. Time enough to watch Jeanne Moreau's lover-thief stranded in the elevator, aghast at his perfect crime undone due to a minor unforeseen detail.

The little things, she thought. Check and recheck, her father had always said. What detail was she was missing?

She watched the movie, waiting for time to pass.

Out in the lobby, she tried Gassot's number again. This time someone answered.

"*Oui*," he said.

"Can I speak with Gassot?"

"We're a café, not a message center."

"But this is the only number I have for him," she said.

"I haven't seen him," he said.

"I'll call back."

She made her way to the club, keeping to the unlit side of the cobbled street. Lush might live up to its name on other nights, Aimée thought. It boasted alternative nights of raï, reggae, jungle, techno, R&B, and tango, but this late evening crowd of semi-heavy metal and Rastas, interspersed with media types, spoke to the *mixte* life of the *quartier*.

And she, with her torn black fishnet stockings, Balenciaga jacket, and Moroccan shirt, would fit right in. *Nouvelle slut*.

Lush felt more *louche* than metallic, the type of place club-bers went after leaving Pink Platinum, a techno striptease, or else en route to a squat-club in an old theatre.

There were DJs on several floors and sofas and harem style rooms with net curtains and canopies over the alcoves for privacy. Inside the old metal-framed glassed-in industrial space, billowing gauze in pastel colors separated the areas. A curtain of metallic pebbled blue lurex material beckoned dancers to lean into it: shimmering and seductive. On the right were low tables and pillows with model-types, assorted rock royalty, and a well-known aging rocker in leather pants, sipping mint tea.

"How old am I?" she overheard him saying to one of the models. "I'm eighteen. The rest is experience."

She found elbow space at the end of the bar, ordered a glass of mineral water with lime, and eyed the stage on the main floor. Mado's set should start soon.

"Come here often?" asked a voice next to her.

She grasped her glass, reached for the bartender's knife, and turned.

Pleyet stood next to her, holding a beer. The smoke and hanging blue halogen lights didn't obscure his eyes: cold and expressionless. Not even a blink. A jagged scar was visible along the hairline of his temple. She doubted it came from a face-lift; more likely a machete.

"I like the band," she said.

"You would," he said.

"I guess Charles Aznavour's more your style."

He shrugged. "This is music?"

The twang of a sitar, accompanied by a curious mélange of mandolin and oboe, pulsed in the background. The wide dance floor filled up and a sweet spice scent of sandalwood wafted from the corners.

"You might want to let go of the knife," he said, pointing to the bartender who was scratching his head and muttering. "Looks like he needs it."

"Pardon," she said, setting it back on the bar.

She wondered if Pleyet had followed her or had come to question Mado. But it only made sense for him to reveal himself if he wanted something.

"Think back to the Place Vendôme affair. Remember the surveillance firm your team contracted with?" she said. "That was me. The little explosion in the Place Vendôme? Well, that was my father. Remember?"

In the pause she could hear rain splattering on the skylight overhead.

"I know," he said.

"That's all you have to say?"

He waved his hand with a dismissive gesture. He rocked on his heels, staring at her.

At least he'd admitted it. They were making headway.

"I had nothing to do with your father's death," he said. "Our team dealt with security. The rest—" He looked down. "They contracted with firms like yours so if it blew up in their faces, as it did, nothing would be traceable to the Ministry. That's all I know."

"I want names," she said. "Department chiefs. Anyone responsible."

"Let it go," he told her.

"People have said that to me for years."

"We were peons, workers. The whole unit was disbanded afterward. Now another Ministry handles 'sensitive' issues. All new faces. And the ones who left? You know how *fonction-naires* lose their files and can't recollect conversations? All their documents have been shredded, all memories erased."

She knew what he meant. And it was probably true. But that didn't mean she could accept coming to a dead end in investigating her father's death.

"What's that phrase, Pleyet, 'Lay your cards on the table.' Then we might do business," she said. "But then according to you, you're not in business and you're not RG."

He shrugged. "Brands and labels," he said as if she referred to items on the supermarket shelf.

He didn't meet her eyes. The band's shaved-headed drummer was tapping his snare drums, doing a sound check.

"What's your connection to Regnier? He's on suspension."

For the first time he blinked. "Since you know so much, are you aware that he's under surveillance?"

"So that's it," she said. "You are the Circle Line . . . . Why do you want the jade?"

"You still have no manners," he interrupted.

"Did that strike a chord?" She'd make it simple. "Pleyet, you're out of place here; you stick out," she said. "But I can help you."

"Out of the goodness of your heart?"

"We can help each other."

The old zinc counter vibrated under her fingers from the music. How much should she reveal to Pleyet? Wouldn't he use her and move on? Special Ops, the Circle Line, they were ruthless. And the suspicion that he'd had a hand in her father's death hadn't gone away.

But she might be able to barter her information for a detail or name.

She remembered Linh's words . . . how her actions were monitored and her family under surveillance. When Aimée had accosted Pleyet in the café she'd understood why he'd brushed her off; he was afraid she'd blow his cover. But now he'd approached her. She had to find out why he wanted the jade, and for whom.

His cell phone rang but he ignored it.

"*Bon*, give me a lead about my father's death and I just might help you."

"You need something more than that to bargain with," he said.

"Like what?"

"I think you know."

He answered his phone, turning away.

Still no sign of Mado, while her band Metallomix was tuning up on the stage. Pleyet clicked off, leaning forward on the counter.

"Why are you here, Pleyet?" she asked. "I don't have the jade, and I already knew Regnier's been suspended. Will you tell me about Thadée?" she asked, trying another angle.

"Thadée swam with sharks. Big, bad ones," Pleyet said. "He

was a spoiled little druggie from a titled family. *Noblesse oblige* tainted by bleeding-heart liberalism. Thadée promised things. Things I doubt he could deliver. And if that's my conclusion, it was probably theirs."

"Who's 'they' and what did he promise them?"

"That's what I'd like to know," Pleyet said.

"But you have an idea. Blondel?"

Pleyet nodded and drank his beer as he watched people on the dance floor. The heat and perspiration from their bodies mingled with the tang of the fresh cut limes.

"Does blackmail feature in this?"

Pleyet studied her. "Why were you meeting Thadée?"

"To help a Vietnamese nun," she said. "Why are you interested in a druggie?"

There, she'd told him the truth. But his hooded eyes gave away nothing. In front of them, the bartender mixed a coconut-milk scented cocktail with turquoise gin.

"Look, I had nothing to do with your father's death," he finally said again. "You should believe me."

Why had the conversation veered from Thadée?

"Prove it."

"I lost someone, too, in a dawn raid the next day. The whole asinine mission was based on hearsay, from an informer who wanted to save his neck. After the fiasco they reshuffled the whole department and buried the accounts in public works."

Whether it was the way his voice shook for a nanosecond or the look of pain in his eyes, she believed him.

"Who did you lose?"

"My younger sister."

"But how?

"She was cultural attaché at the consulate at Tripoli."

"How does this connect to the surveillance Papa and I did?"

"Don't you get it?" Pleyet said, his eyes narrow slits. "It

didn't. It was all fabricated. Lies . . . the *mec* made up a story.
Got a bunch of our people killed, and himself blown up over
the friendly skies of Libya. No one will admit that." Pleyet
leaned closer to her. She saw his thin lips quiver. "Ever. So
don't expect a belated apology. Or a detailed report. It's all
ashes in the wind."

"They never even sent a wreath," she said. "It took me one
year, but I finally got his belongings."

Pleyet averted his eyes. "Consider yourself lucky."

Pause. She didn't know what to say.

"How can you work for them, Pleyet?"

"I don't."

But she'd seen him visit the Musée Cernuschi in the company of ministry types.

"So, who *do* you work for?"

"I can't tell you," he said. "It's time for me to go."

His cell phone rang before she could press him further.
Still no sign of Mado. Before he turned away this time, she
caught sight of the neon-blue face of his phone. His address
book list was displayed.

She grabbed her eye pencil, the first thing at hand, and
wrote down the number opposite HOME on her arm.

He kept one hand on his beer, the other cupping the cell
phone as he slipped away into the crowd.

She placed some francs on the counter by her glass. Pleyet
claimed the surveillance that had killed her father was bogus.
She'd obsess over that later. At least she'd gotten his number.

She edged through the crowd seeking Mado. On her right,
stairs led backstage. Large black boxes of sound equipment
and amplifiers stood in her way. She heard arguing,
raised voices.

"Mado's not coming," said the shag-haired guy whom
Aimée had seen in the Mini-Cooper. "She's split, I tell you."

"Good riddance," said a skinhead.

"But the recording scout's here," the first one said. "If she doesn't show he'll think we lied and beg off on our deal. He likes a cool female to front a metal band. How could she desert us now?"

"Where's Mado?" Aimée asked, stepping forward. "I was supposed to meet her."

"Timbuktu," said the shag-haired one, looking her up and down.

"Then how come I saw her a while ago?" Aimée said. "Where's Timbuktu?"

The rest of the band turned and stared at her.

"Some new performance space. Seems she's too 'creative' for this," the shag-haired one said.

Aimée looked over his shoulder. Her eyes found Jacky's leather bomber jacket bobbing among the lighting technicians. Another *mec* she recognized from the pool hall blocked the exit. Had they seen her? But their eyes were on the crowd. Not the stage.

Aimée saw a gold trimmed silk sari and a Cleopatra headress, gold and black, hanging from a peg. She thought fast. What if she wore that, bided her time, and then. . . .

"Whose costume is that?" she asked.

"You could fill in for Mado," said the guitarist. "Help us out."

"Me?"

He set the bass guitar in her arms. "Put your fingers here, here and here."

Aimée held the silver-faced guitar low against her hip.

"*Non*," said the drummer, his tank top with a skull and crossbones on it. "Did you ever take piano lessons?"

She nodded.

"Keyboard. Watch me. When I nod my head, play the A scale. Can you do that?"

At this point, hemmed in from the front and side, it seemed the best choice. The only one.

"If I can wear that," she said, pointing to the sari.

"Just do it over and over."

She stuck her jacket in her bag, tried winding the sari around her waist and over her shoulders as she'd seen New Delhi women do. No go. In the end she bunched it together toga-style and draped it over her hair. Found dark glasses in her bag. The skinhead readjusted his guitar strap.

"Whatever you do, don't sing," he said. "Look cool. Stand in the shadows. We need to land this contract, or we're in deep shit."

"What's the first song," she asked.

"*Un classique américain*, 'Louie, Louie,' " he said.

She could handle that standing in the background shadows. Couldn't she? And her stomach knotted.

"Showtime," the shag-haired one said, pushing her forward.

Friday Evening

GASSOT WOKE UP SCREAMING, his arms tangled in something and his undershirt drenched with sweat. Pounding throbbed in his ear. Red-pink bursts of tracer bullets arced, flashing above him. Instinctively, he ducked and clutched his leg. His phantom leg. And remembered. This was no red mud foxhole. No dying men of his regiment moaned; there was no thud of distant artillery pounding the thatched huts of a village. The neon lights of a Clichy bar tattooed his wall and the pounding came from the trains hurtling north in the night. His chest heaved.

"Quiet down!" a voice yelled from somewhere next door.

He punched the wall, clutched his cane and hobbled to the

table. The nightmare again! Haunting him, after all these years.

Perspiration beaded his forehead and he reached for what was left in the *Pastis* bottle. Swallowed it. The smell of grease rose from the café below, nauseating him. Who ate in the middle of the night?

His body shook and the phantom pain in his leg ached. The damned leg that wasn't even there.

And those faces. He couldn't get his comrades' faces from his mind. The Expeditionary Force was a decimated, exhausted army even before Dien Bien Phu, despite the psychological warfare strategized by the Fifth Bureau in Paris.

Landless peasants listened to Ho Chi-Minh's ideology and the Vietminh, not to French colonials and fresh-faced graduates from St. Cyr, the elite military academy. Nor to General de Castries who'd relabeled the peaks ridging the heart-shaped valley of Dien Bien Phu, with his mistresses' names: Dominique, Eliane, Claudine, Françoise, Huguette, and Béatrice.

The regiment's annihilation proved it. Even Gassot's work with Tran had been sabotaged. Old World thinking had been outwitted by Asian natives, in a battle to survive.

A knock at his door. The *flics*? Had Picq implicated him?

He grabbed his cane and eyed the open back door where his prosthesis stood, ready for a getaway.

"Who's there?"

"Phone call in the café, old man," someone said. "Hurry or your girlfriend will hang up."

Girlfriend? He wiped his brow. Must be a new code of Nemours's.

"I'm coming."

He slipped on the stocking, then the bandage, eased his stump into the artificial leg, and attached it. By the time he had navigated the backstairs and reached the café's zinc counter, the pockmark-faced youth shrugged his shoulders. "She hung up."

Gassot wanted to hit him.

"But she's calling back," he grinned. "Must like you. Eager, eh?" And he made an obscene gesture.

"Give me a *pastis* and shut up," Gassot said.

"You're not very nice. The *flics* were asking about you, but I—"

Gassot slammed five francs on the counter and shot out the door.

Friday Evening

THE JASMINE CANDLES, CARDAMOM scents, body heat, and smoke made Aimée want to sneeze. Perspiration dampened the sari she'd wrapped around her forehead, and her heels dipped precariously on the low, tilted platform. With any luck Jacky's eyes would be centered on the crowd, not the stage.

The lead guitarist's licks soared as he riffed and jumped around in the spotlight. She swayed in the shadows, the sari covering most of her face, aimed at "cool," and kept her head down. By the third song, her ears hurt. So much for the rock star life.

At least her dark glasses dimmed the flashing strobe lights. She kept the beat, playing the same chords over and over on the keyboard, watching the drummer whose head never stopped moving.

"Shake." The bassist threw her a tambourine. She beat it with one hand and with the other kept palming the three chords. As she watched the drummer, she darted looks at the crowd. The dance floor wavered, glittering with swirling dancers. A throbbing disco-ball descended, shooting rays of blue light.

Aimée's hand at the keyboard was bathed in a blue glow, the hypnotic beat echoing through her body.

"Hey Bombay *chérie!*" someone yelled, another joined in and then the crowd. "Bom-bay *chérie*, Bom-bay *chérie*," they chanted, stamping their feet. The skinhead caught the rhythm, chording along with the chant. The crescendo rose.

And then her eyes caught on Jacky edging close to the low stage. She panicked, slipped further back into the shadows. When she looked again, he'd become one with the pulsating crowd intent on dancing. And then the lights went out.

Candles sputtered. And for a moment, Aimée and the drummer kept the beat amid laughter, then there were shouts and confusion.

Someone pulled at her shoes and she kicked them off. Fear coursed through her. Her ankle was grabbed again, and she kicked harder. Jacky's slicked-back pompadour caught the candlelight as the crowd surged toward the stage. She had to make her legs move, get away. She fumbled by the guitarist, dropped the tambourine, and dove offstage toward the pillows.

Tea sprayed and legs flew. A brass tray shot out from under her. She scrambled forward, intent on getting out before Jacky or the other guy, caught in a knot of people by the exit, saw where she'd landed. On her hands and knees, she crawled through mini-skirt clad women and somehow pushed her way to the door.

"Let me out!" she shouted up at the security guard.

"Wait your turn like—"

"I can't breathe!"

He took one look at her perspiring face and shoulders convulsed with fear and unbolted it.

She dodged into a wet *allée*, the cobblestones slick beneath her. Women of a certain age stood in the street, then retreated to the doorways as men passed them by.

"Slow down, *ma cocotte*," one of them said, "you won't get business that way."

Aimée pulled the sari above her knees and took off down Passage de Clichy. Then around the corner of the winding passage. A door opened to a dimly lit courtyard with leafless trees. She ran inside, panting, and paused by a sign that said PIANO RESTORATION SINCE 1921. A Schubert étude drifted through the air, soft and lingering.

At the side of the high glassed-in workshop, a green metal half-door was open and someone was lugging a box through it. She caught her breath as a white-haired man came into view.

"Monsieur, Monsieur!" she said. "I'm sorry to disturb you. May I join you?" she asked, and slid through the door without waiting for an answer. "I need to go out your back door."

He put his finger over his lip. "Shhh, listen. But the Bechstein's not ready. These things take time." He gestured toward a black piano, the light catching the ebony wood. "You young people get so impatient!"

She closed the door behind her and scanned the interior of the workroom.

Inside the gaping piano, bronze-toned piano wires skewed in circles, a frill of confusion.

"Eh, *doucement*, take your time," she said playing along, wanting to find an exit other than Passage de Clichy that would lead her to Timbuktu.

She rifled through her leather backpack, pulled out the alternative paper, and found Timbuktu's address, then grabbed her Paris map, and scanned it. "Your shop's other exit leads to Passage Lathuille, *n'est-ce pas?*"

The tinkling notes of Schubert wafted through the chill workroom. Lyrical, with pauses so deliberate it felt as if the music was working its way under water.

"Can you believe this piece was played on this piano?" His eyes were elsewhere as he stuck his black smudged hands in his blue workcoat pocket. "From a 1938 Prague recording. This piano! And I will repair it and craft that sound again."

She edged past the workbench with its thin chisels, pliers, and tuning forks.

"It's played from the soul," she said. And it was.

"You hear it, too," he nodded, running his hand over the mirrorlike black surface. "I'll bend and shape the wood the same way, make the sounding boards to the same specifications. The strings and pins, hammers and keys: there will be no variation."

"Monsieur, please, where's the exit to passage Lathuille?"

"No time. None of you have time anymore." He gave a snort of disgust. "Over there. Don't slam the door on your way out."

Aimée made her way through the darkened showroom, felt the sharp edges of pianos, and saw the dim EXIT sign. She unlocked the heavy metal and glass door and relocked it before shutting it. She slipped between the building into a walkway, remnant of a medieval lane, so narrow her shoulders scraped against the damp buildings.

At the end, she turned left into cobbled passage Lathuille. Along the graffitied walls by the tobacco brown, 1930s-style hôtel de passe that rented rooms by the hour, she saw the silver and green fluorescent spray-painted sign TIMBUKTU on an old storefront.

So this was what the band member had meant by "Timbuktu."

No one stood outside. Deserted? But as she got closer, she heard the thrum of a generator. Some kind of squat, or place for band practice?

She knocked several times. Tapped her feet on the wet cobbles. At last the door opened. The person standing there had his face hidden in shadow.

"We're closed," said a man in a low voice.

Closed? It didn't look like they'd ever been opened.

"I'm looking for Mado," she said.

From inside came the acrid smell of kerosene lamps and low flickers of light.

"Who are you?"

Aimée realized the sari still hung, bedraggled, from her shoulders and she still wore dark glasses. If she told the truth, she doubted if he would let her in.

"Mado's sister, Sophie," she said.

"Liar." He shut the door before she could stick her foot inside.

Bad choice. She should have said something else.

She huddled close to the stone wall. A cat slunk by her feet. Moments later, the blue lights of a police car were reflected in the puddles veining avenue de Clichy, as it flashed past. She pounded on the door.

Several minutes later the door opened a crack to reveal Mado's silhouette framed by her rhinestone tank top dress.

"I have something of yours," Aimée said, "let me in."

Mado opened the door a crack wider.

Aimée edged in beside her, unwound the sari, and put it in Mado's arms. "Your band's upset you didn't show up, but I helped them out."

"*Quoi?*" Mado's mouth opened in a violet circle of surprise.

"We have to talk," she said. "People are chasing me and I must reach Sophie. I have to contact her in London."

Mado's eyes widened. "But she's here. How did you find this place?"

Aimée bit back her surprise. "Show me."

Mado gestured toward a room with a wooden counter. Shelves, left from an old *pharmacie*, labeled with Latin pharmacological names, reached the ceiling. Mado's rhinestone-trimmed dress glittered in the dim light, the floor creaked, and dank smells came from the corners. Sophie sat crosslegged on the counter, an army-green blanket over her shoulders, murmuring into a phone.

If she was surprised to see Aimée, she didn't show it. There were dark circles under her smudged, mascaraed eyes. Her blunt-cut brown hair hit the edge of the army blanket.

"The gallery's line of credit's used up," Sophie said, snapping her phone shut. "The bank's recording says we've borrowed beyond our means. Why didn't Thadée tell me?" She shook her head. "I can't even pay the customs duty we owe in England. The show's gone bust!"

"Thadée needed money, Sophie. That's why he tried to sell the jade to the nun," Aimée said. She pulled out the fifty thousand franc check. "This belongs to you."

"Me?"

"For the gallery, or whatever you need it for," she said. "But I have to find the jade."

"As I told you, I've never heard of this jade. And I can't take this check."

Aimée pressed it into her hand.

"He meant it for you."

For the first time Aimée saw a lost look in Sophie's face.

"Good for nothing," Mado said, her voice low. "Thadée never changed."

"Don't talk like that," Sophie snapped.

Aimée saw the jawline the two sisters shared and sensed their rivalry, stemming from childhood, almost palpable in the chill air of the old *pharmacie*.

"Sophie, I think he stole the jade; he needed money. At least, it makes sense. But what doesn't make sense is where he got it and who has it now."

"A mess. I didn't go back to London," Sophie said. "I'm trying to work out a deal with the British gallery. If only he had told me! But he had heart. He tried to help people; he never wanted me to worry."

"Didn't he talk about some big deal?"

"For the past two months I've been flying back and forth, letting him run the show here. In London, the lorry drivers went on strike; we couldn't even get the wood for shipping crates." Sophie buried her face in her hands. Sobbed. "I can't believe he's gone."

Aimée stroked Sophie's hand, comfortingly. Waited until she calmed down. "What about his connections with old families, old collectors?" Aimée prodded. Couldn't Sophie remember some connection?

Sophie shook her head.

Aimée wished she had a drink, and one to give to Sophie. She pulled on her jacket but it was made for the runway, not a frigid, unheated turn-of-the-century *pharmacie*.

"But he was murdered and it has to do with the jade," she said. "What about Asian art collectors or the Musée Cernuschi?"

Sophie shrugged.

She hated to keep prodding Sophie but if she didn't, her chance of finding a link to the jade disappeared.

"Sophie, how would he have had access to a jade collection looted years ago from Indochina?"

"I don't know. We'd grown apart; we only spoke about business the last two months."

"Did Thadée let old veterans stay in that back building?"

"How do I know?" she said. "I never went there."

Aimée had to take another tack.

"Think, please. What did Blondel want from him?"

Tears welled in Sophie's eyes again. "Not dope. He quit cold turkey. Went through hell, did it himself. I was proud of him."

"You make him sound like a saint, Sophie," Mado said, disgust in her voice. "He owed everyone. Past bills in Clichy don't go away until they're paid." Mado paused. "*Non*, you talk like he was a martyr to dope!"

"What do you know? The craving, it's a sickness," Sophie said.

Aimée heard the sadness and something more in Sophie's tone. An echo of real experience. She sensed a subtle change in the two sisters. As if they'd exchanged roles, Sophie with her conservative exterior, more forgiving than Mado with her wild outfit and narrow mind.

"He promised everything would work out."

Frustrated, Aimée leaned close to Sophie, putting an arm around her shoulder. She tried not to wince as the stitches in that arm smarted. "Don't you want to find the killers, bring them to justice? I do."

"But you were the target, *non*?"

"I thought so too, but we both could have been set up." That thought had kept Aimée up at night. "And then *you* were attacked. It could make some kind of sense if Thadée owed money." She thought of what Pleyet said about owing "big sharks." "He gave me the jade to give to a Cao Dai nun, but it was stolen from me. Stolen by someone who knew he'd had it. How will we know who unless you think hard? Tell me whom he dealt with."

"Thadée had pretensions. Ever since his second wife, the one from the chic family," Mado said. "You didn't mention Pascale, the rich one who wised up and moved to Bordeaux."

"I don't want to talk about—" Sophie said.

"Of course not," Mado said, "But at one time, Pascale de Lussigny was your best friend!"

Aimée knew Sophie swung a good punch from experience and shoved Mado to one side, just in case. But the name registered. So Thadée had had a connection to the de Lussigny's. Was it the branch related to Julien de Lussigny, who wanted her to spy on PetroVietnam?

"What's their address?"

"That big mansion overlooking Parc Monceau."

That narrowed it some.

"There's a lot of those. Which one?"

"Gold filigreed gates, by the museum."

"Musée Cernuschi?"

Mado nodded.

"We'll find it." Aimée punched in the taxi request number on her speed dial. "First we're taking you to a safe place. You can stay with my friend."

"Not that old *flic*. . . ."

"In the 16th near the Bois de Boulogne," she said. "More your style. This time you'll remain there for your own good." Even if she had to chain her up.

MARTINE, AIMÉE'S best friend since the *lycée*, answered the tall apartment door wearing a Tintin costume, a cigarette dangling from her mouth. Her orange wig was askew.

"We're having a party for Gilles's children," she said, her voice husky as she looked them over. "I've got an extra costume."

"Don't worry," Aimée said, "we'll set her up in a back room and lock the door."

"Don't tell me." Martine raised her hands. "I don't want to know."

In the gilt-edged white hallway, Aimée heard murmurs of conversation and laughter. Several dinosaur-costumed children ran into the dining room.

"*Nom de Dieu*, we haven't eaten yet and it's midnight . . . lots of hungry natives," Martine said, ushering them to the back of the long apartment. "Great dress," she told Mado. She opened the door to a suite of rooms with Louis XV furniture.

"Things going smoothly with Guy, Aimée?" Martine asked.

Aimée shook her head. She avoided Martine's gaze.

"What did you do now?" Martine asked, lifting Aimée's chin and looking in her eyes.

"Something stupid. Now he's with a blonde."

"And he seemed to be such a good catch! But I guess he's not your bad boy type." Martine exhaled a puff of smoke. "*Bon*, this will work, I've done it myself. Set off the fire alarm and you'll meet big, strong men who can cook."

Aimée grinned. "You seem happy now."

"All men come with baggage." Martine shrugged. "I like Gilles despite the nagging ex-wife and his kids every other week. I'm getting used to living in the eye of the storm."

Aimée noticed the tired happiness in Martine's eyes. And her pointed look at Aimée's torn fishnet stockings. "How about another pair? I've got purple."

"*Merci*, Martine."

AIMÉE SAT Sophie down. Pinpricks of car lights snaked through the Bois de Boulogne outside the window.

"Please stay here. It's not safe for you anywhere else right now."

"Look, Aimée, forgive me for the way I've acted," Sophie said, "but I can't keep this check."

"Thadée meant it for you."

"I can't help you much," Sophie said, hesitating, "but maybe there's something in the computer records." She sank deeper on the low ottoman. "Instead of hindering you, I should try to help. My computer password's 2297jil," she said. "The safe's behind a Jean Basquiat charcoal in the office."

Of course. And the first place anyone would look.

"I'll have to bury Thadée. Someone has to."

Sophie still loved him, that much was obvious.

"Let me find out about the arrangements. But don't move from here," Aimée said, not wanting to add that she'd join him if the men who were after her found her this time.

Late Friday Evening

AIMÉE AND MADO PULLED up in the taxi outside Avenue Velasquez. The gilt-edged gates surrounding Parc Monceau's exclusive enclave confronted them as the taxi stopped.

"You're sure it's this house, Mado?"

Mado nodded. "Nice to see how the other half lives," she said.

Couples walked down the wide front stairs to waiting cars. Several security men spoke into headphones on the driveway. White catering vans lined the back drive.

"Looks like the party's over."

"It's just beginning," Aimée said, hiking her bag onto her shoulder. "I'll call you later; go back to Timbuktu."

Instead of using the main entrance, Aimée wound her way past the catering vans. In the third van she found what she needed. Black-and-white-checked chef's trousers, clogs, a white shirt with side buttons, and a long white apron. She tucked her hair under a white cap, left her bag in the rhododendron bushes outside the service entrance, and joined the chaos in the hot, steaming kitchen.

She kept her head down and made a beeline for the pantry.

An army of caterers loaded huge roasting pans on trolleys, piled hot trays, scrubbed dishes in the stainless steel sink, and loaded glassware in cardboard cartons.

"The LÉGUMES! The *LÉGUMES!*" a florid, flushed man was shouting at her, pointing to the carved rosettes of zucchini. "How many times do I have to say it?"

Aimée nodded, picked up the heavy tray, and aimed for the dining room.

"*NON!* In the van!"

She turned and headed out the kitchen door. When his

head was turned, she backed up right into the pantry lined with Sèvres dishes and linens. She pulled the sliding pantry door shut, latched it, set the tray down, covered it with a table-cloth, then slipped off the shirt, trousers and apron, putting them into a drawer, and exited the other side of the pantry.

A few couples huddled under the chandeliers, standing on the Aubusson carpet, saying goodbye to the hostess, a young blonde woman.

"*Bonsoir*, Madame de Lussigny," Aimée said.

The woman frowned.

Had she made a *faux pas?*

"I see you've met Lena, Mademoiselle Leduc," said Julien de Lussigny, wearing a tuxedo and looking ready to step onto a *Vogue Homme* cover. In fact, many of the guests were faces prominent in the pages of *Elle*.

"So, you feel better?"

"Thank you for asking. Monsieur de Lussigny, I'm sorry to come uninvited," she said, "but spare me a few moments."

She gave him a huge smile. And he returned it, eyeing her outfit, muttering "Too bad, you would have made this more interesting."

Aimée wasn't sure how to take that. When she looked around, Lena had disappeared.

"Let's talk out there," he said.

He escorted her to a glass-covered walkway looking over an interior garden. Small white lights and candles flickering in bubbled-glass holders lit the way.

"I was worried about you," he said. "But you look much bet-ter. Have you come to tell me you've spoken with your partner and Verlet?"

"Right now what I'd like to know is how you're related to Thadée Baret."

Her heels echoed on the stone and a white moth beat its wings imprisoned in a candle-holder.

"Did you know Thadée?" de Lussigny asked.

"I asked first," Aimée said.

"Thadée was my brother-in-law," he said, folding his arms, "but he and my sister Pascale divorced."

Aimée stared at de Lussigny in the dim light.

"Your family were prominent colonials in Indochina," Aimée said, "so I presume you know about the looted jade astrological figures."

De Lussigny took a deep breath. "You've done your homework."

She and Mado had stopped en route at the art gallery, where she'd sent Thadée's documents via e-mail to herself and René. Too bad she hadn't enough time to research further. But half an hour on Sophie's computer had been enough to give her some background. Why hadn't she done this before?

"And you haven't answered my question."

"My father knew stories," de Lussigny said. "Stories he'd heard from the workers on the rubber plantation."

"Stories about jade looted from the emperor's tomb? Or the one where the last Vietnamese emperor entrusted the collection to the Cao Dai, to keep it safe?"

"You continue to impress me, Aimée. Persistent as well," he said, smiling. "I'm not a collector. It's not in my nature. My father had more than enough acquisitive genes in his body for all of us."

So his father was the one?

"So you're saying your father acquired this collection?"

"He dreamed of it, I know," he said. "But no one has seen it since the fall of Dien Bien Phu."

Disappointed, Aimée wondered how this could be true.

"But the jade was put up for auction at Drouot last month," she said. "Then withdrawn. Wouldn't your father have known about this?"

"You're sure?" he asked, seeming truly surprised. "*C'est*

incroyable! I'll bet Papa's turning over in his grave. He passed away in October, at the dinner table. Heart attack," he said.

"Your brother-in-law Thadée had this." She pulled out the auction catalog page. "Then he was killed."

"They're beautiful. But I don't understand," de Lussigny said, puzzled. "How does this involve you?"

Should she tell him? Something held her back.

"I'm helping his former wife, Sophie," she said. "She ran the gallery with him."

"Then she knows that Thadée was always chasing dreams," de Lussigny said. "An artist, such a shame, with all the talent he had."

She'd hoped he would know more about the jade, but she'd struck out again! Aimée pulled her jacket close, wishing she had a warmer one.

"Why would someone kill him?"

"There are some things we want to keep private."

"You mean his habit?" she asked. "According to Sophie, he'd cleaned up."

De Lussigny's eyes darkened. "He's been in and out of rehab for the past year. I loved him like a brother, he was still very much a part of our family, but I had to pull away. It hurt too much to watch."

"I'm sorry," she said.

Was Thadée a victim of a double-cross scam? Or had Blondel used his thugs to send a message about paying debts?

She didn't know what else to ask. The hour was late and de Lussigny looked tired, but if she didn't press him, what other leads were there?

"Was your father acquainted with Dinard, the curator at the Musée Cernuschi?"

"You know a lot about my family," he said. "Dinard's my godfather."

They were all tied together.

De Lussigny was buried in thought. "That's strange. He was supposed to attend the benefit tonight," he said.

"Where does he live?"

"Just across the park."

Lena stood at the door, casting a shadow over the stone. "Your guests want to say good night."

"I'll let you get back to your wife," she said.

"My ex-wife," he said with a sigh. "It's in bad taste to have this affair right after Thadée's death, but last year I promised to host it again. I sponsor this charity event for the land mine victims organization she heads. We have to help people who need help."

How civilized. She saw something very sad in his eyes. Brief and passing, and then it was gone.

"I don't mean to change the subject, but there's a business meeting tomorrow evening at l'hôtel Ampère. Can you bring me the Olf project files and join us?"

She nodded and watched de Lussigny slip back into his gracious host mode.

A IMÉE WANTED to avoid the kitchen and security out front but she had to recover her bag. She'd noticed the entry to the rear wing had what looked like a handicapped ramp. If she continued on the glass-covered walkway, she figured she'd run into a rear outlet to the garden.

It led straight to a door which she opened to find herself inside the dark rear wing of the house, near a small, high-ceilinged kitchen that smelled of lemon grass and sesame oil, warm and inviting.

A small boy with button black eyes, wearing Superman pajamas, perched on a stool, eating with chopsticks. Beside him, an older Asian woman with shiny black hair imprisoned in a bun, spooned rice into his bowl. Her hairpin caught

Aimée's attention. Lustrous, green jade. But what took her breath away was its shape: a dragon.

"*Excusez-moi,*" she said,

"Are you lost?" asked the little boy.

Lost *and* clueless, she wanted to say.

"I'm avoiding the big kitchen and looking for the back door."

He nodded, his look serious. "I avoid it, too. So does *grand-mère.*"

The hiss of steam escaped from a kettle on the stove and a clock ticked above the spice canisters.

She hoped her stomach wouldn't growl.

"Are you hungry, too?" asked the little boy. His grandmother's hand cupped his shoulder as if protecting him. Around his neck a red string was visible; suspended from it was a small jade pendant.

"Very kind of you but *non, merci. Bon appétit,*" she said. "Madame, what a exquisite hairpin!"

The woman touched her hair, then reached for the lid of the rice cooker. "The boy growing, wake up hungry. I feed him."

Aimée smiled. "I see. So big and strong. He's very smart, too, I'm sure."

"*Non, non,* he too small. Weak. Worthless!" she said, horror in her eyes.

Confused, Aimée didn't know what to say.

She saw the little boy grin. "*Grand-mère* always says that, to keep the bad spirits away. So they won't think I'm strong and smart, and steal me."

Aimée nodded. "Forgive me, I didn't think of it that way."

"She says things like that," he said. "That's why we live back here. My *maman* calls it a cultural land mine but I thought those were things that blew up."

Aimée suppressed a smile.

"Where's your *maman?*"

The woman's hand tightened on the boy's shoulder. "Finish rice, Michel. Very late, time for sleep."

Michel yawned. "*Maman's* like a butterfly. Sometimes she comes when I'm asleep." He took one last bite, set his chopsticks down, aligning them with the bowl, put his small hands together, and bowed his head. Aimée saw the pride in the old *grand-mère's* eyes.

"Proper way. Good boy," she said, ushering him toward another room.

If Aimée didn't do something, they would disappear.

"Excuse me, Madame, I love your jade," she said. "It's exquisite. A one-of-a-kind piece?"

"From my country," she said. "No good. Old-fashioned."

"You're from Vietnam?"

The old woman averted her eyes. "It is. Michel tired."

"Of course. I've seen a dragon like that before. What does it symbolize?"

The woman paused at the door of a room suffused by red light. The musk of incense wafting from inside. An old Chinese chest overflowing with Legos and toys stood by the door.

"The dragon mean strong, smart, and patient."

She shut the door. But not before Aimée had seen the Cao Dai shrine on the wall.

AIMÉE STOOD in dense fog outside the locked and silent Cao Dai temple. She saw no sign of surveillance. There was no sign of anyone in the deserted street. Linh hadn't answered her phone, but Aimée had to ask her questions. Important ones.

Down here in the 13th, she didn't speak the language, didn't know the customs. *Merde!* She didn't even look like anyone here.

A video store plastered with posters of Hong Kong action

movies, the only sign of life in the quiet, narrow street, stood a few doors down.

She opened the shop door to the sounds of gunshots and explosions, and flinched. On a screen above the counter, Jet Li karate-chopped a gang of black-suited Ninja assassins.

"Monsieur?" she asked a young Asian man, with spiked red-tipped hair and an earring. He sat behind the counter, engrossed in *rapido Bac histoire*, the study text and notes for the Baccalauréat exam. Aimée knew the *rapido* well—but not well enough, since she had failed her first Bac. She had passed the second time around.

He glanced at his watch. "You're the last rental, I'm closing."

She needed to thaw him out, get information. She leaned on the counter. "*C'est difficile*, eh, the Bac. I didn't pass the first time."

He rolled his eyes. "This is my second time."

Aimée nodded knowingly. "You'll make it. My friends and I did, on the second try."

She tried to keep the conversation going, hoping he knew something about the area. "I meditate at the Cao Dai temple," she said. In theory, anyway. "I need to reach one of the nuns from the temple."

He shrugged. "I've got no clue about what goes on around here in the daytime. I only work evenings."

"Any idea where the nuns live?"

He used a receipt to save his place and shut the book. He shook his head.

"Have you seen Cao Dai nuns in this *quartier?*"

"Never."

The sound of Jet Li's karate chops, brisk and thumping, filled the store.

"What about the concierge of the building next door? Would he know?"

He stood, rang the cash register and cleared it. "I can't help you."

Someone must rent them the space. "Sorry to ask so many questions, but do you know who owns the building?"

"There's a mah-jong game the video store owner goes to sometimes, behind the Cao Dai temple. I've seen the man who sweeps out the temple go there, too. Other than that, I wouldn't know."

At least it was a place to start.

"Thanks for your help," she said. "Good luck on the Bac."

The building next door to the temple had shuttered windows and a dark green oval door with a digicode. She stood, rooting through her bag for a screwdriver with which to unscrew the plate, when the door opened. A man came out with a fox terrier pulling on a leash, his collar raised against the fog.

"*Bonsoir*," she said, smiling. "I forgot my friend's code."

He nodded and Aimée slipped inside and walked toward the rear. She heard the slap of mah-jong tiles before she saw the lighted concierge loge and smelled the cigarette smoke trailing out to the narrow strip of concrete between the apartments.

Several Asian men sat around a table in the small room whose walls were tinged with brown and yellow. Everyone smoked. She recognized the squat man with a withered arm who swept the floors. A charity case, she'd figured, but he played his tiles as fast as the others.

"*Pardonnez-moi*," she said, stepping inside the open door and smiling at him. "I don't mean to interrupt your game, but I wonder if I can have a private word with you, monsieur. I've seen you at the meditation sessions next door."

His eyes shuttered.

"Say it here," he said, looking down. "I'm involved in a game."

A man next to him nudged the man's ribs. "Don't want to spoil your luck, Quoc?"

She saw the pile of francs next to the ashtray, small porcelain tea cups, half-full, tea leaves floating in them, felt their eyes on her.

"Forgive me, but I'm looking for Linh, the nun," she said. "She helped me to meditate. Can you tell me if she's staying nearby?"

"Why ask me?" Quoc said.

"Since you work there. . . ."

"Never saw her before last week," he said.

Was he just trying to brush her off?

"But you're there all the time. Surely you would have noticed her."

He paused, irritation on his thin face. "Ask the priest," he said.

"Monsieur, that's a good suggestion, but in the meantime. . . ."

He covered his tiles, anxious to get rid of her.

"I take it back," he said. "The week before last I saw her. That's all I know. Now, I need to finish this game."

She'd only noticed Linh at the temple a few times herself, but figured not all nuns attended every session. Why would they?

"Can you give me the address of the nuns' residence?" she asked, hoping they lived nearby.

He slapped his tiles down. "But when I saw her, she wasn't a nun."

Startled, Aimée noticed the grins on the men's faces as they smacked tiles down on the wooden table.

"You mean she wore street clothes?"

"Sure, she wore street clothes. Now, if you'll excuse me."

"Eh, Quoc," the man next to him grinned, "you mean she's too pretty?"

He shook his head. "She reminded me of that café actress in the sixties, the one who sang the French go-go songs in Chinese and Vietnamese." He winked at the man next to him. "You remember, eh?"

"Sorry, I don't understand," Aimée said.

"Are you saying she's not a nun?"

"I'm not saying anything. Not many nuns here," Quoc told her. "Only old ones."

"But she could have come from another temple, *n'est-ce pas?*"

Quoc lit a cigarette from a burning stub in the ashtray, a Vietnamese brand, lapsed into Vietnamese and shuffled the white tiles, ignoring her.

What about Priest Tet, who ran the meditation sessions, Aimée wondered. Would he be more helpful?

"Do you have the priest's residence telephone number?"

"Priest Tet?"

She nodded and he wrote it down on a piece of paper.

"That's all I know." He refused to answer any more questions.

She made her way back to the street. Bone-chilling fog swirled around her legs as she ran for the late night bus. If Linh was petitioning the International Court of Justice for her imprisoned brother, she wouldn't necessarily wear her nun's robes all the time. But Quoc's words disturbed her. She telephoned the Cao Dai priest's residence.

"Forgive me for calling so late but I need to speak with Linh," she asked. "The nun who helped me with meditation."

"Nuns? No one here now," Priest Tet said. "Not many nuns practice at our temple. Try Joinville-le-Pont," he said. "They can help you."

But at the Joinville-le-Pont Pagoda there was only an eighty-six-year-old nun who knew of no Linh or any other Cao Dai nuns in Paris. Unease filled Aimée. Where was Linh?

In the taxi back to the Clichy hotel, yellow lights reflected on the wet pavement in Place de Clichy. A line snaked out of the only *tabac* open at this hour. She called Martine.

"Martine, how's your guest?"

"Asleep," she said, her husky voice tired. "I checked. Tomorrow, I work at home and will keep my eye on her."

"I'll owe you double if you check out the Gulf of Tonkin's untapped oil sources, and who looks like the leader in obtaining oil drilling rights."

"You're kidding, right, Aimée?"

"And those rumors that Olf's an unofficial arm of the Ministry of Foreign Affairs."

"My piece on the European Commission's in revision," Martine said, "and I have to fact check twice before tomorrow's deadline."

Martine wrote investigative freelance for AFP—Agence France Presse—and Reuters now, too. She enjoyed it more than her editorship at *Le Figaro* or the doomed magazine *Diva* she'd spearheaded for a brief two issues, until Aimée had discovered her backer was financing *Diva* with laundered arms money.

"Nose around. You've got contacts in that world," Aimée said. "There's a Dom Pérignon with your name on it. Isn't Gilles's birthday soon?"

"A magnum of Dom Pérignon, did you say?"

Aimée groaned. Quick, Martine was quick.

"And those petits fours from Fauchon that he loves."

"Deep background, Martine."

She heard Martine yawn. "*D'accord*, the usual."

Saturday Morning

NADÈGE BLINKED. LIGHT CAME through the shutter's slits and wavered across the floor. Her bag had vanished, her jewelry, and the old lady, too. She felt sore, itchy, and cold.

The old woman had slipped something into that liquid. Like something she'd heard making the rounds of clubs. A tasteless, odorless substance men put in women's drinks, knocking them out and causing them to forget what happened after. But her head felt clear though she remembered drinking and no more.

Footsteps sounded below.

Had the old woman returned?

The wormholed armoire lay open, papers and old clothes strewn around. But her body wouldn't cooperate. She rolled over and was face to face with the smudged baseboard.

"Where did she put it?" a loud voice was saying. "Thadée owes me."

What did they mean? Thadée's stash? Or the old key she'd found? But it had gone with her bag. And she hadn't known what it opened. Her plans for flight had gone up in smoke.

Nadège crawled, her muscles protesting, and gripped the edge of the armoire. She must get inside, hide under piles of clothes. But she felt so tired. Her hand loosened, fell.

"Where the hell did she go?"

Nadège knew that voice. The Bonbon King. Panic gripped her. She owed him. She forced her legs, made them crawl. Somehow she got inside, curled into an embryonic position, pulled an old crocheted shawl over her, and closed the armoire door halfway. Like she'd hidden when she was small and her parents fought, trying to drown out her father's accusations and her mother's tears. But she never could.

Only her *grand-mère*'s warm arms that rocked her, and her inexhaustible supply of ginger candy, had made it better. For awhile.

Several men argued in the doorway. "We find her, grab the kid—"

One of them kicked the bedstead, then the old desk, splintering it to pieces. Nadège shuddered. He'd smash the armoire next.

Saturday Morning

THE VANILLA-HUED LIGHT, UNUSUALLY clear for November, haloed René's head. Aimée blinked and opened her eyes wider. Everything fell into place. There was no fogginess or blurring. She breathed a sigh of relief and smelled something wonderful.

But where were they?

And then she remembered their Clichy hotel room.

"Your espresso's getting cold," René said.

"*Merci.*" She sat up, untangling her purple fishnets and Moroccan shirt.

"You mumbled something last night about running a virus check on the Olf account and duplicating log entries and e-mails before a meeting with de Lussigny later," he said. "I'm printing them out now."

"*Fantastique.* And good morning to you, partner." She smiled, stirring two lumps of brown sugar into her cup. "How do you feel?"

"The mattress came with the hotel in 1830," he said, jerking his thumb toward the bed. "But after the hard earth in the air raid shelter, I loved it."

"We can't go back to the office."

"Or my apartment," he said. "Saj got us some new cell phones. He's bringing my scanner later. Look at you. Nice outfit."

She grimaced, checking the stitches on her arm. "Perfect for escaping through garbage chutes, playing in heavy metal bands, and also for attending elegant *soirées.*"

René swallowed his espresso the wrong way and choked. "Going to tell me about it?"

Aimée handed René a napkin and told him about Regnier's suspension, her encounter with Blondel and Pleyet, Sophie, and the old Chinese *grand-mère*. She didn't mention meeting de Lussigny.

"Blondel? How's he involved?"

"Thadée owed Blondel; his henchman Jacky made my skin crawl," she said. "Gassot's hiding. Afraid. But I don't know why. And I'm no closer to the jade. I need to discover Pleyet's motive and what exactly the Circle Line *is*."

"Aimée, if Pleyet once worked with Regnier," René said, "stands to reason they're in this together now."

"But Pleyet intimated he's surveilling Regnier," she said. "And somehow, I buy it. He didn't have to reveal himself last night. Or tell me about the past."

René hit SAVE on his laptop.

"You mean about the Place Vendôme surveillance? He could be leading you on. But how is that relevant? What you need to discover is who had the jade originally. Then you can question them."

Good point! But so far she'd run into dead ends and silence.

"I e-mailed Thadée's files here. Can you look them over? The Drouot won't release the name of the consignor," she said. "It's in data storage on the île de la Jatte. What's important is, who wants it now? That should point to who killed for it."

René rubbed his bandaged wrist. She noticed his right leg propped on the chair and pillows below his hip.

"Are you with me on this, René?"

He shrugged.

"No choice," he said. "But be careful."

She switched on her laptop.

"This might help," she said. "I've got four digits of Lars's password. If we get the rest, we can crack the Circle Line."

And figure out why the Circle Line was looking for the jade.

She heard a knock on the door. "Who's there?"

"Didn't you say you needed a hacker?" someone asked.

She opened the door.

Saj stood there in flowing Indian pants and wool Nepalese sweater.

"Perfect timing," she said. "Got a challenge for you two."

He rubbed his hands together, taking in the three computers. "My pleasure."

She typed in the digits she'd written on her palm.

"There's four of the twelve numbers Lars entered," she said. "I need the complete password. Want to try a brute force attack?"

René shook his head. "A brute force attack with every possible combination of letters, numbers, and symbols to try and duplicate a password? That could take two days. Aren't we in a hurry?"

"What about a *dictionnaire* attack?" asked Saj. "Try common words found in a *dictionnaire* starting with pets' names or others commonly used in passwords."

"Most ministries use heavily encrypted passwords," Aimée said. "Like we do. Changing them constantly."

But in this socialist system, with the endemic work overloads, she knew little time was spent on such safety procedures.

"Lars's system, I figure, like all the ministries, uses a stored 'hash' of the password in a file," she said.

"Right," said René. "One-way encryption uses a common algorithm which manipulates the password."

"But breaking a twelve-digit or letter password could take a whole day," Saj said, sitting down. "If we use two computers, it will take less time, of course.

"*Bon*, you've got this under control. I've got to follow someone," Aimée said, pulling on her coat.

"Not one of those *mecs*."

"An old Chinese *grand-mère*," Aimée said. "A Cao Dai member. We should have a lot in common."

THE OLD *grand-mère* dropped Michel off at the nearby *école maternelle* and Aimée followed her. The Asian woman, her padded silk jacket flapping in the wind, walked with a quick step across busy Place de Clichy. She paused at the Vietnamese restaurant, fronted by a flashy aquarium proclaiming CATCH OF THE DAY. Gunmetal gray storm clouds bracketed the last slice of blue sky.

Now was her chance.

"*Quelle surprise*, Madame!" Aimée smiled. "Why, I'm just going in for lunch. May I invite you to join me?"

The woman backed away in surprise, fear in her eyes.

"Eat at home," she said.

But a group of black-suited Asian businessman, their voices raised in singsong Vietnamese, blocked her way. The skies opened, pelting down hail, slivers of ice, which bounced on the cracked pavement.

"Quick, you'll get wet. Please, be my guest," Aimée said, steering her inside. Flustered, the woman was herded forward by the smiling *maître d'hôtel*. With a flourish, he showed them to a table in the well-lit restaurant and proferred menus. Once this had been an old style workers' *bouillon* canteen, Aimée thought, noticing balconies several floors high, all filled with tables.

A fragrant pot of jasmine tea appeared on the table with two celadon green cups.

"Please," Aimée said, reaching for the cup and pouring the tea.

"*Merci*," the old woman replied, her manners taking over. "But I must go."

Out of the corner of Aimée's eye, she saw people huddled in the doorways in Place de Clichy, shielding themselves from the hail with their umbrellas.

"Of course. Drink some tea and go when the hail stops. Right now, it's too dangerous; you might slip on the pavement."

Cornered, the woman nodded. Despite her slight build, Aimée imagined a rod of steel in her backbone. She was strong, like the bamboo which swayed in the wind but clung with tenaciousness rooted in rock.

"My name's Aimée Leduc, I know Monsieur de Lussigny through business," she said, desperate to establish familiarity. "He told me his father died last month. So sorry to hear that. And now, his brother-in-law is gone, too!"

The woman clasped her cup and took a single sip. Perhaps this was a good sign. From around them came the orders shouted by the waiters.

"And so sad for you, I'm sure," she said. "Madame . . . ?"

"Madame Nguyen. I live in France long time," she said. "Know Métro very good. I take Métro home."

Try anything, Aimée told herself, to get this woman to stay and talk.

"Madame Ngyuen. You look too young to have a grandson! He's just a boy you take care of, isn't he?"

A smile escaped the woman. She displayed a full set of white-capped teeth. "My *great*-grandson. Michel, good boy."

"I can't believe that," Aimée said, hoping she wasn't laying it on too thick. "Impossible!"

"Possible. My granddaughter his mother," Madame Ngyuen said, nodding.

"You help her," Aimée said. "She's lucky!"

"I raise her, too." There was an enigmatic expression on her face.

"But how? *Non*, you have so much energy, like a young woman."

She nodded. "More energy in my country."

"So your granddaughter works . . . ?"

"Nadège. She stays somewhere else."

Nadège. The other name Thadée had uttered.

"How can I find her?"

"Don't know. I take care of Michel now."

"Of course, but—"

"Gone," she shook her head. "In Indochina I run big house with servants, all day, and raise five children, too. Dead, all dead now."

"I'm so sorry," Aimée said. "Did that happen here, or in Indochina?"

"Indochina, long time ago," she said.

"I'm practicing meditation at the Cao Dai Temple," Aimée said. "Trying to. The nun Linh helps me. But I'm sure you know her, *non?*"

Madame Nguyen's eyes narrowed. "Eh, what you mean?"

"I mean Linh's so helpful. Do you know the nun I'm referring to?"

"No temple. Pray at home."

Disappointed, Aimée tried another tack. She remembered the few Vietnamese words she'd learned. "Má," she said. She hoped it was close to the Vietnamese word for mother.

"Inflection wrong," Madame Nguyen said, shaking her head. "Listen, 'ma' can mean ghost, *má* mother, *mà* because, *ma* rice seedling, *ma* tomb or *ma* horse."

"What's the word for dragon?"

Madame Ngyuen looked away. "You nice French lady. Not like most *gweilo.*"

"*Gweilo?*"

" 'White devil,' but meant in nice way," she said.

"Isn't that Cantonese?"

Madame Nguyen nodded. Her black hair shone. She wore no ornament this time, just a tight bun, with small jade dots in her long lobes.

"Indochina all China once," she said. Shrugged. "Rape and rule like all conquerors. We kick Mandarins out in tenth century. People stay."

This could be an opening, Aimée thought.

"They looted emperor's tombs, didn't they?" she said, eager to keep the woman talking. She pulled out the auction catalogue page. "And stole things like this. Or was it the French?"

Aimée saw her companion shrink back against the leather banquette.

"Do you recognize this treasure? Weren't the Cao Dai guarding it?"

No answer. Madame Nguyen still stared at the photo of the jade figures.

"Take your order now?" a waiter asked.

Madame Nguyen shook her head.

"Give us a few more minutes, please," Aimée said.

The waiter shook his head and walked away.

"Thadée gave me this before he was murdered." Aimée leaned closer and showed her the disk she held in the palm of her hand. "But I don't understand why. You said the dragon symbolizes—"

"He give you this?"

Aimée nodded.

"Don't understand."

For a moment, Aimée thought she saw fear in the old woman's eyes.

"Neither do I, Madame Nguyen," she said.

"No good. Belong to Vietnam."

"The Cao Dai nun, Linh, wants to thank the man who saved her father's life at Dien Bien Phu."

Madame Nguyen said something in Vietnamese.

"What's that?" Aimée asked.

"Hiêú," she nodded. "Filial respect. Confucian way. Not like *him*, the owner's warlord uncle." Her face crinkled in disgust. "Warlord, steal land."

Aimée stared. "You mean the owner of this restaurant?"

"No respect for emperor."

Aimée knew the deposed Vietnamese Emperor Bao Dai had lived in French exile since the 1950s. She remembered that much from studying for the History section of the Bac. Did this relate to the looting of the emperor's tomb?

"Could the owner's uncle have looted a tomb in Dien Bien Phu?"

"Grave robbers never change."

A cell phone beeped somewhere under the table.

Madame Nguyen pulled out the smallest cell phone Aimée had ever seen.

"*Oui . . . allô*," she said. She blinked several times as she listened, the lines around her mouth tightening.

Bad news?

Madame Nguyen stood. "Must go. Michel have school trip earlier. Must go."

"Let me find you a taxi," Aimée said, rising and laying some francs on the table.

Outside, by some karma Aimée figured she or Madame Nguyen had earned, a taxi idled at the stand. She helped the old woman inside. "Take my card; I'm trying to find this jade. Perhaps you may be able to help me."

Madame Nguyen's face remained expressionless. But Aimée thought she'd mask her terror, having been well-schooled in concealment in Indochina. Disappointed, Aimée closed the door, and the taxi took off. She remembered her coat left inside the resto and ran back for it. The waiter handed it to her, his mouth turned down in a frown.

"I'm sorry we aren't staying for lunch," Aimée said.

"She never eat here," he said. "Understand."

"Pardon, but what do you mean," she asked surprised. "You know Madame Nguyen?"

"Cochin Chinese have long memory. Like elephant."

"But Madame Nguyen—"

He lapsed into what Aimée took for a Southern Chinese dialect. Several of the waiters around him laughed. Rude and disgruntled, she figured, since she'd taken up his time.

"They're not saying nice things," said a frowning young Asian woman, seated by the aquarium. "I'm sorry. No need to act rude, people change their minds."

"What are they saying?"

"Forget it," the young woman said. "They're nervous underneath."

"But why?" Aimée asked.

The young woman's frown deepened. "They're saying the health department visited last week. One man says he's afraid the health department will close the restaurant and then he'll be out of a job."

A good thing they hadn't eaten here, Aimée thought, running to the bus. She had an idea and somehow she had to get back into her office.

AIMÉE KNEW Leduc Detective was being watched. Yet everything she needed was inside the office. She walked up rue Bailleul, entered an apartment building foyer, and kept going to the rear garages she knew corresponded to the back hall window of their rue du Louvre office.

The garage and back alley were deserted. She pulled down the fire escape, hiked up her skirt, and climbed. On the landing, she took the fire extinguisher from the wall—just in case—and unlocked Leduc's frosted-paned door.

No one.

She had to make this quick. In their storeroom she found the Health Inspector badge from the *Direction de la Protection du Public*. She changed into a navy blue wool suit, grabbed some underwear and her black heels. The answering machine light blinked.

Two messages. Both hangups.

In the mail stacked on her desk, she found a letter addressed to her in Guy's writing. She took a deep breath and opened it. A court summons for damage to his office?

Flyers from Neuilly real estate agents and several full page ads describing apartments for rent fell out. Guy had circled one of them in red.

> *Neuilly sur Seine—four rooms, light and with southern exposure, near Métro, 150 m²* facing park.*

Below it he'd written: Perfect for my photo lab and your home office. Even a guest bedroom, and the park nearby for Miles Davis!

She looked at the postmark. The day before yesterday. Was this all a misunderstanding? Should she swallow her pride and call him?

Never.

Yet after a moment, she punched in his office number. Four rings later his secretary, Marie, answered.

"I'm sorry, Dr. Lambert left an hour ago," she said.

"Left. When does he return?"

"Let's see," she said. Papers rustled in the background. "I purchased return train tickets for him and Madame Bélise."

"Madame Bélise?"

"Can you hold on, please?"

She put Aimée on hold.

"Returning tomorrow," she said in a businesslike voice when she came back on the line. "Any message?"

"*Non, merci.*"

Gone with his new woman.

And for a moment she had thought it could work out. Wanted to make it work out, even if she'd have to live in the suburbs. She tore the real estate flyer into little pieces.

*mètres carrés, square meters

She switched on their remaining computer and quickly consulted the Direction de la Protection du Public online site. The Vietnamese restaurant's several infractions were listed. She switched the computer off, locked the office door, and climbed back down the rear fire escape.

A half-hour later, she stood at the service entrance of the resto, behind Place de Clichy, having been careful to avoid the rue de Clichy and Académie de Billard. Steam billowed from the resto back door.

She stepped inside and saw pots of boiling water and colanders draining translucent rice noodles, and heard the hiss of frying sesame oil filling the kitchen. Piles of limp bean sprouts and broccoli sat in aluminum bowls. A radio blared Chinese pop songs.

"I'm looking for Derek Lau, the owner. Where's his office?" she asked, holding a file folder in front of her.

A cook, his face beaded with perspiration, took one look at her badge and pointed toward an open door.

Aimée knocked and peered into the cluttered, low-ceilinged fluorescent-lit office. Derek Lau, facing several phone books on his desk, was scratching his head. His eyes protruded, a classic thyroid condition symptom, and he had a crossover parting of his black hair to cover his bald spot.

"Monsieur Lau?"

"*Oui*," he nodded, taking in her outfit and setting the phone books aside. "You people weren't supposed to come until next week. We have one week to comply."

"Monsieur Lau, we use our own discretion in timing our visits."

"Eh, what does that mean? Where's the usual inspector? Let me see some credentials."

Aimée pulled out the form she'd printed out from the site. Areas of hygiene were checked off.

"It means, Monsieur Lau, if I see compliance, we won't make a formal visit next week. We have plainclothes staff checking up often. Catch my drift?"

A dawn of understanding crossed his worried eyes.

He reached in his drawer, pulled out an envelope, and stuffed franc notes inside.

"This should take care of it," he said.

She waved aside the profferred envelope.

"So far we've noted meat stored and transported without containers, dirty ceilings, bacteria festering in the tile cracks, and inadequate freezers."

He snapped his fingers and the cook entered bearing a tray with tea. Had he stood at the door waiting?

"Look, let's smooth this out, eh," he said, pushing the envelope toward her again. "I run a little business, struggle to make ends meet."

Let him think she was going along with him.

"I'm referring to the farm-raised sea bass you serve," she said, thinking back to the regulations. "A flagrant health violation, as you know. Your dossier's full."

"Just jealous restaurateurs complaining I'm sure. I told my uncle we should have stayed in the 13th." He shrugged. "The old coot wanted 'prestige' but this was the closest we could get to the *bon* 17th."

"This form indicates that a Ming Lau owns this. . . ."

"My uncle, *oui*," he interrupted. "He retired to Hong Kong, but I manage his investments here."

Derek Lau closed a tall metal file cabinet and what Aimée saw framed on the wall made her blink. She suppressed a gasp, stood, and edged toward the piled account books. How could she find out what she wanted without looking too obvious?

"*Bon*, show me your vendor receipts," she said, shooting for a businesslike tone. "We're doing a full-scale investigation this time. You know that means a temporary shutdown."

"*Ecoutez*, eh, don't get so serious," he said, his words conciliatory, but alarm in his eyes. "It's all here, nothing out of line."

He rummaged through his files.

"We'll have to close your business unless you provide immediate proof of compliance and proper documents."

Sweat beaded his brow. He pressed a buzzer on his desk. "Bring the Crédit Lyonnais files." He turned to Aimée. "Drink your tea, it will only take a moment."

She pointed to the sepia-tinted photo on Lau's office wall. Under the title 'Lai Chau,' the twelve jade zodiac figures were pictured. "Your family treasure?"

Instead of the fear she expected, Derek Lau shrugged.

"Just an old photo," he said.

"Of stolen treasure."

Surprise turned to amusement. Then he sneered. "You've been talking to that crazy old lady. She has no right to complain!"

She said, "Maybe you had to sell it to pay your debts?"

"Debts?"

"According to the records, this restaurant's heavily mortgaged."

"Ridiculous. We have a line of credit," he said. He looked at the photo on the wall. "You should be talking to the French soldiers who stole it."

"What do you mean?"

"Like I told the old cow, according to my uncle, the French took everything, even what was hidden in the ground."

"The Sixth Battalion?" Aimée asked.

"I don't know details," he said. Derek Lau smoothed the hair combed over his head. "Anyway, black crude's more valuable now."

"What about your emperor? Doesn't this jade belong to him?"

"To some branch of the Imperial family, but it's hard to say which, since they intermarried. All of them trace their lineage back to the first Emperor. Now Bao Dai's ill and penniless after a life of Monte Carlo gambling and many wives, but the

French government keeps him," Derek Lau said. "His old mother in Saigon sold the Imperial porcelain to pay for his child support. Spoiled to the end."

"But isn't this jade more important than its price in money? Doesn't it mean something?"

"It guarantees the patrimony. The possessor is the ruler ordained by heaven, according to my uncle."

"Patrimony?"

Derek Lau patted his thin strand of hair into place. "The right to the land, promised by the first Chinese emperor. We've had many emperors, but what the first emperor ordained remains law."

She stood, put the health violation list on his desk and shoved the cash-filled envelope back to him.

"I don't take bribes."

His calculating eyes took in her interest in the photos of the jade.

"But ancient treasures interest you, eh?"

She grabbed her clipboard.

"I'm sure I'm not the only one who appreciates beautiful objects, Monsieur Lau," she said.

He shrugged. He wanted to make a deal, it was in his eyes.

"Who else is interested, Monsieur Lau?"

"My memory's not what it used to be," he said.

It seemed fine to her.

"I could delay this report," she offered. "If I sense your cooperation."

He paused, weighing his answer. From the kitchen she heard the crackle of oil in a hot wok.

"A man from a museum," Derek Lau said. "He'd been talking to the old lady, too."

"Did you catch his name?"

"I run a business, not an information service," he said.

"Tall and thin?"

Derek Lau combed his hair with his fingers. "Plump, round glasses."

"Did he wear a bow tie?"

"Bow tie? Is that how you call it? On his neck. Yes."

Dinard.

"It's yours," he said, unhooking a picture frame from the wall. "Take it."

Aimée shook her head, she'd seen and heard what she needed. "*Merci*, Monsieur Lau, we'll be in touch."

"What about the credit reports?"

"Next time," she said.

Saturday

HIDDEN DEEP IN THE armoire, Nadège heard the faint beep of a cell phone. The kicking stopped.

Mumbled words, then footsteps descending the stairs and the start of a car engine below. She crawled out of the armoire. Water . . . so thirsty. She had to find water for her parched throat. Weak afternoon sun slanted across the floorboards.

How long had she been out? All she remembered was the old grande dame's long kid gloves. Then a smoothness like she'd felt at the rehab clinic when she'd been given sedatives for several days. Part of a cure that had almost worked.

What had Thadée told her? A *child condemns one to live*?

She steadied herself and, despite the tremors, made it to the window. A car backfired on the street. The men's words echoed in her mind. *Find the kid*. Michel. Her child. In danger.

Her eyes watered as she held the handrail, making her way down, careful to avoid the rain water pooled on the steps. On Avenue de Clichy, she found a taxi. When the taxi pulled up to her father's, she asked him to wait and made her way inside, shaking. No one was there except stooped, old Ngoc, the last butler her *grand-père* had brought from Indochina. She knew her father was embarrassed by the colonial flavor that still pervaded the house. Perhaps it would not for much longer.

"Ngoc, lend me twenty francs, would you?" she said.

"*Désolé,* Mademoiselle," he shook his bald head. A wisp of a gray beard was tucked into his cardigan, a castoff of her *grand-père's.* "I'm not supposed to give you money."

"For the taxi, Ngoc," she said.

Ngoc crinkled his eyes.

"Tran, Tran!" he called.

To her surprise, she saw Tran, their retired gardener, appear.

"Let me help, Mademoiselle," Tran said, and pulled a bill from his pocket.

"I hope you're a good girl, Mademoiselle," he said. "Not getting into bad ways, again."

"The best I've been in a long time, Tran," she said, her heart beating fast. Her body had cleared the knockout drug and something had lifted inside her. Michel's life was at stake. That was more important than anything.

But she had to find a sedative to tone down her craving. Like in rehab. She slipped into the bathroom, searched the drawers. Found the clonadine and valium her father had wangled from her last rehab, and paid the doctor for privately. It would ease the chills and pressure; it couldn't make her feel any worse. She needed help to function through withdrawal.

Inside her grandmother's room, she called for *grand-mère* and Michel but there was just the burnt toast smell of incense, its thick powdered ash on the red lacquer altar beside the five fruit offerings for good fortune. She stumbled over one of the toys scattered on the floor. Horror hit the pit of her stomach.

"Ngoc, where are Michel and *grand-mère?*" she called.

Tran appeared and took off his cap. Why was he in the house now? Something felt wrong.

"She's upset with him; he's worried," Tran said. "Your *grand-mère* won't talk to Ngoc."

Her *grand-mère* ruled the back wing. Poor Ngoc. Over the years Ngoc had been her ally. But he forgot things. Little things. There was always a commotion in the back wing when her *grand-mère* discovered Ngoc's forgetfulness.

"*Grand-mère* upsets easily, Tran," she said. "Then it's over."

Ngoc appeared next to Tran, leaning on the door for support.

"I can't remember where I put the chest for Madame Nguyen, and she refuses to speak with me until I find it. But—"

"Perhaps they're at school, Ngoc?" she suggested.

"Mademoiselle," he said, "Now I remember!" He grinned. "At the science museum in La Villette. Some school trip."

Nadège breathed a sigh of relief. They would be safe with so many others. She called her *grand-mère*'s cell phone. No answer, just a message in Chinese. She told her, "Take Michel to the country house in Fontainebleau. Don't come back here."

She went back into her grandmother's bedroom and lit a handful of incense, and propped it in the blue and white porcelain holder on the shrine. She bowed her head three times as she had been taught. Prayed, "Keep my baby safe, keep my baby safe, keep my baby safe."

She reached for the thin red cord around her neck. Gone. Of course, and her luck with it, courtesy of the old grande dame. Then she felt something tangled in her purple braid. She combed through her long hair with her fingers. Her lucky red cord with the jade disk came back between her fingers. Maybe the gods would answer her prayers after all.

She had to think. But her mind had slowed. A wave of nausea rose and subsided. Thadée wouldn't have left something valuable in that building, where anyone could get at it.

She sniffled, rubbed her running nose with her sleeve. *Think.*

Thadée must have kept his stash here. Her stomach cramped and then it subsided. Right under everyone's nose. He'd told her it was big and would take care of everything. The key. She remembered her old grandfather's dressing room. She'd seen Thadée there once.

She stumbled to the other wing, her heels clacking on the marble, and into her grandfather's rooms. They were still cluttered with his things, as if he'd left for a moment, not an eternity. His white helmet was still on his desk, the overhead ceiling fan and white mosquito net still hung over the canopied bed. He'd sworn he couldn't sleep without it, even here in Paris.

She opened the changing room door. It was windowless and dark. A wave of sleepiness came over her. She ran her hand along the wall, found the light switch, and hit it. The suits and overcoats were flooded with brittle white light. An old-man smell and the sight of medals imprisoned in dusty, glass shadow-boxes greeted her. His ties, belts, and slacks hung in straight lines. In the corner, she saw his steamship chest plastered with an old label: HÔTEL MAJESTIC, SAIGON. It lay open. Empty. She grabbed for the closet rail, fighting her fatigue, and fell.

Saturday Afternoon

Aimée knew Dinard wanted the jade. What if he'd found it?

She approached his home in the fashionable part of the 17th where celebrated courtesans like la Belle Otero who'd counted kings and ministers as her "benefactors," had lived, where Debussy had composed. Not Aimée's stomping grounds. Impersonal, with deserted sidewalks where the affluent still dwelled behind steel-shuttered windows. Dinard's street was cornered by the Banque de France in a former neo-Gothic mansion. Opposite, the Nazi Kommandantur had melted the statue that had once stood in the square, like so many monuments in the city, for the German war effort. Now, honey-colored leaves skittered across the desolate excuse for a square.

Her cell phone rang.

"*Allô?*"

"Aimée, Saj and I speeded the program up a bit," René said. "But we're knocking on the door of Interpol. Do you want to go there?"

She chewed her lip. So the Circle Line was part of Interpol. Pleyet had told her the truth. He didn't work for the RG, he belonged to Interpol.

Interpol was the information gathering center dealing with international crime. Contrary to popular belief, there were no Interpol officers traveling around the world investigating cases. The member countries employed their own officers to operate in their own territory and in accordance with national laws.

"Aimée, did you hear me? It's embedded in the structure; if we go in, we leave big hacker footprints," he said. "I thought I'd check."

"Good thinking, René," she said. "Make a gracious exit. I know what I need to, now. But can you keep checking on Thadée's files?"

She hung up and put in a call to the number she'd seen on Pleyet's cell phone. An anonymous voicemail recording answered.

"Pleyet, I know who you work for," she said when she heard the beep. "Let's combine forces. Call me."

She hoped she could trust him.

AIMÉE KNOCKED on Dinard's glossy-blue door. A middle-aged woman with short dyed-blonde hair, wearing a wool houndstooth-checked suit, answered. The woman kept her hand behind the door.

"Madame Dinard?"

"*Oui?*"

Aimée showed her ID, noticing the women's red-rimmed eyes and the alcohol smell wafting from her.

"I'd like to speak with your husband," Aimée said.

"He's not here," she said, stepping back inside.

"Madame, I haven't been able to reach him at work. May I take a moment of your time? I need your help."

"You need my help?" she said, with a hoarse laugh. "He's gone. Left with his twenty-something *cocotte*. *Pfft*, like that."

"You know that for sure, Madame?"

Madame Dinard rolled her eyes.

Tessier had said that Dinard was on the way out at the museum, but she hadn't imagined him taking off with another woman. Doubt crossed her mind.

"What do you want?" Madame Dinard asked.

"May we talk inside, please?" Aimée suggested, glimpsing a long hallway lined with paintings through the partly open door.

"Ask your questions here," Madame Dinard said. Her hand, coming from behind the door, held a full wine glass, from which she took several sips. Aimée wondered how coherent Madame Dinard was, but she had to question her.

"Monsieur Tessier indicated he'd tried to ask Monsieur Dinard about this jade." Aimée stood in the doorway and unfolded the page from the auction catalogue. "Have you seen these before?"

"Not again!" Madame Dinard said. There had been a flash of recognition in her eyes. "Leave me alone."

Again? She couldn't let this woman close the door on her.

"Forgive my persistence," she said. "When did you see these jade figures?"

"Did I say I'd seen them?"

Aimée detected the slight slur in her voice.

"But I think you recognize them. When?"

"Persistent's not the word. You're annoying me," Madame Dinard said.

"Of course, you've got a lot on your mind," Aimée said. "Think back, was it at the Drouot auction, a month ago?"

Madame Dinard waved Aimée away. She downed her wine, gripping the door. Her eyes narrowed. "If you can find out which young thing went off with my old fart of a husband, and get me proof for divorce, eh, then we could talk. Isn't that what you sleazy detectives do?"

No use explaining it wasn't her field.

"But Madame, I'm not so sure he left you for a woman," Aimée said. "Wasn't he going to the hospital?"

"Hospital?"

"For a hypertension screening."

Doubt crossed Madame Dinard's face.

"I checked," Aimée said. "He had an appointment for an exam but never showed up."

Madame Dinard wavered.

"Please, we need to talk," Aimée said.

With misgiving in her unfocused eyes, Madame Dinard let her in and showed her down the hall.

"Are you sure? He never mentioned it to me." Madame Dinard stood in the dining room. "But then he wouldn't if he was running away with another woman."

Like Guy, Aimée thought.

Glass-fronted cabinets displayed Limoges china, the long dining table held piles of papers at one end and several open wine bottles. On the mantle stood framed family photographs.

"Our thirty-year wedding anniversary was today," she said in a broken voice. Madame Dinard's face sagged, and she looked older than the fifty-something Aimée suspected.

"*Le salaud!*"

But Aimée heard no conviction in her voice.

"I'm so sorry," Aimée said.

Quiet pervaded this room. A vase of hothouse apricot-hued roses perfumed the air: the stillness of sorrow.

"What did you mean when you said 'again'?" Aimée asked. "Has someone been asking you about jade astrological figures?"

Madame Dinard ruffled her hair with her manicured ringed fingers. "It has nothing to do with me."

But Aimée knew it did.

"Thadée, your godson, de Lussigny's brother-in-law, was killed. He had this jade in his possession. Of course, you're upset."

Madame Dinard smoothed down her skirt and poured another glass of wine.

A dog barked from somewhere in the back.

"*Mon Dieu.* Felix! I have to let him into the garden." She stood and wobbled to the back room.

Great. A tipsy, sad woman who wouldn't talk.

"Please, Madame, don't you realize?"

"Thadée was always in trouble," Madame Dinard said, her bleary eyes tearing. "But I couldn't do anything for him."

Madame Dinard had changed her tune. Aimée nodded, encouraging her.

"Creative people see things with different eyes, don't they?" Aimée said. "Such a shame and so sad for you."

"He painted so well." She took Aimée's arm, brought her into the next room, and pointed to an unframed canvas on the wall.

"See?"

A green-hued dragon was surrounded by the astrological figures Aimée had seen in the photograph in Derek Lau's office. It took her breath away. With deft strokes he'd created the ensemble. A little boy peeked at the opalescent dragon from a grove of bamboo.

What did it mean?

"Did Thadée tell you anything about this painting?"

"His last work. So much talent wasted." Madame Dinard let the sentence dangle. She paused. "I don't want to talk about it." Then wobbled to the back stairs and the barking dog.

Aimée pulled out her cell phone and punched in Tessier's number. If she could get him on the phone, he might have better luck with Madame Dinard.

"*Allô*, Tessier?" she said. "It's Aimée Leduc. I'm at the Dinards'. Can you explain to his wife. . . ."

"Not a good idea," he said.

In the background Aimée heard the revving of engines and insistent beep of a truck backing up.

"What do you mean?" Aimée asked.

"I'm in the Parc Monceau."

She heard a nervous edge in his voice.

"Has something happened?"

"Dinard left a strange message on my cell phone. To meet—" the rest of the sentence was lost in the backfire of a bus.

"Where?"

"Boulevard de Courcelles, the men's bathroom," he said.

Aimée knew the Chartres Pavillon, a rotunda housing lavatories at the entrance to the park, the remnant of the old toll house.

"I'm just two blocks away," Aimée said.

She would have to hurry, to catch Dinard. This could be the break she needed. Tessier had hung up.

Madame Dinard sat in the twilight-filled back garden, rocking a small springer spaniel who growled at Aimée.

"I'll say goodbye," she said, handing the woman a glass of water. "Your husband just left a message with his assistant."

Instead of the hope she expected to see on Madame Dinard's face, the woman waved her away. "If he cared, he'd be here."

ANXIOUSLY, AIMÉE hurried down rue de Phalsbourg. The red Métro sign, like a beacon in the dusk, reflected in the puddles and off the gilt-tipped wrought-iron gates of the Parc Monceau. Guards in dark blue uniforms walked the gravel paths, informing strollers the park was closing.

No sign of Dinard.

The worn stone lavatory was at the gate of the Chartres Pavillon rotunda. From the distance came the muted quack of the ducks in the park's pond. She remembered feeding ducks stale baguettes on a hot summer's day long ago. Remembered her mother's strong hands gripping her small ones, and how with deft twists they'd fashioned twigs and leaves into a duck.

Now rain clouds threatened once more. She thrust the memory aside.

The smell of wet grass and Tessier's gaze met her over the hood of a small Renault. His glasses had fogged in the chill air and he brushed at them with the sleeve of his raincoat.

"When did you get Dinard's message, Tessier?" she asked.

"I just found it," he said. "I'd forgotten my cell phone in

the pocket of my other coat. When I took it from the rack there was this message. I hurried over."

Raincoated commuters spilled from the Métro. Tessier's eyes darted over the crowd. "He's not here."

"Let's check inside," she said. "You might have missed him."

They walked through the gate into the park. Bare sycamore branches and oriental plane trees shuddered in the evening wind.

Aimée saw the orange plastic barriers used by the toilet cleaning brigade and a sign reading FERMÉ on the men's lavatory door. No sign of Dinard. Just the scrape of wet gravel as a mother pushed a stroller toward the gate.

"Tessier, may I hear the phone message?"

He handed her his cell phone and Aimée listened. *"Tessier, don't answer the office phone,"* said Dinard. *"Meet me at the men's room at the Parc Monceau gate. No questions . . . now!"*

She took out her mini-flashlight and scanned the phone's display.

"*Alors*, Tessier, look at the date. He called yesterday."

"My mistake. He wasn't in the office today."

She didn't want to let it go. "Come with me."

"But the park's closing."

Guards shooed people toward the gate.

"Hurry," she said, grabbing his arm and running up the three steps to the WC. She shoved the orange plastic stanchion aside and pushed. But the door held. She tried the handle and it turned.

"Help me. Push hard."

"What are you doing? You're not supposed to—" Tessier said.

The door was blocked by something. Mops and buckets, she assumed. She pushed again and it opened partway.

Aimée stumbled forward, shining her flashlight over the simple porcelain sink, then over the tiled floor to the open stalls. A man's shoe stuck up from the metal drainpipe grill centered in the tile.

Dread filled her.

She traveled the light up a twisted trousered leg and gasped. Then further, to Dinard's bulging eyes and to a line of dark red congealed blood across his throat. They hadn't bothered to string him up by the toilet pipes.

"We're too late, Tessier." The smell of putrefaction and the iron tang of blood permeated the air of the cold lavatory.

Tessier peered in and gasped. "But who . . . *mon Dieu* . . . it's my fault!"

And then she noticed what the killer wouldn't have seen. Dinard's swollen fingers, nails caked with blood, and the character he'd scrawled on the tile.

"You read Chinese, right?"

He gagged. "I'm going to be sick."

"Not in here, it's a crime scene now," she said.

"What's going on? You're not allowed in there," said the guard's hoarse voice behind them.

"My boyfriend's sick and then we saw this man," she shouted.

She edged out, but not before grabbing her pen and copying the Chinese character onto her palm. Tessier heaved into the bushes and the guard muttered "*Nom de Dieu!*" and made the sign of the cross.

"Quick," she said to Tessier as he straightened up. She took his arm again and left through the gate.

"*Attendez*, wait," the guardian raised his voice. "You're witnesses."

"We should cooperate, poor Monsieur Dinard," Tessier said.

"Not on your life," Aimée interrupted. "Trust me." The last thing she wanted was another encounter with the *flics*. They'd lock her up this time. Ronsard would throw away the key and Morbier would say, *I told you so*.

She led Tessier down the Métro steps, battling the onrush of the exiting crowds. They rode one stop, Tessier pale-faced, to exit at Villiers, then doubled-back two blocks to the dark Musée Cernuschi.

"We have to get into Dinard's office."

"But—"

"Quick. Before they identify him." Aimée saw the horror on Tessier's face.

"What kind of cold creature are you!" Tessier backed away.

"It horrifies me, too, but we have to find out who killed him." *And what Dinard had known*, but she didn't say that.

"Do it on your own, I don't have the stomach for this," he said.

"Yes, you do. Or else, you could be next," she said. "Didn't someone follow you the other day?"

"What? It's related?"

She wished he wouldn't argue. The shadows moved, night sounds rustled in the bushes. She wanted to get inside.

"You're his assistant. He's told you things, or they'll assume he did. Odds are they're still following you."

The African night security guard at the museum's back entrance gave them a big smile, showing several gold teeth. Tessier signed in; a fevered discussion on Radio Liberia raged in the background.

"I forgot my files," Tessier told him.

"No problem, Monsieur, cleaners going to offices much later," the guard said.

By the time they'd rushed up the back stairs and reached Dinard's office, Aimée had broken out in a cold sweat.

She pulled down the blinds, drew the cloth curtains, and turned on the desk light, then worked plastic gloves over her fingers.

"I'm going to call the *flics*," Tessier said, lifting up the phone.

"Put that down," Aimée said.

"*Non*, it's my duty, I have to give them information," he said.

Great! Tessier wanted to assuage his guilt. And get them in trouble.

"It's important to tell them about Dinard's call, and how—"

"The phone's tapped," she said.

"What?"

Using her Swiss Army knife, she pried open the black phone case.

Open-mouthed, Tessier stared at the small black knob Aimée pried out of it. "Don't use the phone! There might be others, and I don't have time to dismantle them."

"You mean, someone has heard our conversations?"

She put a finger to her lips and scanned the room's elegant *boiserie*. Plenty of hiding places and no time to hunt for bugs.

"Did Dinard keep a safe in here?" she whispered.

"A lock-up, downstairs," he whispered back.

She nodded, turned off the light, and motioned for Tessier to lead.

The underground level, the museum's basement, could use restoration, Aimée thought, noticing the dank watermarks and chipped stone. Rank humid air hovered. She took off her coat and tied it around her waist. Weren't works of art supposed to be kept in climate-controlled storerooms?

"We don't have room to store much here. We have an agreement with the Musée Henner," Tessier told her, taking off his glasses and wiping off the condensation. His voice trembled.

Tessier led her through a warren of coved passages with

doors leading off them. "This used to be a mansion. These were storerooms."

Tessier paused at the what looked like a meat locker.

Hurry, she wanted to say, seeing him hesitate. "Tessier, continue, it's vital."

He wiped his brow and hit some numbers on what resembled a digicode. The metal door clicked and he pushed it open. Inside the antiseptic stark-white painted room, file cabinets and shelving held a Tang dynasty painting on silk, ritual bronzes, and statues on the shelves.

"Part of our collection is on loan in Düsseldorf," he said. "These funerary statues and Buddhist sculptures are part of our permanent collection."

She showed him the character she'd copied onto her palm. "Look familiar?"

Her hands shook and she held her wrist so Tessier wouldn't notice.

"*Wu*," he said, looking at the character 巫.

"That's the character you showed me before," she said, excited. "The character for Shaman." She pulled out the jade disk, with its primitive etched dragon. "Dinard tried to tell me it's the disks that are valuable. Rare." She stared at Tessier as she thought of the images Dinard had mentioned. "If the other disks bore motifs like the sun, a phoenix, clouds, how old might they be?"

"Such a thing's impossible to date correctly, even with carbon techniques."

"Ballpark, Tessier?"

He shrugged. "Pre-bronze age? It's difficult to prove. But why kill Monsieur Dinard?"

"What was Dinard doing yesterday afternoon? Think back."

"I had a dentist appointment," he said. "I left after lunch and didn't return."

Frustrated, she didn't know what to look for. She lifted up some papers. Underneath lay files and museum correspondance.

"Roll up your sleeves," she said. "We have to check everything."

"These shelves deal with maintenance and building codes," he said.

"Let's try those." She pointed to shelves filled with bulging folders and binders and sat down to tackle the first shelf. In a binder labeled Miscellaneous, what she read made her bolt upright. A Drouot photocopied receipt, made out to Monsieur D. Inard, for "Heavenly Jade Astrological Pieces." D. Inard . . . of course, Dinard.

Dinard had put the pieces up for auction!

Dinard, then Thadée. Had Thadée stolen them from Dinard? If so, where had Dinard gotten them? Where were they now?

"Did your museum handle ancient jade pieces like these?"

"Never." Tessier shook his head. "These types of objects show up every so often: No record of excavation, or history of ownership. No pedigree. Like I told you. Some have sat in a collector's home for years, accumulating dust in their crates, forgotten."

"That doesn't make sense."

"Without provenance there's no verification, no history," Tessier said. "The subtext is, they've been looted. Stolen. With all the scrutiny these days, and the international agreements, we're too wary to buy such objects."

"Did Dinard tell you where the jade figures came from?"

Tessier shook his head. "I never even knew of their existence, until he told me to ask you about them."

She sat down. Studied the Drouot receipt.

"If the Drouot staff had done some research, and concluded items had been looted would they just note 'withdrawn' in the catalogue?"

Tessier nodded. "If they were smart."

* * *

AIMÉE FELT apprehensive as she approached l'hôtel Ampère for the Olf meeting. Did de Lussigny know about his godfather's murder? She didn't relish being the first to tell him that Dinard had been killed.

The four-star hotel was a short walk from the Arc de Triomphe, situated in the prestigious part of the 17th. Too bad she and René couldn't afford to hide out *here*.

De Lussigny greeted her at the door, his shirtsleeves rolled up. The meeting had ended, or so she surmised from the cigarette butts in the ashtray, several used glass tumblers, and a half-empty bottle of vodka in the suite. Stacks of yellow legal pads and charts sat on the table. A fire crackled in the fireplace.

"They made it an early night," he said. "Sorry, but I hope you brought the reports."

Odd. Why hadn't he called and asked her to come sooner?

"Of course, right here," she said opening her bag.

De Lussigny reached over and turned on music. Soft jazz. "Sit down. Have a drink."

What was all this about? But she sat down, took the tumbler he'd splashed with vodka, and drank for courage. Nice, with a citrus punch. He sat down next to her and ruffled his hair.

"Your godfather. . . ." She hesitated, trying to read his expression before voicing the bald truth. Did he already know?

"The investigating inspector called me," he said. "First Thadée, now my godfather, Jacques." He shook his head. "Jacques played around. . . ."

"Played around? We found him dead in the Parc Monceau lavatory and he'd written this in his blood."

She saw the horrified look on his face. "But . . . what do you mean . . . *you* found him?"

She wrote the character on a yellow legal pad: 亜

"Know what it means?"

He shook his head. "I've grown up here. My father read Chinese; in some ways he never left Indochina. . . ." His voice trailed off.

"It's the character *wu*, for shaman," she said.

Did he know about the disks? All she saw on his face was concern.

"Your godfather, Dinard, put a set of jade figures up for auction," she said. "Then withdrew them. But it was Thadée that gave them to me to deliver to a Cao Dai nun. They were stolen from me. What does it mean?"

"You surprise me all the time," he said, taking a big gulp of vodka. "But I'm sorry you had to find my godfather's body."

Sorry?

"It's his poor wife I feel sorry for. And Thadée."

De Lussigny raked his fingers through his hair. "She loved him. What about you, Aimée. Why don't you trust me enough to explain to me how you're involved?"

"I don't know you," she said.

Or anything.

She felt his hand on her thigh, surprised that such a suave man would make such a move at a time like this.

"We can change that," said de Lussigny.

He kissed her. Warm, moist lips. Startled, she pulled back. He kissed her again. Just right, lips a bit open. Nice kisses.

"*Non*," she said, pulling away.

"Why?"

"It's complicated."

A barge pole wouldn't be long enough to keep him at a safe distance.

"It doesn't have to be," he said. "The only way to react to death is with life."

His eyes searched hers.

"But I had no idea you felt this way," she said, uncomfortable. His godfather had been murdered, yet all he wanted was to get into her pants!

She wondered at the connection he'd made to her, that she knew nothing about. His fantasy? The soft jazz in the background, the dim lighting, the half-full glasses of vodka and white Egyptian cotton duvet of the bed conspired against her. She'd better turn to business, then leave, before she did something she'd regret.

"Lena and I are in the midst of divorce proceedings," he said. "And, believe it or not, I don't do this often."

She doubted him, determined to ignore the way his lips had softened on hers, the aura of power and trace of vulnerability that textured his voice. She must keep in mind that he was a powerful and devious insider. Not her usual bad-boy.

"I can't," she said.

He pulled his hand back. Irritation shone on his face as he combed his hair back with his hands. "So what do we do?"

"We talk business," she said, reaching for her vodka glass. Trying to keep her hand steady.

"*Bon,*" he said, checking his watch, stifling a yawn. "You already gave me the reports."

She stiffened at his dismissive gesture.

"I want to know about PetroVietnam."

"Aren't you the one supposed to give me information?"

Arrogant bastard.

"I want to know why you asked me to monitor the Chinese bids. And why the various bids have disappeared."

Surprised, he sat forward. "Who says that?"

"I checked, and they're not here. All records of the bids disappeared from the file and that means—"

"It's on someone's desk under a pile or it's in intra-corporate mail," he interrupted. "And a camel walks faster than that."

Or someone had gotten a hidden kickback. But how to word it with tact?

"Convince me. Put a trace on it."

"You're on a fishing expedition," he said.

"Whoever has the bids, wants to keep them secret. Private. Not to point fingers, but what if someone got a pay-off? I can help you more if I know the truth."

He sat back on the couch. "You really *do* want to talk about business."

"Find the bids. If they're in intra-corporate mail, then you're right. Otherwise, I am."

"*D'accord*," he said, his look pensive. "I will. But I still want you to monitor the Chinese."

"You still haven't given me a reason."

"Haven't you figured it out? We want to match their bids for drilling rights in the Tonkin Gulf."

She stood.

He treated her as he'd treated her before. Like a professional. As she reached for the hotel room doorknob, she met his hand reaching for it at the same time.

"*Excusez-moi.*" His hand recoiled.

"*Au revoir,*" she said. They were standing so close.

He kissed her again. That soft warm mouth. His hands cupped her face, stroked her hair.

She pulled away, opened the door, and left. Outside in the hushed carpeted hallway, she ran, her knees shaking.

Saturday Night

IN THE REAR BOOTH of the cafe below Leduc Detective, Aimée pulled off her Nicorette patch and lit a Gauloise. Her smudged red lipstick was all over the small espresso cup. She slumped, kept her head down, and took a deep drag.

"Why the long face, *mon américaine?*" Zazie, the ten-year-old daughter of the owner asked. Juliette was nicknamed Zazie because she'd begun using strong language at an early age. Her mother complained to Aimée that she'd inherited her grandmother's mouth. Zazie scratched her red curls, set her magazine on the counter, and steamed herself a cup of warm milk. "Can I sit with you? I like your lipstick."

"It's Stop Traffic Red. But isn't it past your bedtime, Zazie?"

Zazie's family lived above the café. "I had a bad dream," Zazie said, rubbing her eyes. "I want to show you something."

"Fine. And then to bed."

She thought about de Lussigny. Lust wasn't love. And it didn't work when you wanted to forget about someone—someone like Guy.

"Look at this," Zazie said. "That man in the big car who gave you a lift, Aimée, remember? When your eyes were bad that day?"

Aimée nodded. De Lussigny. She'd like to forget.

"He came in for a Perrier. He's in the magazine *maman* buys. *Regardes-toi-même?*" she said, with an admiring gaze. "I didn't know you knew famous people, I've been waiting to show you. Look Aimée!"

Zazie turned the pages of *Voilà*, the tabloid magazine that featured celebrities and photos of aristocrats' parties. And there he was, tuxedo-clad, hair brushed back, both arms around young women. Julien de Lussigny.

"Good memory, Zazie."

Well, no surprise there. He hadn't gotten lucky with her but . . . She studied the caption more closely.

Last Year's Happiness:
Julien de Lussigny with his wife Lena, now separated, and

Nadège de Lussigny, his daughter from a previous marriage, at a benefit for land mine victims at their mansion on Parc Monceau where it was held again this year.

The young half-Asian woman, her long black hair entwined in purple braids, was stunning. She looked familiar. That smile! Her mind traveled back to Thadée's words, remembered seeing the woman who'd climbed on the Vespa when she first found Sophie, what Madame Nguyen had said. Could this be her, de Lussigny's daughter, Michel's mother?

Had she been staying with her uncle Thadée? And most important, where was she now?

"Aimée. Aimée!" Zazie was saying. "Yoo-hoo, you there?"

She'd been lost in thought. She stared at Zazie.

"You're a little detective in the making, Zazie," she said, stabbing out her cigarette.

Zazie's eyes shone with pride.

And for a brief flash Aimée wondered what it would it be like to have a child. Would she be like Zazie, and never go to bed?

"Is that a photo of you over the espresso machine, from when you were five?"

Zazie grinned. "It's from the *école primaire*, but I was six."

Close enough. Little Michel was five and had the same smile as his mother, Nadège. Aimée had to find her.

She pulled out her lipstick and slid it into Zazie's hand. Zazie's eyes sparkled.

"For me?"

"Don't tell your *maman*," she grinned. "Someday you'll follow me into the business, Zazie. Until then, get some sleep."

OUTSIDE, ON dark Avenue de Clichy, a lone streetsweeper dealt with the detritus of the local Armistice Day Veterans' Parade. Each year the number of marchers got smaller. With the driver's assistance, an old man alighted from a taxi onto the wet pavement. His wool suit hung from his shrunken frame. A blue, white, and red tricolor ribbon was draped over his caved-in chest; several medals glinted on his lapel.

Aimée guessed he was one of the few remaining veterans from the First World War. His limbs trembled as he hobbled to a door on rue Sauffroy. The taxi driver lit a cigarette and drove away.

Peeling posters of the Nigerian footballer Okocha glistened with rain on the stucco walls. Aimée heard the metal clink as the old man's keys hit the ground. She stooped to pick them up.

"*Monsieur*, your keys," she smiled. "May I help?"

"I always forget the code," he said, his rheumy eyes tearing. "It's in my pocket somewhere. My hands shake so."

"Permit me?" She stuck her hand in his pocket, found a card with his name, address, and digicode.

"Caporal Mollard, that's you, eh?" she said.

He nodded.

She punched in his code. The green door clicked open.

"*Merci*," he said.

"Did you enjoy the parade?"

A lost look painted his hollow-cheekboned face. "That farce?"

Shocked, she saw that he picked at the ribbon as if trying to pull it off. But the effort seemed too much for him.

"Most of me died in the trenches. The mustard gas took one of my lungs. The rest, well. . . ."

"Caporal, you must be tired," she said, not knowing what else to say.

"We were supposed to save the world for peace, *mon enfant*. Fight the war to end all wars," he said. "Did it do any good?"

She shook her head. What had happened in 1914–18 on French fields had just been the beginning. "I don't know. Can I help you inside, does someone wait for you?"

"Everyone I knew is dead," he said. "It's my turn."

*   *   *

RENÉ HAD left a note on the laptop in the hotel room.

"Dining downstairs on Cameroun manioc, fish and rice *aloko*. Join us."

She put her head in her hands, rocked back and forth. Her hands came back sticky with tears and black mascara. She'd lost her man, been tempted to sleep with a chiseled-cheek-bone charmer, and still hadn't found Gassot or the jade. She curled up on the lumpy settee by the window, overlooking wind- and rain-blasted rue Sauffroy, feeling as alone as the old vet.

Sunday Morning

SHE WOKE UP TO her cell phone's ringing. René lay asleep, pale lemon light pooled on the duvet bunched around him. Her stockings were twisted and she straightened them while listening to Serge's voice.

"Sorry, Aimée, I was called to Nantes, just got back to the morgue," Serge said. "I have to work Sundays now."

"Which twin had the fever?" She could never tell them apart, the boys never stood still long enough to enable her to figure it out.

"Both came down with *la grippe*; thank God my mother-in-law came with us."

"Do me a favor, Serge, find me the autopsy report on Albert Daudet."

"Why?" he asked.

"It's a suspicious death."

"You stopped all that, didn't you?"

Not Serge, too!

"I'll bring Miles Davis over," she said. "Let the twins take him for a walk."

"Look Aimée, that's not your field now."

"It never was," she said. "But if I tell the boys you wouldn't let me bring—"

"*Arrête*! What's the deceased man's name again?"

"Daudet, Albert."

"Like the writer, eh? Hold on."

She heard the shuffle of papers, conversations in the background. By the time Serge came back on the line, she'd taken her pills and pulled on her skirt.

"Daudet died under medical care, so it took a while to dredge it up," Serge said. "Hmm, interesting report. Most old men who go in for a cardiogram don't die from cartilage thyroid fractures and hemorrhaging in the neck."

"Meaning?"

"Asphyxiation due to manual strangulation. My guess is it came from a carotid sleeper hold."

She gasped. Regnier and his henchmen. Hadn't René said he'd been caught in a carotid sleeper hold?

"Daudet had a preexisting coronary condition. It didn't help. The compression of the carotid did it for him," Serge said. "I figure it took three or four minutes. That's indicated by extensive bruises to the neck and petechiae."

"Would the killer have to be muscular?" she asked.

"It helps. Hook and hold the neck in the crotch of the arm, apply pressure, and most folks pass out in ten seconds. Hold a few minutes longer and it's the big sleep."

"And Serge, in your professional opinion?"

"The evenness and deep pressure bruises indicate a big guy," Serge said. "But that's off the record."

"Fax it to me, will you?"

"You owe me, Aimée. Count some babysitting in, too!"

* * *

AIMÉE KNOCKED on the door of Albert Daudet's widow, Lucie. She lived in a peeling stucco former *loge de concierge* at the mouth of a cobblestoned courtyard.

The window lace shimmied and swayed as the glass door opened. Crocheted figures danced and then became still forever, caught on the lace panel, as if sculpted by sea-salt spray.

"Madame Daudet?" she said.

"*Oui?*" said a woman with a tightly curled gray perm and reading glasses hanging by a beaded string around her neck.

"May I take a few moments of your time?"

She stared at Aimée, smoothing down her apron. "The coffin's all I can afford right now. Forget the memorial service you people try to cram down my throat. The *anciens combattants* should help bury a veteran!"

"I'm a detective." She flashed her license. "Sorry to impose at this time but I want to ask a few questions."

"The *flics* came by yesterday," she said. "I told them the same thing. It's foul play."

Aimée nodded. "I know. It's in the autopsy report."

"They won't show it to me. Keep telling me to wait."

"But I have a copy," she said. "Would you like to see it?"

Madame Daudet covered her mouth with her hand. "Come in," she said.

The converted *loge*, a suitcase of an apartment, was crammed with shelves of religious statues and plastic vials of holy water from Lourdes. Bronze statues of the Virgin Mary and a kneeling Bernadette were prominent. A small sink with a floral print curtain below stood next to a two burner stove.

"Albert was my second husband, you know," said Madame Daudet, gesturing to chairs around a table which bore a file of *supermarché* coupons. The corners of her mouth turned down in a sour expression. "I never had to do such things before but the pension's not enough."

She pulled her reading glasses on and read the autopsy report. "What's this 'petechiae'?"

"In layman's terms?"

"I don't speak medicalese."

"Red pinpoint hemorrhages in his eyes. Their presence indicates strangulation."

Madame Daudet's brows creased with concern. "I don't understand."

But Aimée thought she did.

"Did he have enemies?"

"Albert?" Though she shook her head, the tight curls budged not a centimeter. "He supervised the tire warehouse for forty years. A joker. Always good with his hands, he was." She pointed to the built-in shelves, like in a ship's cabin. "I told the police the same thing. Don't you talk to each other?"

If she thought Aimée worked with the *flics*, why enlighten her?

"I just need to clarify. Why do you think someone would do this?"

Madame Daudet scanned the report. "Albert talked. 'Big mouth,' I called him. To his face, mind you. He knew what I thought. No lies between us. That's why I wondered. . . ."

She paused, her eyes wistful.

"You wondered if he'd run off at the mouth and it got him in trouble?" Aimée asked.

Madame Daudet nodded. For the first time Aimée saw tears in the corners of her eyes. She brushed them away.

"Was it something he mentioned to his comrades from the Sixth Battalion?"

"Some scam. For the first time, well, Albert kept secrets from me. I thought they were just old men with fantasies."

"Fantasies?"

"Who comes out of war unscarred, eh?" she said, clipping

the coupons, and putting them in the box. "But when the nightmares started again. . . ."

"Madame Daudet, what do you mean?"

"The nightmares Albert had!" Madame Daudet said. "He woke up screaming, bathed in sweat. The first year we were married, it happened every night."

Aimée crossed her legs and shifted the file of coupons. Outside in the courtyard, footsteps sounded on the cobblestones. Despite the cramped warmth inside, a damp muskiness permeated the floorboards.

"From the battle of Dien Bien Phu, you mean?"

"He said odd things in his sleep," she said. "Over and over, about a dragon."

Aimée gripped the edge of the table. "A jade dragon? Did he mention that?"

Madame Daudet took her reading glasses from her nose. "A list of animals, he kept repeating it. But when he woke up, he denied knowing anything about them."

The astrological animals of the Chinese zodiac? Excited, Aimée leaned forward. Was he one of the soldiers who'd looted the Emperor's tomb? Did Madame Daudet know Gassot?

"What do his comrades in the Sixth Battalion say?"

"They're scared," she said. "Afraid the past has come knocking on their door. After I mentioned that his pants cuff was rolled up, Picq had such horror in his eyes. He hasn't been in touch since."

"Wait a minute." Aimée scanned the autopsy report. In the description of Albert's body there was a tattoo, a flower with a dripping knife, on his left calf.

"Didn't you think it odd?"

"More like disrespectful, a careless staff error, so I made my thoughts known to the director."

"I mean his tattoo."

"They all had them. Some drunken Haiphong foolishness, Albert told me."

"Doesn't the Sixth Battalion keep in touch, meetings and so on?"

"You mean swapping war stories of the good old days in Indochina?" She shook her head. "Not like that at all. Albert was in the supply commissary. He hid behind his desk. I think he had seen some combat but he didn't like talking about it. Most of the boys shipped in on transports, dallied with bar girls. But then who didn't? Got shot up and shipped out in wood boxes or on troop transports. But me, I knew the old Indochina."

Madame Daudet's eyes took on a faraway look. "I remember the flame trees and the tamarinds by the grass lawn that spread all the way down to the mouths of the dragon."

"I'm sorry, I don't understand, Madame."

"The Mekong has nine tributaries, like the nine mouths of the dragon, the Indochinese say," she said. "My parents had parties, magical soirées with lantern lights, the banana leaves nodding in the breeze, tables of hors d'oeuvres and so many servants we tripped over them."

Aimée hoped this was going somewhere.

"My father planted rubber trees. Kept big accounts with the tire manufacturers he supplied on the île de la Jatte."

Aimée tried another tactic. "Was your husband a rubber planter, too?"

"Paul, my first husband, was a naval attaché." Her eyes misted over. "I polished his épaulettes, kept the gold braid just how he liked it. We'd go to Café Parisien, you know, where the right types were seen: the governor, and everyone of importance. Such a scent of frangipani in the courtyard! At one time they called it the Paris of the East. Gustave Eiffel designed the post office, can you imagine?"

Aimée didn't think she expected an answer.

"But there's no more rue Catinat now. Our beautiful ochre villa's a community center, someone told me. They don't even call it Saigon anymore," she sighed. "We wore hand-sewn silk tea dresses. No one wears things like that anymore. And we changed several times a day, *très élégantes*. The humidity, you know. Dense, heavy like a wet blanket all the time. I'll say one thing for the natives, they knew how to dress for the weather."

"Did you know the de Lussignys over there?"

"My dear, we dined with them at the Café Parisien," Madame Daudet said, a trace of hauteur in her voice.

To Aimée it sounded sad, so long ago and so far away.

"Was the old man a jade collector?"

"He loved everything native, including his mistress," she said. "Life seemed perfect until the guerillas bombed the café. As far as I'm concerned, it ended then. All the guerilla warfare that followed, attacks on us by the Hoa-Hoa and Cao Dai."

"Cao Dai? But it's a religious sect."

"Religion cloaks many things." Madame Daudet shrugged. "A political vehicle for *les asiatiques*. Paul always said that. The Cao Dai had an *army*. At first, I didn't blame them. Starving on the streets, well, we could see that. With all those green shoots in the rice paddies, I wondered where the rice went but the guerillas took it. They brainwashed the peasants. Our servants, too. Imagine, after all those years, and how generous we were! Those betrayals hurt. But I prefer to think, well, not everyone."

A true colonial childhood, Aimée thought. And now she had come to this. Aimée noticed the small armoire, the door ajar, which held only a few housedresses on hangers.

"When my old nanny died, a devout Buddhist, they laid a banana on her stomach, as a guarantee of an afterlife. Imagine!" she said, sighing. "The Cao Dai bury their dead sitting up."

"With jade?" Aimée asked.

"Wouldn't surprise me," she said.

Outside the weak sunshine slanted on the wall. The voices of children and the bouncing of a ball echoed from the recesses of the courtyard.

"How can I get in touch with Picq and Gassot?"

"Bad lot," she said. "I always said it. They proved me right, the *flics* did."

Frustrated, Aimée wished the woman would give her facts, not hints. Gassot might have the clue to the jade she needed. "What do you mean?"

"They were arrested for possession of explosives," she said. "Last I heard, they were in jail due to their crazy scheme."

"Gassot, too?"

"Seems he can move fast despite his peg-leg."

"So he escaped. Where could I find him?"

Madame Daudet pulled back.

"I think he knows why your husband was killed," Aimée said. "Please, tell me how to find him."

Madame Daudet blessed herself and kissed the gold cross around her neck. She pointed across the narrow yard to a five-story hotel with peeling shutters, that displayed the sign HÔTEL, and a phone number with the old-fashioned prefix BAT 4275. There was a shuttered café below it.

"Are they ever open?"

Madame Daudet rolled her eyes. "A money-laundering front for some gang. At least that's what Albert said. No wonder Gassot lives there cheap."

And then Aimée remembered the address she'd gotten from the police. The building Thadée owned in the back of the gallery courtyard: What had the faded old blue sign said? A warehouse or manufacturer?

"Either your husband, Picq, or Gassot left a contact phone number at the *anciens combattants*. Was it the telephone number of the tire warehouse?"

Madame Daudet nodded.

"Were there other men from the Sixth Battalion in their group?"

"Nemours. He's a gourmand who loves food more than life itself. We all thought he'd go first, with his cholesterol!"

"But your husband was the first. And someone's after his remaining comrades, aren't they?"

Madame Dinard looked down. "I don't know."

Aimée tapped her heels on the wooden floor wanting to steer the conversation back on track.

"What about Nemours?"

"He follows Picq. They'd meet with Albert at the tire warehouse. When Albert retired, he became a part-time custodian. After work, they'd go to play belote upstairs in the café on rue des Moines."

Now it made sense. She'd met them already. The day she confronted Pleyet in the upstairs room of the café, the day after Thadée was killed. She shivered with fear.

Could she have it wrong? Had *they* killed Thadée, then their comrade Albert, out of greed?

"Did Albert ever mention Thadée Baret? He was related by marriage to the de Lussignys."

"*Mais bien sûr,* all the time!" she said. "Albert loved talking to Thadée about Indochina. Thadée ran the gallery. He received it in the divorce settlement. Once the de Lussignys owned the tire factory. They were rubber barons who intermarried with the natives," said Madame Daudet, her mouth crinkled in a *moue* of disgust.

"May I keep the autopsy report?" she asked.

Aimée nodded, wondering if it would wind up on the shelf next to Bernadette of Lourdes. She thanked Madame Daudet and left. But now she'd learned of the old men's connection to Thadée and where Gassot lived.

Outside on the street, she ducked into a doorway and checked her cell phone. Two messages.

The first was from Pleyet, finally returning her call.

"We need to talk," he said. "Call me back."

She'd call him *after* she found Gassot. If she worked it right, she'd have information to barter with Pleyet.

The next was from Martine.

"*Allô*, Martine. How's Sophie?"

She heard Martine inhale on her cigarette.

"Safe in her room. The valium helped," Martine said. Her husky voice rose. "Interesting news, Aimée," she said. "The Brits dropped out of the oil rights bidding. And seems the Chinese have transported impressive drilling rigs to the bay off Dingfang, on Hainan Island. They're raising territorial issues. But right now it looks like Olf and the Chinese are neck in neck."

"Great, keep going, Martine."

"There's a rumor of fat 'commissions' for the inside track to the oil rights. I'm still on it."

AIMÉE ENTERED the narrow corridor of Gassot's hotel, her shoulders brushing against the peeling, fawn-colored walls. A single bulb lit the hall. But she imagined that the pensioners who lived here appreciated it. Better than a cardboard box over their heads in an abandoned lot.

The smell of grease from a nearby kitchen hovered. Chirping came from the reception booth, a particle board structure, under a Art Deco sign advising NO EVENING VISI-TORS ALLOWED AFTER DARK. FULL AND DEMI-PENSION WITH CAFÉ MEALS AVAILABLE.

Judging by the grease smell, she doubted the inhabitants chose full pension if they could afford to dine elsewhere. A tall man wearing a raincoat and holding a watering can stood in the doorway leading to a concrete rear yard.

"Looking for someone?" he asked, in a hoarse voice, the guttural roll of consonants betraying his Russian origin. His eyes took in her legs and he grinned. "I'm available."

A stab at Slavic humor?

She gave him a big smile.

"Which room is Monsieur Gassot's?"

"Eh? What's that?" he said, blocking the doorframe in a swift movement.

"You heard me," she said, keeping the smile on her face. "Which room does he stay in, Monsieur?"

"Spell that name for me, eh. My hearing's gone. Everything else works fine."

She reached for the cell phone in her pocket. As he set down the watering can, she punched in the hotel's number. Seconds later the phone rang in the small reception area.

He glanced at the phone, his eyes unsure.

"Go ahead, I'll wait," she said, still keeping the smile on her face with effort.

"Please sit. Wait over there," he said, entering the reception cubicle to answer the telephone.

Fat chance. She ran past him and into the back yard, skidding on the wet concrete in time to see a white-haired man slipping into a dilapidated lean-to shed. Rabbit hutches covered with wire-mesh lined the old wall, celery stalks peeking through the holes. She slammed the hotel door shut with her booted heel, found her Swiss Army knife, and wedged it between the door jamb and door handle. The Russian gorilla would have to kick the door down to open it. She had no intention of losing Gassot now.

"Monsieur Gassot, I'm not a *flic*," she called. "I know you've been avoiding me. You were an engineer at Dien Bien Phu. I read your article about the looting of the Emperor's tomb."

The shed door scraped open. A knife blade glinted.

All she had in her bag was a can of pepper spray and Chanel No. 5.

"Who are you?" he asked.

She had to get him to listen to her. "Aimée Leduc. Your friend Albert was murdered. You could be next."

What if he'd been responsible? But whatever he'd done she needed to gain his confidence. Convince him to talk to her.

He edged out of the shed. Even under the 1960s-era gray twill raincoat she saw his well-built frame and muscular arms. And his limp.

"What's that to you?"

"I was hired by a Cao Dai nun to find a set of jade astrological figures. Let me do my job. Talk to me."

The Russian kicked at the door.

"Call this *mec* off," she said. "Or I'll treat him to pepper spray."

"Where's your gun?" Gassot asked.

She shook her head. The gutter dripped. Big splats of water landed on her boots. "I'm a private detective. No gun."

Too bad it sat in the hall drawer of her apartment.

Gassot stood, rain glistening in his white hair, holding the knife with an unreadable expression.

"Why was Daudet killed? Why are they after you?" she asked.

And by his eyes, she knew she'd said the wrong thing. She'd lost him.

"I've lived this long, so you should know I'm not stupid enough to fall for your approach. I know you were hired to avenge the past."

"Avenge? Wait a minute, you're confusing me with someone else."

Gassot's mouth twisted. "It was a mistake. We never meant to do it."

Do what? She had to reel Gassot in. Get him to trust her. She remembered what Linh had said.

"War's a series of mistakes," she said. "But you couldn't have been more than nineteen or twenty years old. What did you know? The important thing was you saved a Vietnamese man's life. The life of this nun's father."

"What nun?"

"A Cao Dai nun named Linh asked me to bring her the jade figures."

"She wasn't a nun then." Gassot flexed his knuckles but he still held the knife. "Not when we fought at Dien Bien Phu."

"His grandchildren are in need of the jade hoard. One's in a Vietnamese prison for protesting the régime and his sister's this nun who is petitioning the International Court of Justice to bring about his release," she said, embellishing. "And you were in the Sixth Battalion, one of the men who looted the jade treasure after the battle."

Gassot's mouth trembled.

Aimée lifted the absinthe-green disk into the dull gray light. It glowed.

"Didn't you find this?"

Gassot's mouth trembled. He stepped closer and let out a deep breath. "And a lot more. We were surveying, digging trenches, but we hit an old ammunition box. There were twelve figures inside. The next day they were gone."

She'd been right. She placed the jade disk on the rabbit hutch ledge, staying far away from Gassot's knife.

"There's another, isn't there? It's called the Dragon. The most sacred."

Gassot turned over the small jade disk in his hands, then punched the rabbit hutch, his shoulders beaded with rain.

"You have it, don't you?" she said. "And the dragon makes the set complete."

"By rights they're *all* ours. But I never saw them again."

"A museum director put the figures up for auction here in

Paris a month ago," she told him. "Then they were withdrawn. He was murdered in the men's bathroom of Parc Monceau. You know that, Gassot, don't you?"

Silence. She saw defiance in his eyes.

"If the jade is stolen from its true owner, bad luck follows the thief," he said.

"So you killed Thadée, then Albert, because he wanted a bigger share. Demanded it." She was guessing. "Did you arrange to meet Dinard and murder him, too?"

Gassot shook his head. "Think what you want." He turned the jade piece in his hand again.

"You're not the only ones who want the jade," Aimée said. "Albert's wife said you and the others concocted some scheme."

"But the rumor. . . ." Gassot hesitated.

Had she put it together wrong?

"Go ahead, Gassot. What rumor?"

"The man I saved told me the de Lussignys had stolen the jade. I never saw him again, so I couldn't question him further. Albert insisted Thadée knew something, but he couldn't get it out of him."

The door splintered and the Russian stood there. And so did Blondel.

The spillover from the broken rain gutter beat a pattern on Aimée's boots. She wished she had René for backup. Though she'd found Gassot, she had walked into the eye of the dragon.

"Time for that talk, Mademoiselle Leduc," Blondel said. His zipperlike mouth and dull, flat gaze bothered her, but not as much as his clenched fists.

"About your dope running in Clichy?" She had to deflect him, get out of here. But how? Keep talking. "So you pay off someone in the Commissariat. I'm not interested."

"You weren't nice to Jacky; he remembers that," Blondel said, motioning to someone behind him. "But I'm on someone else's franc."

He worked for someone else? She glanced at Gassot.

"Thadée owed you money," she said, "Why kill him, and Albert? Whose side are you on, Gassot?"

"My own."

"Meaning you double-crossed these *mecs,* and they're after you?"

"Something like that," Blondel said.

"I never did business with you, Blondel!" Gassot said.

"But your comrade did. And look what happened to him."

"Albert? He talked too much but he'd never deal with the likes of you," Gassot said, a quiver in his voice.

"Think again," said Regnier, stepping into the doorframe. His riveting black eyes locked onto hers.

Aimée stifled a gasp. Why hadn't she put that together? But the truth, as Oscar Wilde had said, was rarely pure and never simple.

"You work for Olf don't you, Regnier?" she asked. "You hired Blondel to do your dirty work."

His eyes never left her face. A small smile painted his thin lips. "Took you awhile, didn't it?"

"You killed Thadée, Albert, and Dinard. And kidnapped René, to force me into—"

"A little too late for those observations, isn't it?" Regnier interrupted. "But you two make a nice couple. Now we're going to get the jade."

"Why? To get back at the Ministry and the RG?"

He shrugged. "You know what the RG's like. Thanks to them I wear a hearing aid," he said. "Once I fell for their line about honor and service. But I came to my senses, and now I work for the highest bidder."

Did he expect sympathy from her? She remembered Martine's comments on how close Olf and the Chinese were in the bidding for oil rights. Now it made sense.

"Interpol's infiltrated your group," she said. "That should

screw up Olf's plan to use the jade to get an edge on the Tonkin Gulf oil rights."

Regnier's eyes widened. "What do you mean?" His phone beeped and he turned away to answer it.

"Pleyet's with Interpol," Aimée said.

Would that knock him off balance, at least for a moment? But he'd disappeared.

She looked for another door, another way out. High walls dripping with rain and the rabbit hutches hemmed them in. She was trapped in this postage-stamp-sized concrete yard. How had Regnier managed to vanish so quickly? Well, it was one less to face.

Could she take on these *mecs*? Her pepper spray would disable one. Maybe. Gassot had the knife but she didn't like the bulge in Blondel's coat pocket. And would Gassot back her up?

She pepper-sprayed the Russian, who yelled and put his arms up to his face. Gassot, lunging with his knife, tripped against the rabbit hutches, sending them crashing to the ground. She got Blondel with her Chanel No. 5 purse-size atomizer.

She raced past them, aiming for the street. Scrambled down the corridor. She heard Gassot panting right behind her. And for a moment, she thought they'd make it.

A stinging blow from Jacky threw her into the reception booth. Hands tightened around her neck.

"Shall I take care of you now or wait until you tell me what I want to know?" Regnier said, sticking his blunt-nosed Mauser in her ribs. "You choose."

Aimée froze.

Gassot, careening from a punch, was held spreadeagled against the wall. Frightened rabbits skittered over their feet. Gassot's knife fell, clattering on the cracked tile.

"Outnumbered and outgunned, I'd say," Regnier said.

"*Stupide*. No escape route," Gassot said, his breath heaving. "One should always have a way out."

"So let's talk," Aimée said, trying to think fast. "You've got it all wrong, there's—"

"We will talk, and you'll give me the jade," Regnier said, watching her lips. "But not here."

A plumbing van waited on the curb, a yellow sign PLOMBERIE 24/24 painted on the side panels.

"And you looked like a nice girl," said the Russian rubbing his red eyes as he shoved Aimée and Gassot down the hall. "Nice legs, that waif-look, half-wild and free. I like."

"You're not my type."

"You never know until you try," he said, feeling her up under her sweater.

"Later, Sergei," Blondel said, opening the back doors.

"Keep your hands off! Help!" She screamed and kicked, hoping someone on the street would hear them. But then Jacky blocked the view in the three seconds it took to bundle her and Gassot into the van.

She and Gassot were thrown onto the van floor, the door locked. The engine gunned and the van took off, throwing them against the metal racks of supplies. No side windows. Just a small back window.

Jumbled thoughts came to her. Linh's father had known about the jade! What a world class liar Julien de Lussigny was, acting as if he'd never heard of the jade! He'd said his father would turn in his grave if he knew of its existance. Liar! When his godfather Dinard had put it up for auction, De Lussigny had probably helped him.

The van swerved and she rammed into the wall.

"Gassot, you ok?"

"Are you kidding?"

"Think!" she said.

But he shook his head, defeated.

Maybe not this time.

She scanned the dim interior of the van. The divider between the driver's compartment and the rear of the van, where a window had been, was blocked by a metal panel now. Had Blondel used this van to kidnap René? She didn't think they were going far, otherwise they'd have tied them and taped them up. A whiff of pepper spray wafted from the front so she knew the Russian was up there. Jacky? Where were Regnier and Blondel?

White plastic pipe, hoses, and plumbing equipment were scattered over the van floor.

"The pipe's not strong enough to break the rear window safety glass," she said, rooting through the equipment. "We need a wrench, a pair of pliers, something made of metal to shatter it."

Nothing.

She noticed Gassot's old-fashioned flesh colored wooden leg.

"How much does that weigh?"

"Enough."

"If you took it off, would it be strong enough to smash the glass?"

"Then how would I run away?"

Good point.

The van careened around a corner, throwing him against her.

"You jump first, then I follow," she said, "I will pick you up." If neither of them broke any limbs, it might work.

He shook his head.

"Got any other ideas?"

"No wonder our plan backfired," Gassot said, his eyes far-away. "The jade was not meant for us. It's sacred."

Perhaps. But she had to get him back to earth. They didn't have much time.

"The old Cao Dai priest was right," Gassot said. "Remember the old saying, *Ngoc linh phai . . .*"

"Don't go mystic on me, Gassot. That lock's rusted," she said. "Lean on the side and try kicking it. You need a new artificial leg anyway."

The van slowed down. She had to galvanize him to action.

"Quick, Gassot. Brace yourself against me. Now! Kick!"

And he started kicking.

He missed the lock. Pounding came from the driver's compartment.

"Try again."

Gassot kicked. Again and again. Only a small bulge where the doors joined. But a thin lick of streetlight showed through. "Keep kicking." She grabbed several white plastic pipes from the floor and wedged them into the opening he had created.

"Harder, Gassot!"

She braced him and worked the pipes back and forth. One cracked and splintered and she shoved another in. At each corner, the van slowed, then shot ahead, to throw them off balance.

The door buckled. But the lock wouldn't give. She felt the gears downshift, heard the brakes screech. Then a sickening crunch of metal and a crash that sent them sprawling. They'd run into another vehicle. The van shuddered to a halt.

"Get up, try again, Gassot." Her cell phone vibrated in her pocket. "Give it all you've got."

He strained, hammering the lock with quick jabs of his foot. She twisted the pipes back and forth and the door burst open.

"Now," she said, pulling Gassot up and dashing out the door.

They landed on the surprised Russian, his eyes still red and tearing, in a crosswalk on rue Legendre. Smoke billowed from the mangled van now enmeshed with a small truck. The angry red-faced truck's driver had Jacky in an armlock on the pavement.

"Run, Gassot," she said, kicking the Russian in the head.

No passersby. Only a shuttered violin shop and a *boucherie*.

An old woman peered out from the *boucherie* in the dim evening dusk.

"Call the police," she yelled.

But the old woman shut the door.

The rumble and clack of a train below reminded her that rue Legendre bridged the rail lines. A black Peugeot screeched to a halt behind them. Regnier and Blondel loomed on the pavement.

Blocked in both directions. And a prime shooting target. Gassot stood immobile, like a frightened deer in the car headlights. They had to take advantage of the confusion.

"I hope you can climb, Gassot," she said. She grabbed him by the shoulder.

"What do you mean?"

"Hurry. Metal criss-cross beams support these railway bridges." At least they did under the Pont Neuf outside her window. She prayed this bridge had them, too.

Chunks of concrete flew as bullets hit the ledge. She moved her hands, her toes reaching for footholds on the metal struts, trying not to look down and see the huge drop beneath them.

Gray-green criss-cross beams ran below. Dizzied, she held tight to the faded green steel span. Electric freight trains with yellow lighted windows clattered below on the dark, glistening metal tracks. A narrow gray-ribbed walkway for workmen ran parallel underneath, spanning the rail lines.

"Now, Gassot . . . here!" she said, reaching with her legs and finding solid metal.

And somehow he did it. Landed next to her on the narrow walkway.

"Keep moving, Gassot, we can make it. It's not far." She pointed to a ladder built into the stone side wall. At least they could climb it instead of getting picked off like flies.

Grit flaked off the steel girders as bullets peppered the steel, pinging and sparking.

Bad idea.

"Get down, Gassot."

And then her feet slid and she tripped on metal rebar scraps. Airborne, she grabbed the rusted railing and fell against it. Rebar pieces sailed past her. She grabbed one before it fell and crouched down, pulling out her cell phone, and punched in the number.

"*Allô*. Pleyet! We're under the rail bridge on rue Legendre," she shouted, hunching down.

"Sightseeing?"

"Regnier's men are shooting at us. Isn't Interpol interested in the jade?"

More shots pinged on steel and Gassot fell, knocking her phone into the air. *Merde!*

The snub nose of a pistol edged around a metal girder. And then she saw a blue-sleeved arm. She lifted the sharp, cold rebar piece and swung with all her might. Only air. She tried again, this time hitting something solid. Heard a yell muffled by the sound of clacking train wheels. She pulled it back. Swung again.

A hand with a pistol appeared in front of her face. She banged the rebar into the knuckles. Heard a clanging and the crunch of flesh.

And then Blondel whipped past her, flapping his arms like a bird. The wind took his scream. She fell back against the girder. When she looked down, the blue of his jacket lay sprawled on the roof of a freight car rumbling into the night.

She grabbed Gassot, pulled him toward the ladder in the stone wall a few steps away. Sweat ran down between her shoulders.

"Climb, Gassot," she said, pushing him up.

"My leg. . . ."

"You can do it."

Gassot stopped. Shuddered.

She looked up to see Regnier straddling the ladder. And Gassot crumpled back on her, falling onto the narrow walkway.

She clutched the metal cross strut, rusted flakes covering her hands.

"We're worth more to you alive, Regnier," she shouted.

A stinging kick at her jaw. But she held on, grabbed at some twisted wires hanging down. Regnier had one leg on top of Gassot's head. "So where is it?"

She clenched her fist around the flashlight in her bag, "I'll take you there."

"Look at me when you talk," Regnier yelled.

She felt her collar grabbed and then her shoulders pulled. Her feet slipped and she hung suspended, her legs dangling. Her arms flailed in the cold air.

"Hurry up, or I drop you."

She tried to look up but her coat tore with a loud rip. She saw the glistening wet tracks below her twisting boots. Her father's face flashed in front of her, a black and white image of her mother, the little apartment with a blue table they'd once lived in.

Her hands struck a steel girder and she grabbed. Her fingers slipped, and she grabbed again. Caught the thick edged steel. Her heel struck the stone wall and slid. She swung back, hit the wall again with her foot, and pushed off.

And then Regnier let go. Pounding and yelling sounded above her. Then a scream and a sickening thud from below.

Her right leg reached the girder and she caught her heel in a hole. She grabbed higher with her other arm, finding the steel beam, and scrambling with the other leg, she pulled herself up.

"Gassot . . . Gassot?" No answer. She kept reaching and climbing. The train whistle screeched below.

And when her shaking hand couldn't hold the metal grid columns anymore, she realized that now sirens were wailing overhead. And Gassot was singing. Something in Vietnamese.

She peered over the steel girder. Caught her breath. Regnier lay sprawled below on the train tracks. And then a train flashed by. Gassot leaned over. She was afraid he was about to jump.

"Gassot, it's all right," she said, rubbing his shoulder. "Help me. We've got to recover the jade."

"I should never have touched it," he said.

"YOU TOOK your time, Pleyet," Aimée told him.

"I try to keep a low profile," he said, shielding his face from the photographers on rue Legendre. The whirr and flashes of photographer's lights shot off like fireworks until the *flics* shooed them away. Blue lights from the police cars and ambulances played kaleidoscopically over the balconied buildings overlooking the train lines. Jacky, handcuffed, spit in Aimée's direction as he was escorted into a police van.

"Nice view," Pleyet said, pointing to the rail line walls. One read PARIS in white letters on the blackened stone.

"There's a better one," she said. "In the Parc Monceau. Get us out of here."

"I'd like to, but the *flics* want to question you. . . ."

"Use your clout, Pleyet," she interrupted. "Don't international oil rights and looted art take precedence? Call headquarters in Lyon, make your buddies smooth this over. Or it will be too late. I know where the jade is."

SHE HELPED Gassot into Pleyet's blue Renault, borrowed Pleyet's phone, and called René.

"What did you find, René?"

"Interesting stuff, Aimée," said René. "The oil bid the French Ministry made contains a unique offer."

"The jade figures?"

Aimée saw Gassot's hand stiffen.

"Bingo. But here's what's even more interesting. The Chinese bid includes it, too."

Whoever had the jade would claim the oil rights by virtue of patrimony. Just as Derek Lau had told her in his restaurant. The ancient jade disks, older than the animal figures, were the guarantee of legitimacy for the claimant.

"You have proof in written form?" she asked.

"It's all printed out in the e-mails and ministry documents. The jade's supposed to be returned by the Ministry of Interior to the Vietnamese people in a munificent gesture in consideration for oil rights. The vast untapped reserves in the Gulf of Tonkin."

"Good job, René. So the People's Republic of China and the Vietnamese Government both claim to be legally entitled to the oil," she said. "No wonder Julien de Lussigny wanted me to monitor the Chinese and hired Regnier."

And tried to seduce me, she thought.

"Martine left you a message," René continued. "Since you didn't answer your phone. Olf pays secret commissions from a fund that funnels back to politicians and officials."

No wonder de Lussigny could afford the Parc Monceau mansion.

"Do me a favor, overnight everything to Interpol in Lyon. Put down Pleyet's name as the sender."

"All in a day's work," René said.

"Good job, partner."

The windshield wipers kept time to the pounding of the rain as Pleyet drove. The gray-misted Clichy streets were haloed by red-orange traffic lights.

"Thanks, Gassot," she said, taking in his huddled form in the back seat.

But his eyes watched the wet cobblestone streets.

"You owe me, Pleyet," she said.

"Want a job?"

"You know what I want," she said. Her peripheral vision fogged and she clenched the door handle. She reached for her pills, swallowed them. Took the vial of mint oil, rubbed it on her temples, and closed her eyes.

"Tell me when we get there."

AIMÉE LED them around the back to the mansion's rear wing. An older Asian man, in blue pants and work jacket, smoking a cigarette, answered the door.

"We're here to see Madame Nguyen," she said. Odors of lemon grass wafted toward them.

"She's not here," he said, blocking the door.

"Tran, it's all right," Gassot said.

Aimée noticed the quiver in Gassot's voice, the hesitation.

"Since you know each other, won't you let us wait inside?" Aimée said.

She walked past Tran into the kitchen and toward Madame Nguyen's room. A woman stood by the red-lighted altar where incense was burning. As the woman turned, her silk red scarf shimmered in the light of the votive candles.

Aimée saw Gassot lean against the doorframe and heard his swift intake of breath.

"What's the matter, Gassot?"

He took a few steps. Stopped.

"Bao?" Gassot asked.

Aimée blinked. She saw a stunning Asian businesswoman of indeterminate age. Shocked, she stepped closer. Linh looked different in makeup and wearing a black pantsuit, a Hermès silk scarf around her shoulders.

"But . . . aren't you a nun?" Aimée said.

"Half-right," Linh said. "I was a nun. Once."

No wonder Aimée hadn't found her at the temple. The words

of Quoc, the temple cleaner, came back to her. *He hadn't seen her before; she wore streetclothes*. She should have paid attention.

"You've changed, Bao," Gassot said, haltingly.

"Everyone changes, Gassot," she said. "Except you."

"You know her, Gassot?" Aimée asked.

"In another life," he said. "As Bao—"

"Bao Tran, the Chinese recruited you in the labor camp," Pleyet said. "They schooled you and your cousin Tran as saboteurs."

"We're an old-fashioned country," Bao said. "We have to go far to catch up to the next century. But the jade will make it possible. We want what's ours."

Aimée quailed. She'd believed *her* . . . Linh . . . Bao. Been taken in by her warmth and calculating patience.

"And I was a perfect tool for you," Aimée said. "Everything you told me was a lie. You made everything up."

"Not everything," Bao said, her voice wistful. "My brother is in prison and my country is in chains."

"So you betray your country by helping China to win the oil rights? How can that help Vietnam or liberate your brother? You set me up, and Thadée, too," Aimée said.

"It should have worked," Bao said. "You would have brought me the jade. Simple!"

"Simple, except that Thadée owed Blondel," Aimée said. "And Regnier, in Olf's pay, knew that. He paid Blondel's henchmen to do *his* dirty work. But Albert got in the way."

"Albert wasn't that big a fool," Gassot said, his voice shaking. "I don't believe it."

"Albert worked in the tire factory—the de Lussigny's factory—next door to the gallery for years. He knew all about the lost treasure. When old de Lussigny died, Thadée found the jade. Albert suspected that Thadée had taken it."

Gassot hung his head. "It was my old comrades. They'd concocted a plan to use Thadée."

"Linh, or should I say Bao, you promised Thadée money. Money he needed for the gallery and to pay old drug debts.

"And you played on Thadée's sympathy," she continued. "You told me yourself he had a good heart—you promised the jade would help the Cao Dai. It's the ancient disks the Chinese government wants."

Bao raised an eyebrow. "You lied to *me*," Bao said. "Madame Nguyen used the surly one with the withered arm—"

"Wait, do you mean the temple cleaner?"

"Don't play dumb." Bao's eyes flashed. "He took the jade from the doctor's office where you hid it. You planned it that way. You know where the jade's hidden now. So you will lead me to it."

It made sense. Quoc, the mahjong-playing temple cleaner had followed her after Thadée's murder, and stolen the jade.

Did Bao truly believe she was in league with Quoc, and knew where he'd hidden the jade?

"Tran, what's the matter?" Gassot asked.

"Now it's my turn to use you, the way you used us," Tran said.

"But Tran, it wasn't like that—"

"It's not enough you French colonized us, salted the fields, raped our women, firestormed my village . . . but to take our beliefs—"

A door slammed. Small footsteps crossed the tiles. Aimée saw Pleyet's shoulders tense and his hand bunch in his pocket.

"*Maman? Maman's* here!" Michel ran in and dropped his bookbag. "She called us. Where is she?"

Everyone froze.

Madame Nguyen stood behind him, staring. Aimée followed her gaze.

"Michel, come here," Madame Nguyen said.

But Aimée had knelt down by the old chest filled with toys and lifted out the Legos. She had to get Michel engaged.

"Michel, can you finish this?" she asked, keeping her voice steady with effort. "Looks like you were building a truck."

Michel grinned. "Fire engine, silly."

"Show me, we'd all like to see."

Bao moved nearer. Something glinted. Was that a knife blade under her silk scarf? She shot Pleyet a look.

Michel pulled out the red, blue, white, and yellow pieces. One by one. Aimée sensed weight shifting on the wooden floor behind her as Bao moved closer.

"Michel, let me help you get the big green one down there."

Madame Nguyen said something in Chinese. Aimée reached down, lifted a silk scarf, and something that it had hidden under the layer of toys.

She lifted out the green jade monkey.

"This belongs to my people," Madame Nguyen said. And screamed, as Tran grabbed Michel and held a knife to his throat.

"*Maman*, where's *maman*!" Michel's eyes were wide with fright.

Aimée's heart dropped. She heard scuffling, saw Nadège's purple black hair, outlined against the doorframe.

"Let go of my son!"

And then Tran's eyes bulged; a red cord was pulled tight around his neck, cutting into his skin. Nadège was strangling him from behind with the silk cord from her jade pendant. Aimée lunged, pushing Michel aside.

Pleyet sprang, but Tran turned, and plunged his knife into Pleyet's side. Aimée got to her knees and knocked Bao off balance, pinned her on the floor, and twisted the woman's silk scarf around her flailing hands.

"In here," Nadège shouted. Aimée saw blue uniforms, raised billy clubs.

By the time Aimée got to her feet, the *flics* were cuffing

Tran. All eyes were on Gassot, who'd leaned down to staunch Pleyet's bloody wound. Aimée stood in front of the toy chest, blocking it from view, as she scooped the figures into her bag.

"*Maman*'s here," Nadège said, folding Michel in her arms.

"You saved me, *maman!*" Michel said.

"*Mon cœur*, you saved me," Nadège breathed, shaking.

"No *hiêú*. Young people. No tradition," Madame Nguyen observed.

But Aimée disagreed, looking at the three generations. The old grandmother had held them together and imbued them with tradition. At least, she'd done her best.

Now Aimée would finish the job.

Monday

THE WAN NOVEMBER SUN slanted through the skylight onto the Cao Dai temple floor tiles. The all-seeing eye seemed to follow Aimée. Miles Davis curled beside her feet.

"These were in your care once, I believe," she said, handing the bag to the priest Tet. "What you do with them is your decision."

He nodded, his eyes grave. "Our government has changed, despite what you've heard. After your message, I spoke with the Director of the National Museum in Hanoi. They will display the jade with the dragon disk, recovered last year in Seoul. Our people, and visitors, will appreciate the jade. It will all be back where it belongs."

One by one, he set each jade piece crowned by a disc on a side altar. "They don't belong to China, nor to anyone else. They are our patrimony."

The jade figures glowed. They took her breath away.

"The zodiac figures symbolize the animal hidden in one's heart," the priest said. "They help one to know oneself and to divine the path."

Aimée knew that she could find her path only by putting one foot in front of the other.

"Very auspicious," the priest said, grinning at Miles Davis. "Your dog."

Miles Davis wagged his tail.

The gong sounded. "Please," he said, indicating a meditation mat. "Join us."

She sat, folding her legs. Sometime later Aimée opened her eyes and grew aware of the wind rustling over the soot-stained chimney flues on the roof, students putting their mats away, and René.

"Did you experience Mindfulness?" René asked.

She grinned. "Something close. A small shining moment."

IN THE temple foyer, Aimée found her coat.

"Olf and the Chinese will be upset," she said. "But right now, what they don't know won't hurt them."

"A subtle way of putting it," René grinned.

She stared for the last time at the jade. The figures, bathed in the afternoon's last light, emitted a sea-foam green glow. And she drew inner strength knowing they'd return to their rightful place.

Her stitches hardly ached today as she slipped her arm into the sleeve of her coat.

"No one suspected how ancient the disks were," Aimée said, "except Dinard and Bao who knew their value, financially and historically."

"And Bao?" René asked.

"Interpol's file on her only goes back to Oslo, 1992," she said. "Before that, in the late sixties, she was a Chinese agent acting with traveling troupes along the Vietnamese border."

René stroked his goatee. "And the older de Lussigny stole the jade right after Gassot discovered it."

Aimée found her scarf and wrapped it around her neck.

"In the 1930s the last Chinese Emperor, Pu Yi, is thought to have sold the jade disks to warlords in the south to finance his private opium patch," Aimée said. "Rumor was that a local French governor stole the disks and hid them by having them fastened to the jade astrological figures that were being held in safety by the Cao Dai. He planned to prop up the failing colonial rubber industry by selling the disks, piece by piece. The governor was Julien de Lussigny's father."

René rocked on his feet. "Ironic that Julien de Lussigny tried to use them just as his father had earlier."

She nodded. "After the colonials fled Indochina, no more was heard of them," she said.

She picked up her bag. Put the leash on Miles Davis. Aimée stretched her arm and winced.

"Dinard and Julien de Lussigny planned to sell them at auction," Aimée said, "but then they withdrew the jade for a 'private sale' to the ministry."

"From what I saw in Thadée's files," René said, "it seemed that Thadée counted on selling the jade to settle his and Nadège's debts to Blondel."

"And the gallery's, but Blondel not only had drug debts to collect, Regnier had hired him. He shot Thadée," she said. "And strangled Dinard. But it was Gassot's comrades who strung up Sophie. They all wanted the jade."

René reached in his coat pocket. "I'm sorry I gave you a hard time, Aimée." He flipped his wallet open. Despite his misgivings, he put a creased business card with a man's name on it in Aimée's hand.

"Pleyet left this at the hospital for you," René said. "This man's retired, Pleyet said. But he worked with your father."

She stared at it. *"Merci."*

"Pleyet told me to tell you 'Sometimes in life the answers we want don't make sense.' " René buttoned his coat. " 'Or make the sense we'd like them to.' And to remember that."

OUT ON the quai, the apricot-hued setting sun filtered through blue-gray tree branches. Aimée paused under a quay-side light, its pinprick of illumination reflected in the sluggish Seine. The Métro rumbled over the Austerlitz bridge, looped past the red stone Morgue, and hurtled toward Bastille.

"I'm off to my Hacktaviste class," René said.

"See you later. Miles Davis needs a walk."

Down on the quai, Miles Davis barked and sniffed a man's pants. He turned. Surprised, Aimée stared into Guy's eyes. She didn't know what to do. Had he come to accuse her, hand her a summons, or inform her of the bill for his damaged office?

She stood tongue-tied, wishing it had happened differently. And that she was wearing more mascara.

Guy shifted his feet. "Don't forget, you need to have those stitches taken out."

His gray eyes and lopsided smile were the same. And his wonderful hands, that ruffled Miles Davis's neck fur.

"Let me write you a check for the damages," she said, pulling out her checkbook. But her newly bandaged hands impeded her progress. "Please forgive me. I owe you an explanation."

"That's not why I came," he said. "And we don't owe each other explanations."

But once they had. "Look, Guy, let's try to settle this out of court."

He reached out and touched her cheek. "I tried, but I can't stop thinking about you."

How could she say this the right way? Was there a right way?

"Why pretend, Guy? We're too different. We both know I'm not what you want," she said. "You have someone, I know. Work it out with her."

"What?"

"Like you said, we don't owe each other explanations."

Something glimmered in his eyes and he laughed. "So you're the one who telephoned. I'm going to be an uncle!" He pulled her over to the street. He waved and a blonde waved back from a Renault, a bouquet of white roses in her arms. "Do you see Cécile? She's my sister! She's been trying for years. We went to the Savoie to tell my parents."

Aimée stared. Her mouth hung open.

"Speechless for once, Aimée?"

How could she have been so wrong? Stupid again!

"My schedule's crazy. Like yours. Cécile keeps telling me that I should accept you as you are," he said. "Big eyes, torn fishnet stockings and all. Do you want to try this again?"

Aimée saw the last glint of the sun hitting the rooftiles.

Did she?